The Dying Seconds

CANADIAN PLAYED
BOOK EIGHT

CYNTHIA GUNDERSON

With Gratitude

Editing and Critique
Jordan Truex, Scott Gunderson

Cover Design
Ink and Veil

Assistant and Sanity Support
Kyra Schroeder, Desri Wulandari

CHAPTER

One

Present Day

THIS WAS THE NIGHT. The one she'd dreamed about for almost eight years. Her whole life, really. Not that she subscribed to the cultural dialogue that a woman's crowning achievement was watching a man slip a ring on her left hand. *Theoretically.* It was more that her life wouldn't be considered whole by the people she loved most—her parents—until she walked under a wedding arch.

Kelty wanted to please them. Not because they nagged her, though her mother definitely did that, or because she felt like she needed to jump through hoops to earn their love. That was given freely and always had been. No, her desire came from a more wholesome place.

She'd never gone through the teenage battle so many of her friends had. Sometimes she wondered if her parents had installed the voice of a wise old mentor in her head at the moment of birth. Anytime she'd felt the urge to throw a fit or lash out, that little voice in her mind would remind her that her mom had packed her lunch for school or that her dad went to work with the stomach flu because they were saving up for a Disneyland trip.

They had sacrificed so much for her over the years, and thanks to that Gandolf in her brain, she was fully aware of it. After finding out her older brother wasn't interested in or planning on having kids, she was their only hope for carrying on the family line. If she didn't check the marriage and children boxes, her parents would never be the mother and father of a bride. Or groom, for that matter. They wouldn't have the gauzy photos or the arguments over flowers or the something borrowed and something blue.

And if she didn't have kids? Well. That dragon's hoard of toys and clothes her mother had packed under the stairs since the nineties would die untouched.

She wanted to give her parents every single one of those dream moments. And, truth be told, she wanted them, too. A piece of paper didn't solidify commitment, but there was something about having the man she loved declare his devotion to her and make promises in front of their friends and family.

Maybe it felt especially imperative because the man she loved was more skilled with a hockey stick than words of affirmation. Or, you know, words in general.

"Are we turning here?" Kelty shifted in the passenger seat, her puffy coat squeaking against the leather like a dying balloon. The soundtrack to every winter date she'd ever had. Outside, the city was a snow globe someone had forgotten to shake. The grey sky pressed flat against glass buildings. It was technically spring, but the cold had circled back. It was day three of a February weather repeat.

Sean's eyes stayed glued to the road. "Next light."

Kelty exhaled through her nose, fogging the passenger window. He was always quiet, but tonight his silence was charged. The inside of the truck cab seemed to hum like it did when they drove to the rink together before a game, and she was pretty certain she knew exactly why.

Sure, part of it could've been that they were on their way to see Mason, Sean's partner, at the offices where their startup went belly up. But the most compelling evidence for Sean's flexing jaw muscles and fixed glare was his own credit card statement.

She hadn't been snooping, just logging in to contribute some money toward their bills for the month, and it was the first line item. A jewelry store. *The* jewelry store. Bow and Stirling. It had sleek branding, frosted glass windows, and no prices on the display tags. The charge was $4,636, and just the sight of it was enough to make her drop her phone down the side of the sofa.

She hadn't said a word, but that number was burned on her retinas, thrumming inside her all week like a second heartbeat. Everything clicked into place. Why he'd been spending more time at the rink, why he felt more closed off. In short, why he'd been such a stodgy ass for the past couple of months.

Sean Thompson was a workhorse, a nose-to-the-grindstone kind of man. He had a soft heart hiding under his rough edges, and he was loyal as hell, but he'd rather rewire a truck than his habits.

"You okay?" Kelty turned her head to look at him.

"Yeah. I'm fine." Sean turned at the light as discussed, and Kelty kept her mouth shut.

Normally, she'd tell him to figure his shit out before they got up to the party so he didn't scare people away with his resting bitch face. But tonight, she let it slide. "You sure you want to do this? We could go grab dinner instead." She waggled her eyebrows.

Sean blew out a puff of air. "I kind of have to go."

She scoffed. "You don't have to go to anything." His mouth quirked as he pulled into the parking garage and retrieved a ticket from the turnstile. "Though, I guess if you don't show up, Mason will think you're butthurt."

Sean chuckled at that. "Pretty sure he's already convinced of that."

"Well, you were a little."

"Yeah. I know." Sean grunted.

The situation was pretty shitty. Sean and Mason had gotten in on the ground floor of a startup together during undergrad after both of their hockey dreams crashed and burned. One of their mutual friends, Andrew, was the technical brainchild. He created software for medical companies.

Since they weren't together at the beginning of it, Kelty hadn't wasted time trying to understand the logistical details. But since she helped with the acquisition, she'd been there when it went under. She knew all the gory details on the back end.

They'd been trying to build an interface to streamline patient data between diagnostic machines and hospital records. A noble idea that sounded fantastic over beers but crumbled when funding dried up and the health system's red tape strangled them.

When it all went belly up, Sean, Andrew, and Mason parted ways. Sean jumped into a more practical field after graduation, taking a job with Prairie West Insurance in corporate risk management. It was steady, respectable work. Later, he moved into compliance at Foothill Financial, where he spent most of his days making sure mid-level managers didn't tank the company with dumb-ass decisions.

Mason, on the other hand, landed a position with a technology firm in Edmonton that specialized in data analytics for oil and gas supply chains. The contacts he made there turned out to be gold.

Three years ago, Sean got word that Mason was back in Calgary, but his friend hadn't mentioned the new project he was working on. Or that he and Andrew were back in business together. Now their small company, Northern Vector Solutions, a logistics software provider for mid-sized energy firms, had grown its market share by fifteen percent. Tonight, they were celebrating millions of dollars in profit and an initial public offering. If the *Calgary Sun* was to be believed, because none of that came from Mason himself.

Now, despite Sean's unwillingness to talk about it, Kelty was piecing together his story based on the nearly eight years they'd been together. It wasn't that Sean expected his friends to come back offering him scraps. But it was a punch to the throat to find out they'd hired someone to do his literal job and hadn't sent so much as an email. It never felt good to miss the boat. But this was a frigging yacht, and he'd been iced out.

Sean found a parking spot on the third level. Kelty's heels clicked against the concrete floor of the parkade, the sound bouncing off the cement pillars. She tugged her coat closer around her shoulders, the puffed fabric rustling like a sleeping bag.

"This isn't tacky, right?" She squinched her face, motioning at her coat over the sleek, black cocktail dress that hit her mid-thigh.

"What?"

"Babe. The coat." She waited a moment, but when Sean only looked more confused, Kelty grabbed his hand and started toward the elevator. "I didn't know if I was supposed to have some, like, sexy trench coat or something."

"Are we role-playing? You're a detective—?"

"Stop!" She laughed, bumping into his side.

He tugged her to the right, and she fell into step next to him. Her skin buzzed, like her bloodstream had been replaced with soda water. "We haven't been here in, what, two years?"

Sean scrubbed a hand over his jaw. "Didn't go into the building."

Kelty nodded. They'd come to the hotel once for a friend's wedding reception, but hadn't gone back to the office. Why would they? None of their friends worked there anymore since the acquisition. Or so they'd thought at the time.

The steel doors slid open with a groan, and they stepped inside, greeted by the scent of stale perfume. Kelty glanced at Sean's breast pocket, willing the outline of a ring box to appear but nothing obvious materialized.

The elevator deposited them in a hallway where they walked to a set of revolving doors. As they passed through, commercial tile gave way to plush carpet, swallowing their footsteps.

"What is that smell?" Kelty whispered.

"Hm?" Sean scanned the lobby.

"I swear, it's in every one of these hotels. It's not quite floral—"

"Like the soap at the gym."

"Yes!" She gripped his arm tighter, her eyes lighting up. "Exactly! They must buy it from some wholesaler or something."

She flipped her long, loose curls over her shoulder, grateful she'd worn black. On light colours, every stray, dark strand of her hair turned her blouse into a CSI crime scene.

The lighting in the hotel lobby was low and sexy. Soft chatter swirled between the upholstered seating vignettes and the bar. Towering arrangements of faux lilies and orchids were draped over the concierge desk.

Sean guided her toward the back, through a set of glass doors. They spilled into an outdoor courtyard lit with strings of fairy lights. The stone pavers were damp from errant spray from the fountain, glistening under the glow.

They crossed the courtyard, Sean's palm pressing against her lower back, before pushing through another door into the connected office building. The atmosphere changed instantly. Less fairy tale, more corporate gloss.

A doorman in a tailored suit greeted them with a tablet in his hand. "Welcome. Can I—?"

"Northern Vector Solutions. Sean Thompson."

The doorman scanned his list. He nodded once, then escorted them to the elevator and pressed the button. Kelty caught Sean's eye and raised a brow. *Fancy.* His lips twitched. They'd been together long enough that he understood her subliminal messages.

As soon as the doors closed, Kelty whirled. "They hired a greeter."

"Yeah."

"Who does that? What is this, a British apartment complex? Or . . . Walmart?"

Sean's jaw twitched. "Is this what we're doing?"

"Obviously. Isn't that why you brought me?"

"No."

"No?" She levelled a stare at him. "We're not going to mock Mason and all his bougie-ass friends while stuffing shrimp cocktail into my bra cups?"

Sean snorted. "That's a bonus."

"Uh-huh."

"I brought you because Mason always had a thing for you."

Kelty snorted. "He did not." *Did he?* Her mind sent out feelers searching for any proof of that statement in their past interactions. She was old enough that any flattery, current or prior, was more than welcome.

Sean shoved his hands in his pockets. "I told you to wear the black dress, didn't I?"

The doors opened, and the hum of the party swept over them. Laughter, chatter, the clink of glasses. The whole floor had been cleared of cubicles and was now filled with cocktail tables, pop-up bars, and floral arrangements. Music pulsed through the room, jazzy and probably live.

"I thought *you* liked the black dress," Kelty hissed as they strode toward the coat check.

"I do." He winked at her. "It's short."

Kelty raised an eyebrow and smirked. Okay. Sean wanted to show her off. That meant his normal abhorrence of PDA was taking a backseat. She got to be handsy.

She leaned in as they waited for the couple ahead of them to extricate themselves from their tailored jackets. "Watch out, Thompson. I'm ovulating."

Sean pretended to ignore her, but his cheeks were noticeably pink as they handed off their coats. Kelty adjusted the fabric of her dress. The neckline dipped into a dangerously low V—wearing that was the one benefit that came with having a small but enthusiastic chest—and the hem settled across her upper thighs.

She had great legs. Her quarter-Korean heritage had made her virtually hairless, and, as had been well established in her various friend groups, gave her perfectly shaped knees. Sean laughed at her the first time she brought his attention to that fact until his sister Emma corroborated her analysis.

"Yours are straight from an anatomy textbook, and mine look like— like the face of that Spiderman villain." Emma snapped her fingers. "What's his name?"

Kelty tried to breathe through her laughter. "What!?"

"Ooh! KINGPIN!"

Kelty looked up to see Sean watching her. "What?"

"You're thinking about it."

"Hm? I'm not—"

"Kingpin."

Kelty pursed her lips, stifling the full-blown guffaw itching to get out.

He shook his head. "I can't take you anywhere."

That was kind of what made the two of them work. Sean kept his mouth shut in social situations, and Kelty made up for it by having no filter.

But this was important to him. She could at least try. Kelty blew out a breath. "I'll be good, I swear."

"Uh-huh." He pulled her to his side, his hand brushing down her hip and landing squarely on her right cheek. "I make no promises."

CHAPTER

Two

I MAKE NO PROMISES. Could that have been intentional? Was Sean dropping hints, waiting for her to connect the dots?

After their heated discussion in Edmonton, Kelty hadn't broached the topic of commitment. Not even to update their phone plan. Sean needed time to process things, and the only reason they were still together was that she was stubborn enough to wait him out.

Kelty checked the back pocket of his pants. Nothing. She frowned. *Where was the ring?* He couldn't have put it in the coat. No way he'd hand over something that important to a stranger. His left hand was in his pocket. Probably holding it.

Her heart galloped as they meandered. The room hummed like the world's most pretentious beehive, everyone pollinating with buzzwords about seed rounds and burn rates.

"Sean!" a voice called.

They turned. Mason waved from across the room, weaving through guests as he made his way over. How long had it been? Since he first moved back to Calgary?

Mason was classically handsome. Broad shoulders, clean jawline. An easy smile and brows that had to be manicured.

"Long time." Mason gripped Sean's hand.

"Yeah." Sean clapped him on the back.

Mason's eyes turned to Kelty, and his lips parted. "Uh, Kelty. You look—" Air hissed through his teeth. "Damn, Thompson. How'd you manage to hold onto this one?" He laughed, his eyes dropping to her left hand.

"Nice to see you, too." She reached for Sean's hand, giving it a squeeze. She'd spent plenty of time with Mason in years past, but had only seen him a couple of times when he visited Calgary since. She'd never responded to the DMs he sent her before moving to Edmonton.

Mason adjusted the rolled sleeve of his button-up shirt. "So how's life? You still working for Prairie West?"

Sean shook his head. "No, moved on from that a while ago." He rocked on his feet. "Looks like you built something good here."

Without me, Kelty added in her head on his behalf. He had to be thinking it. She scanned the room, searching for Andrew. If he was there, he wasn't making it obvious.

Mason exhaled. "I mean, you know how it goes. Doesn't always work out to take the risk. We got lucky this time."

Sean bristled beside her. "Good for you, bud."

Nice. That was big of him.

Mason ran a hand through his hair. "Thanks. It's been insane. We're onboarding three new clients this quarter, I'm flying to Houston next week, then Chicago—"

Kelty pounced. "That must be exhausting. All that travel. No time for hockey these days?"

Mason shook his head. "Not really, no."

"Did you know Sean's captaining?"

Mason's brows lifted. "Hell yeah, the Snowballs still?"

Sean's jaw tensed. Okaaay, not the reaction she was hoping for.

Mason reached out and took a flute of champagne from one of the passing servers. "I'd love to get back on the ice.

Can't be a priority right now, obviously." He motioned to the tray, and they both plucked up a stem.

Obviously. Kelty plastered on a smile.

Someone called Mason's name, and he held up a hand. "I'm being summoned."

Kelty lifted her drink. "To your big win."

Mason met her eyes, clinking his glass against hers then Sean's. "I hope we'll get to catch up more later. I should be able to escape the merry-go-round after about eleven. Maybe get some food, relax, and we can pick this up then?"

Kelty smiled, wrapping her arm around Sean's waist. "Might be past our bedtime."

Mason laughed, already moving into the crowd. "If you managed to tame Thompson, I'm impressed."

Sean waved him off, and Kelty turned him to her, taking a sip of her champagne. "Mm. He's worse than I remembered."

"You don't have to say that."

She kissed his jaw. "Arrogant ass."

Sean smirked. "He's a decent guy."

Kelty leaned closer. "He's probably hiding bodies in his basement. Like that movie with Hugh Jackman."

"What movie?"

"The magic one. Where he drowned himself every night."

"What—?"

"No, remember? He clones himself."

Sean shook his head. "Yeah. I remember the ending of the movie—"

"Shh. Don't think too hard about it. Just accept the immorality of Mason's rise to success." She circled her fingers around his wrist and pulled him toward the table next to the windows. "Now we're going to eat all the food purchased with his blood money."

They filled tiny black plates with aged cheeses, olives, marinated kebabs, and fruit skewers, then made their way to one of the couches past the bar.

"Right there." Kelty settled her plate on her lap and pointed to the far end of the room where lights glinted off dark glass. "That was the conference room, wasn't it?"

Sean popped an olive into his mouth. "The one and only."

"Does it still have tintable glass?"

His mouth curled. "You want a do-over?"

"I want you to *do* me over. The table. Yes."

Sean grinned, turning until his knee bumped hers. "Thank you."

Her chest warmed. "For what?" He raised an eyebrow, and Kelty flashed a cheeky smile. "Yeah, I know, but I want you to say it."

His hand slipped over her bare thigh. "For being here." He squeezed.

"Mm. You forgot 'for being super hot and hilarious—'"

Sean's hand slipped higher, and her breath caught. "Roof?"

Kelty's ears started ringing. The roof. Of course. That was where he was going to do it—the only place where it made sense for him to do it. That was where they'd first kissed. Damn it, that kiss still took up permanent residence in her brain. How he hadn't said a word, just pushed her up against the bricks and—

"Hey. You okay?"

Kelty blinked. "Hm?" She glanced down, realizing she held her plate in front of her with both hands like she was doing reps with a kettlebell. "Oh, yeah. Sorry. Definitely the roof."

Her pulse skipped as she tugged on Sean's hand, weaving them through the crowded room toward the coat check. There wasn't a line since it was still early in the evening, and in less than two minutes, they stood in front of the elevator with their coats on.

Another greeter intercepted them. A young woman in a

tailored suit, clipboard pressed to her chest like a shield. "Heading down?"

Kelty leaned into Sean. "Actually, we were hoping to sneak up to the roof. Just for a minute. We won't cause trouble."

The woman's brows pinched. "The roof isn't really—"

"Listen." Kelty leaned in conspiratorially. "I'm a lifestyle influencer, and I rank city skylines all over the country. If you don't let us up, Calgary won't get the opportunity to compete."

Sean coughed into his fist, disguising a laugh.

The greeter hesitated, lips twitching. "Fine. Straight up and straight back down. Five minutes, max." She hit the button, and the doors opened.

"You're amazing, thank you." Kelty tugged Sean toward the open elevator before the woman could change her mind.

The doors slid shut with a whisper, enclosing them in chrome.

Sean smirked. "You're going to have to see her again on the way down."

"I didn't say I was a *successful* influencer." Kelty grinned. "I could start a YouTube channel right now. Be legit."

"I'll be your first subscriber."

She leaned in and slipped a hand under his coat. "Founding members get special benefits."

Sean's thumb brushed over her hipbone as his hand curled around her waist like it was molded to fit. "Obviously."

She tipped her chin and peered up into his eyes, wondering if after seven and a half years she had them memorized. Could she properly describe them to a sketch artist? The exact color of green? The deep olive edging and the starburst pattern of umber around his pupils?

Kelty was going to marry him. Her heart fluttered. This couldn't be a more perfect night, Mason be damned.

The elevator dinged, and they exited. "Does that sound ever make you want a corn dog?" Kelty whispered.

"Ah, no."

"Right. Me either." Her dad always used to put them in the toaster oven, and the ding was disturbingly similar. She was classically conditioned.

The wind whipped her hair around her face as they pushed through the door to the rooftop. Sean grabbed her hand and pulled her to the railing, weaving around the industrial fans and boxes planted in the concrete.

The city was quieter than expected for a Friday night. No sirens or music, though lights were on in the office building across the street. Looking through the bright, shrunken windows with minimalist furniture and fake plants made her existential. Seeing a highly curated life through a snapshot, disconnected from time and space, no beginning or end. Pretty much how she felt every time she walked through Ikea.

Kelty sighed, taking in the snapshot in front of them. "That's depressing."

Sean gripped the railing. "Working late on the weekend. Who does that?"

She huffed a laugh. "I don't do it anymore."

He smirked, his eyes still trained straight ahead. There had to be a thousand things swirling through his head, but she'd learned that trying to force Sean Thompson to talk about something when he wasn't ready to was about as effective as nailing Jell-O to a wall.

"I'm sorry," she whispered. "It sucks that they didn't bring you in."

Sean grunted. "Probably would've said no."

She wanted to make some joke about how his ego couldn't have taken another hit like that, but bit back the comment. Instead, she sidled closer, leaning her head on his shoulder. "I love you."

The words were laced. *Talk to me. Let me in.* They were

good at sarcasm, excellent at banter. But the real conversations?

Kelty's cheeks heated. She knew the exact moment those started to feel off-limits.

"Come here." Sean tugged her into his arms, wrapping her in warmth. This feeling had to be her favourite. Like she was tucked behind the walls of a fortress. Sean's chin rested on the top of her head, and she closed her eyes, breathing in the crisp, clean scent of him.

His fingers threaded through her hair, pressing her cheek against his chest. The solid ba-dump of his heartbeat was almost hypnotic, pulling her out of her head and into that physical moment. It was strange. She could almost exist in two places at once without ever realizing she'd left her body.

Sean blew out a breath and relaxed his grip. "Ready?"

Kelty pulled back to look at him. "For what?"

He nodded toward the door.

Her mind zoomed in, feeling everything. The chill seeping into the tips of her ears, the end of her nose. The prickle of gooseflesh on her bare legs. "Leave?"

He blinked. "Unless you want to go back to the p—"

Kelty laughed. She stepped back and pressed her fingers to her temples. "You are—I don't even know. Do you enjoy torturing me?"

Sean's mouth opened then closed. His brow pinched. "Don't know what to say to that."

"The commitment is impressive, I'll give you that." She leaned back against the railing, crossing her arms in front of her. "If you're chickening out—"

"I'm a little lost." The confusion on his face seemed genuine. A flash of heat zipped from the crown of Kelty's head to her toes.

"Sean." She said his name with a tone of warning. This was becoming less funny by the second. When he didn't respond, it was as if someone pulled the tab on an inflatable life vest behind her ribs. She couldn't breathe.

The words erupted before her ribs cracked. "I saw the charge."

"What—?"

"On your credit card. For around four thousand dollars?" Was he going to make her spell it out? Beg him to get down on one damn knee and ask her?

Realization fell over his expression like the fade transition on a PowerPoint presentation. "That—" He scrubbed a hand over his mouth. "My dad asked me to buy something for him. For my mom. It's their anniversary . . . "

Sean's mouth kept moving. He was saying words, probably English words, but none of them computed. They rolled through her head like hieroglyphics, in one ear and out the other. *My dad asked me to buy something for him.*

The house she'd built card by card since catching sight of that purchase toppled. His standoffishness? Not because of her. His lack of discussion after the fight they'd had in Edmonton? Not because he was doing something about it.

Had she not made her feelings clear? Had she not broken down enough about what she wanted and how much she longed to take those next steps with him? Or did he hear every word she said and decided he didn't care?

Her legs moved before she gave the command.

"Kelt—"

"Don't." She slapped his hand away as she beelined for the door, her eyes burning, heels scraping against the concrete.

CHAPTER

Three

SEAN DIDN'T KNOW endings had a sound. The paper-shuffling, murmured voices, throat-clearing, and box taping. All the soundtrack needed was an occasional clang of a metal locker and the smell of wet concrete to take him right back to the moments before he'd walked out of the Blizzard locker room for good.

He stepped around reams of copy paper ready to load onto the dolly, muttering under his breath. Sharing space with another startup had seemed like a great idea when they'd set sail. Now it was just another stab of indignity. Their neighbours were still thriving, still holding their Friday foosball tournaments, while his team was dismantling desks and bubble-wrapping monitors.

Mason appeared at his shoulder, matching his stride, with his laptop tucked under his arm. "She's here. On her way to conference room three."

Sean grunted. "And you're telling me this because?"

"You're better with people."

Sean almost smiled. "Hilarious."

Mason flashed a cheesy grin. "That's why you married me."

Sean slowed and grabbed a pile of power strips from the ground. "Is there a reason you can't do this?"

"I need to get on the phone with the bank."

Sean raised an eyebrow, and Mason had the decency to look sheepish. "Fine."

Mason exhaled with relief as resentment crawled up the back of Sean's neck. He loved the guy, but Mason was the king of finding an alibi the second a task came up that wasn't his cup of tea.

But it was Mason who had vouched for him back when no one wanted to take a chance on an ex-hockey player with a patchy résumé. Mason, who understood what they were both missing after leaving their teams. Mason, who welcomed him into this rag-tag group with open arms and gave him a new team to root for.

If it had been anyone else, Sean would've walked months ago, cashed out what was left, and saved himself the humiliation of watching their work get sold off piece by piece. But Mason asked, and that was the difference. You didn't bail on the guy who'd stood by you when you were nothing. Even if it meant sticking around on a sinking ship long enough to make sure your friend got to the lifeboat first.

"Thanks, bud." Mason clapped a hand on his shoulder. "I would—" He stopped mid-sentence, and it only took Sean a split second to figure out why.

A woman with a smooth hourglass figure, tight pants, and dark hair layered in waves down her back stood at the end of the aisle peering at the glass in front of her. Conference room three. *That was the woman he was meeting with?*

Mason's grip tightened as he pushed off Sean, bolting

forward, but Sean saw it coming. He'd already grabbed the back of Mason's pants and yanked.

"What the hell?"

Sean grinned, passing him and turning to walk backward. "You've got that thing. With the bank."

Mason laughed and flipped him the bird. Sean passed a row of cubicles where one of the developers was pulling down her sticky notes. Rows of neon pink and yellow that used to look like strategy, now reduced to confetti. Someone else was folding their office plant into a cardboard box like they were sending it off to foster care.

Walking toward the conference room, his brain did what it always did when things went sideways: it tallied his failures on the scoreboard.

Motorcycle accident at nineteen. Game over on hockey, and with it, his dad's dreams, even though he never would've said as much. His parents had given up on pro hockey when they found out they were having his older brother, Carter. Neither of his brothers had a chance like he did. And he'd screwed it up.

So he went back to school. Got the business degree. Took the safe jobs until Mason pulled him back into the dream. This startup was supposed to change everything. His second chance. And now? Back to the drawing board. Again.

"Hey, is this—?"

"Conference room three. Yeah. You're in the right spot." Sean pushed the door open and held it for the drop-dead gorgeous woman in front of him, trying not to overtly check her out. But damn, she smelled good. The air around her seemed to be a degree cooler, laced with the scent of vanilla and something floral.

He wanted to taste it.

Not the best thought to have before discussing an acquisition.

The woman settled into her seat, opened her laptop, and

uncapped her pen with a flick before setting a notebook on the smoky glass table. "So. Inventory, hardware, software licenses, IP. I'll need the breakdown of what you've paid off and what's still leased."

Sean blinked. Straight to it then. "I didn't get your name."

"I didn't give it."

Before he could come up with some witty response to that, the door swung open behind him.

"Oh, hey. Just thought I'd check in and make sure you both connected." Mason leaned against the door frame, nonchalant, his arm blocking the door from shutting.

Sean's jaw flexed. "All good, bud."

"It's Kelty, right?" Mason's mouth quirked, his eyes warm. It was the same look he gave the woman at the Tim Hortons on the corner when he got his coffee in the morning. The one he slept with two weeks ago.

"Correct." The woman tapped her pen on the notepad. Her shoulders were ramrod straight, her hair tossed over her right shoulder.

Mason pushed off the frame and strode forward. "I'm Mason C—"

"I know who you are." Kelty smiled, ignoring the hand he'd thrust toward her. "Did you need something, or . . ."

Mason chuckled. "Nope. Just wanted to introduce myself."

"Hm. Thanks." Kelty never dropped eye contact.

Mason's confident facade slipped. "Alright, well, I'll leave you both to it." He turned and shot Sean a look that said, *I'm conceding the round, not the match.* Sean smirked, then took a seat across from Kelty as the door closed behind him.

He cleared his throat. "That was—"

"Don't say something right now to make it seem like we're buddy-buddy." She cocked her head to the side.

Sean opened his mouth, then closed it. If he thought she

was hot when s he walked in, her Scoville rating was now off the charts. "So."

"So." Her eyebrow quirked.

"Men want to sleep with you."

Kelty's eyes widened.

"I get it. Cockblocking straight out of the gates. Smart move."

She wet her lips. "I'm here to do a job."

"Right. And assholes like Mason don't make that easy." He leaned back in his chair, setting his phone on the table.

"You're not an asshole?"

"Oh, I'm definitely an asshole."

She let out an involuntary puff of air that bordered on a laugh. "At least you're honest."

"Ask me anything."

The pen stilled in her fingers. "About . . . the acquisition."

"Right." Sean leaned forward, resting his forearms on the table. "About the acquisition."

CHAPTER
Four

Present Day

PENNY'S HOUSE was the definition of cozy. The walls were a soothing grey, the couches in clean modern lines punctuated with pops of colour that brought whimsy into the modern space. In the kitchen, lit candles and spring-patterned hand towels infused the space with warmth. The three pints of ice cream sitting on the island solidified the homey ambiance.

The containers sweated rings onto the quartz as Penny prepared a mountain of toppings: rainbow sprinkles, crushed pretzels, coconut flakes, and a jar of homemade hot fudge.

Kelty sat on a stool, clutching a wadded tissue, trying to stop crying long enough to taste anything but snot.

"Okay." Penny peeled off the lid on the chocolate chip cookie dough. "Any requests?"

Kelty sighed. "Just give me a scoop of all three with fudge."

She nodded and started scooping. When they all had a

bowl in front of them and the ice cream was all safely back in the freezer, Penny and Emma took up their posts around the bend of the countertop.

Right. This was when she was supposed to start talking, but she couldn't figure out where to start. Everything with her and Sean was like the wires behind their computer desk. You couldn't find the beginning or the end, and the more you pulled on one cord, the tighter the tangle got.

"You went to that party tonight, right? The one for Mason's company?" Emma prompted.

Kelty nodded, tears already refilling her eyes. "Mm-hmm."

"Not great?"

She sniffed and forced a spoonful of ice cream into her mouth, wincing as it hit her sensitive front teeth. "No. It was great. That was the problem." She rehashed the night, their flirting, the whole bit about Mason.

"Oh, he definitely wanted you," Emma cut in. "Didn't Sean tell you about that?"

Kelty frowned. "About what?"

"When you first met at the office. Mason wanted you bad. He kept trying to bid."

Kelty thought back to that day. Mason peeking in. Yeah, he'd wanted to try something, but she'd shut it down.

Truthfully, she'd found Mason attractive. Obviously Sean, too. But Sean was intriguing. Mason was always talking, letting it all hang out. Sean sat back. Observed. And when he did speak, it was usually a gut punch. Ironic that his lack of words then had been a turn on. Now it made her want to strangle him with a phone charger.

"Yeah." Kelty took another bite, letting the ice cream melt until she could chew the balls of cookie dough. "They did have a bit of a sword fight back then."

"And when he came to visit." Emma's spoon clinked against her bowl.

Kelty's brows pinched. When he came to visit? That was a couple of years ago. "What do you mean?"

"Sean was pissed after you all went to dinner. He wouldn't say much, but the second I heard Mason was there, I knew that's what it was about. I asked him, and he got all . . . you know. Sean. He said Mason needed to keep his dick in his pants." She pursed her lips.

Penny snorted. "Does he have any other line?"

Kelty laughed. "Nope. That's his favourite." Her mind swung back around to the memory of that night at dinner with Mason. Sean had been standoffish, but that wasn't anything new. He'd tensed when Mason gave her a hug. And touched her knee. And—

Okay. So there were quite a few moments she hadn't been particularly tuned in to. Was that all last night was? Sean one-upping Mason? Showing him he'd won? At the time, she'd been happy to be his trophy girlfriend. Now the thought made her stomach twist.

Kelty's eyes brimmed with tears. She rehashed their moment on the roof and the alternate reality she'd been living in all night because of that credit card statement. "There's nothing I can do. He doesn't get it. I don't think he'll ever get it."

The words cracked something inside her, releasing years of battered and compressed emotions. How many times had she argued with herself? Convinced her doubting inner voice that Sean only needed time? That he *did* want the same things she did.

Now, instead of pushing away the hundreds of times Sean had clammed up or changed the subject when she or anyone else brought up marriage, she viewed them with eyes wide open. Instead of ignoring his avoidance of baby showers or pregnant bellies, even his own sister's, she accepted it for what it was.

Sean didn't want to get married. He didn't want to have

kids. Or maybe he just didn't want to do either of those things with her.

Tears spilled down her cheeks.

Emma dropped her spoon in her bowl with a clatter. "I want to kick him in the balls, you know?"

Penny snorted, then pulled Kelty into a hug. "Ditto."

Ball kicking, as fun as that sounded, wouldn't solve this problem. Kelty wasn't mad. She wished she could rouse anger or hatred or anything that wasn't this dead, empty void threatening to swallow her whole.

She was just sad. Deeply, soul-crushingly sad. "I love him," she whispered.

"Oh, babe. I know." Penny rubbed her back in slow circles.

The ice cream helped a little, but by the time Emma was yawning so hard she couldn't finish her sentences, Kelty still felt like road kill. How was it possible to be torn open and numb at the same time? To be both buried and floating outside of your body?

Emma straightened with a stretch, her sweatshirt riding up to reveal a slice of her growing stomach. "I need to go," she said, making a face. "I have a shoot with Lindsey and Vaughn first thing in the morning."

Kelty stood and hugged her, and a new, terrifying thought sent a shock down her spine. "Will I lose you?" she whispered, the words barely forming.

"What?" Emma pulled back to look at her. "No! Are you kidding? If Sean is too stupid to figure this out, we'll still be friends, Kelt. You're like family to me."

Kelty nodded, grateful for the words, but not fully buying it. Sure, they'd be friends now, but what about if Sean met someone new? What if he decided to marry her? Would Emma really want to hang around with his ex?

They walked Emma to the door, waited for her to text Tyler and tell him she was on her way, then watched until she was in the car and pulling away from the curb.

Penny led her back down the hall. "Guest room's ready. Fresh sheets."

Kelty snagged her bag from beside the couch. "Ironic."

"What?"

"A couple of years ago, it was you crashing on my couch."

The guest room was more than inviting with a plump duvet, soft lamplight, and a small vase of daisies on the dresser. Kelty needed to know they were fake. If Penny was procuring fresh flowers for her guest room on a regular basis, she wasn't sure they could still be friends.

"It's funny . . . " Penny stalled inside the door. "Sean always seemed . . . I don't know."

"Seemed what?"

Penny looked up. "Remember when he had that hamstring injury?" Kelty nodded. "He was so protective—said he'd knock some sense into Brett, and I told him it was me that was the problem. He said something about how that didn't matter. Brett didn't know how it worked yet." She winced. "I thought you two had it all figured out."

Kelty's eyes stung. "Yeah. So did I."

Their situation was idyllic on paper. Everything in their lives aligned. Their work schedules, their preferred recreational activities, their favourite restaurants. Over the past seven and a half years, their two separate lives had melded into one. All of her best friends were Sean's friends. Or his family, which was even worse. If she lost him . . . she lost all of it.

Kelty stared blankly at the off-white comforter, biting the inside of her cheek to keep from breaking down as the colourful life she'd curated faded to black and white. No more hockey games with the Snowballs. No more Sunday suppers. No more inside jokes or nights at the Dusty Rose or—

Penny stepped close and squeezed her elbow. "We're just down the hall. Text if you need anything."

Kelty nodded and shut the door behind her, then set her overnight bag on the chair and dug out a toothbrush. She pulled out her phone to find a text from her mom. Her stomach flipped.

Back at the hospital. Don't panic. Just wanted to let you know

Don't panic. That was laughable.

More info pls????

She watched the phone, every second stretching to what felt like ten. A minute went by. Two. Kelty started to pace. She could call, but if they were talking with the doctor, she didn't want to cause more stress.

Her whole life was falling apart. She should've gone back to Penticton the minute her dad was diagnosed. She waited for Sean instead, but now that had hit the fan, so what was the point? What was the point of any of it?

Kelty dropped her phone on the bed, beginning to hyperventilate. She grabbed a honey-mustard decorative pillow, pressed it against her face, and screamed.

CHAPTER
Five

SEAN bent low on the backcheck, legs pumping, the roar of the crowd fading into white noise in his head. His calves screamed. Lungs burned. He wanted it to hurt.

He hadn't slept more than half an hour the night before, the image of Kelty walking out the front door with a backpack playing like a highlight reel in his head. That and the expression on her face on the rooftop.

When he was sixteen, he'd contracted a doozy of a stomach bug. Knocked him out for a week, and even once he could keep food down, the idea of food gave him the shakes.

Walking back to the elevator and down to the parking garage felt like that.

Garrison, a winger for Mills Hoodie, cut across the blue line, but Sean shadowed him, stick angled, lungs clawing for oxygen. His body was half a second behind his brain, but he forced it, slashing to cut him off. The edge of his skate bit, his knees quivering under the strain, and the puck careened off his stick into the corner. He should have peeled for the bench. Every cell in his body was begging for it.

But that meant he'd have to think. Feel.

Instead, he slammed the boards and pinned the kid just

long enough for Darcy to scoop the puck and clear. By the time Sean pivoted back, his chest was a furnace, spots crowding the edges of his vision.

"Get the hell off the ice, Cap," Country chirped as he sprinted past.

Sean choked on a gasp. He gave in, nearly stumbling as he cut to the boards.

"Shit, Thompson. Whose dog did you kill?" André shoved a water bottle into his hands.

"It's almost playoffs."

André was already leaning over the boards, shouting something at Bowen.

He was glad he didn't hear the comment. The fact that they were gearing up for playoffs was exactly why he shouldn't be dragging his ass on the ice. A hundred percent effort, fast shifts. Wasn't that the speech he'd barked in the locker room?

The horn finally blasted. 1-0. Not the score he'd hoped for, but they'd pulled it out. That secured them a bye in the first round.

He threw off his helmet and forced himself off the bench and back onto the ice to tap gloves. Sweat dripped off his nose and chin. His only goal was to not puke on the centre line.

"Turn it up!" André was already grinding to a K-pop song in the dressing room when he pushed through the door and stalked to his locker.

"Hey, not sure if you noticed, but we won, bud." Suraj clapped him on the shoulder.

Brett gave him a sympathetic smile, and Tyler's eyes darted away as he grabbed his towel and strode to the showers. Sean yanked his locker open. He hated that they both knew, but it wasn't like he could expect Kelty to go radio silent with her friends. Thankfully, both of them had kept their mouths shut. So far.

Kelty hadn't texted or called all day. She was probably waiting for him to say something, but what the hell was he supposed to say? It wasn't his fault she misunderstood the situation. Probably his fault for not telling her, but with Mason's thing and the end of the quarter at work, they'd barely communicated about what time they were leaving for downtown.

He stripped off his jersey and gear, heaped it on the bench, and found an empty shower stall. He felt like an insect about to molt. His skin was too tight, everything inside him roiling and hot.

Thoughts rolled into his head as he washed the sweat off his skin. He couldn't let Kelty stay at Penny's, sneaking back in the house to switch out her clothes. He couldn't tell her to come back with him. But he could go to his parents so she could stay at their place. Though that would require him to endure an onslaught of questions that he couldn't come close to having any answers for.

He rinsed the shampoo from his hair, the suds slipping over his shoulders and stomach.

Then what?

The question clogged his throat. He coughed and scrubbed off the rest of his body, rinsed, and towelled dry.

"When were you going to tell us about the anniversary pot, eh?" Country sat on the bench, shirtless, a comb in his hand.

Sean frowned. The only anniversary he was aware of was his parents', and they definitely weren't involved with any kind of pot.

Boyd nodded. "Nora couldn't stop jabbering about it when I came in. Said it was a shit-tonne."

Sean shoved his gear to the side and reached for his boxers. "Sounds like a shit-tonne of nonsense." When was the last time he checked the league chat board? Was there something in there he'd missed?

Once his skivvies were on, he pulled out his phone and scrolled to the app. Then had to re-download it. He checked the boards religiously at the end of summer when they were leading into a new season, but playoffs were starting. He couldn't afford to get sucked into their chatter and head games.

" . . . No, I think she said it was best out of three."

"So the same?"

"Best out of five for the finals."

Boyd and Country went back and forth. When the last piece of the download pie filled, he opened the boards and scrolled. The announcement sat at the top, pinned in red.

Elite League 30th Anniversary Surprise

He squinted and skimmed. Holy shit.

Please disseminate to your teams! Elite League founder and commissioner Madelyn Wilson will be appearing for the playoffs held in Calgary this May. To celebrate thirty years of the league, there will be cash prizes for 1st ($50k), 2nd ($20k), and 3rd ($10k). The league will also invest up to $100k in your home rink for renovations.

Sean let out a low whistle. No wonder Nora was running her mouth. The pot *was* a shit-tonne, and renovations for the rink? He scrolled past the sponsor acknowledgements, noting that the Blizzard was listed as one of them, and honed in on the comments stacking up under the post.

Country leaned over his shoulder to read. "Am I reading that right? Fifty thou?"

"That can't be right, bud. More than double?" Darcy pulled a clean T-shirt over his head.

André raked a hand through his damp hair. "Is this on the team boards?"

Sean shook his head. "Captains only." He didn't know why the league made announcements like this private. They were all going to show their guys anyway.

André held out a hand, beckoning with his fingers. "Pretty please?"

Sean grunted and tossed him the phone. "Don't believe me?"

André smirked. "I want to see what Jord said about it."

Sean scoffed. "You two have nicknames for each other now?"

"I'd give you one if you let me." André waggled his brows, then peered at the screen. "All logistics, no trash talk. I'm disappointed in our leadership."

"No, that's perfect," Boyd leaned over to tie his shoe. "You can start the chaos."

Sean didn't have to say no for them to get the message. After what happened with Jordan, after everything Rhonda said to the team (but mostly to him), he hadn't chirped Wheatfill on or off the ice. It took all of his willpower, but Jordan and Rhonda were still together, and Rhonda was basically a part of the team.

"I know that look in your eye." Tyler slung his bag over his shoulder.

"Murder on his mind." Suraj winked.

Brett snorted. "Just make sure to get their signatures first."

"What would Chelios do?" Ryan held up his water bottle for a toast, and half the guys reached out to thunk plastic against plastic.

Fifty thousand dollars. Their roster was only at seventeen, which meant they'd each get almost three grand. That wasn't in and of itself life-changing, but upgrades to the locker rooms and showers would be.

Something twisted in his gut. *Playoffs.* The rush. The fight. And then nothing.

The end of the season always felt like a letdown, but the summer now loomed. He and Kelty had flights to Paris in June. It had taken her a year and a half to convince him that a ten-hour flight was worth seeing old cathedrals and eating the same chocolate croissants he could get from Éclaire de Lune.

The fact that he was thinking past the finals, that he was already puzzling out how they could cancel the trip, sliced deep between his ribs. Why wasn't he assuming the trip would be on? Why was he mentally erasing every plan they'd made when Kelty had barely walked out the night before?

He turned to face his open locker, rifling through his shit as if his clothes weren't sitting there in plain view. The answer to his question came quickly.

Because deep down, he'd known this night was coming.

Ever since Edmonton, the timer had been ticking. He just hadn't known exactly when the clock would run out. The hardest piece to swallow was that he could put the pin back in the grenade with one question and a gold band.

He knew exactly what he needed to do to fix this. He just couldn't do it.

"Oh, shit, sorry." André handed his phone back. "It popped up right as I clicked."

Sean rotated the phone and read the text from his brother.

> Hey. Been thinking about the parents' anniversary. I'm coming out with Alix and the girls for two weeks mid-April
>
> Taking advantage of cheap flights since our spring break is off norm

Remember Mom's dream? I want to make it happen. You in?

Emma responded before he finished reading the last sentence.

HELL YES. She'll never expect it since this is a random anniversary. Their 40th, they'd see it coming

Three dots. Another text from Carter.

Waiting to hear if Nate and Naomi are in. You, Tyler, Sean, and Kelty have the easy gig since you're local

Alarm bells went off in Sean's head. Mom's dream. Shiiiit, no. They were not—

"All good?" André slung his bag over his shoulder.

Sean glanced up, realizing the guys were all staring at him. "What?"

Tyler dropped his eyes, clearing his throat. "Ah, nothing. Just—if something's going on—"

"Nope." Sean clicked off his phone screen and set it on the bench next to his gear. He bent over, shoving his foot into his pant leg.

Brett ran a hand over the back of his neck. "Right. Good game tonight."

"Yep." Sean didn't turn his head. *You, Tyler, Sean, and Kelty . . .* He should say something. Give some words of encouragement. Round one of the playoffs started in April.

Nothing came. Thoughts buzzed in his head, zipping around like drones. None of them hockey or playoff related.

His parents loved the Amazing Race. How many times had his mom mentioned she wanted to be on that show? Then, just like every time his parents were mentioned in a group chat with Kelty, the guilt set in.

"When's the last time you texted them, Sean? When have you suggested we go out and visit?"

Her words were barbs that hadn't released their hooks since Edmonton. It would've been easier to extract them if they were false.

". . . and then I asked my chatbot how to best carb load for the game," Curtis said, laughing as he packed up.

"You specifically?" Suraj looked skeptical.

"Bud, it doesn't have my genetic profile."

André shrugged. "It probably pulled it from Foothills." Curtis frowned. André looked up, buttoning his jeans. "Where you dropped off your test tubes. Because four kids wasn't enough—"

Sean snorted as Curtis threw a roll of tape in André's direction. He finished dressing and waited for the guys to filter out, then picked up his phone and typed out a quick response.

Not sure we'll be available

Playoffs at that same time

It was the truth. At least the truth he wanted to tell. He shoved his phone in his pocket, packed up, and headed for the tunnel. The walk to the parking lot seemed to take half an hour. When he finally got to his truck, he dropped into autopilot, stowing his gear and pulling out of the parking lot. When he stopped in the driveway, he barely remembered any part of the drive home.

He stepped onto the sidewalk, and the haze in his head burned off in seconds. Emma stood on the step, arms crossed over her chest, brows pinched. He scanned the street and found her car parked by the curb.

Sean blew out a breath and pulled his bag from the backseat. "I didn't order pizza."

"You couldn't afford my delivery fee."

He pulled out his keys to hit the lock button, momentarily considering getting back in and peeling out. Staying at a hotel for the night.

"You know I'll follow you," Emma snapped, reading his thoughts.

Fine. Better to get this over with.

CHAPTER
Six

THE CONFERENCE TABLE was littered with lined, yellow legal pad pages. Mostly Kelty's notes, because at a certain point, writing numbers down with a pen and paper was more efficient than duplicating spreadsheet rows. Kelty sat cross-legged in the leather chair, her blazer abandoned on the backrest, sleeves shoved up, highlighter tucked behind her ear.

Across from her, Sean slouched with his elbows braced wide on the table, scrolling through another set of asset sheets on his laptop. His tie was long gone, shirt rumpled. "Tell me again why we're categorizing by purchase year when half this shit is already depreciated?"

Kelty didn't look up. "Because the buyer wants clean buckets." She drew a box around the six-figure number in front of her. "Tidy little boxes."

Sean leaned back, staring at the ceiling like he half

expected an angel to appear and save him. "It's a fire sale, not a showcase."

"Yet they still want it gift-wrapped." She flashed a tired smile.

Sean ran a hand through his hair, and it stayed mussed, boyish and carefree. *She liked it like that.* "Four MRI service contracts, three still active, one terminated." He rubbed a thumb over his lip.

"Expenses reconciled?"

He gave her a sidelong glance, and her mouth quirked sideways. "Kay. I'll write this up and get it to you all . . ." Kelty stifled a yawn while closing her laptop, then checked the calendar on her phone. "Probably Tuesday."

"Unacceptable."

She scoffed. "Mmhmm."

He grinned, and her defences sagged a little. All week, they'd sat in this conference room, and she'd succeeded in keeping things utterly professional. Sean, to his credit, didn't push. He didn't make things awkward. Even when Mason kept popping in with increasingly expensive coffee. He hadn't even bothered to ask whether she drank it or not, which she didn't.

Kelty stood and picked up her bag, repacking her things. "I heard something about you."

Sean's brow raised. "If it's about the thong and the maple syrup, I had nothing to do with it."

She snorted. It was past nine, and her filter was wearing thin. "Oh, yeah, I heard that was all Mason." She slung the strap of the messenger bag over her shoulder. "What about the part where you were drafted to the Blizzard?"

The glint in Sean's eyes faded. His smile slipped. He wet his lips and pushed his chair back from the table. She could see it in him. The build of a professional athlete. He was at least six foot two with broad shoulders and thick arms. His collared shirt stretched in all the right places. Not that she'd been checking him out, it was just hard not to notice. Or wonder what he'd look like in a wet T-shirt contest.

"Yep. Didn't ever hit the ice with them, though."

She'd heard about that too, but wanted to hear the story from his perspective. "Why not?"

He plucked his phone from the conference table. "Motorcycle accident. Took out my wrist."

"Kind of an important part."

"For hockey?" Sean met her eyes and waited a beat before saying, "Yeah. Second only to ankles."

Her stomach swooped like she'd just tipped over the drop on a rollercoaster. Was she making this up? Sometimes he said things like that, and she swore the hesitations, the twitch of his lips, and the held breath were all purposeful. But then he'd move on as if nothing happened, and she wondered if it was all in her head. If she wanted his comments to be laced with subtext.

Maybe she needed to get out more. To go dancing, wear a slutty top, and put on lipstick for the first time in six months. To throw caution to the wind and make out with some guy in the parking lot.

"Something funny?" Sean asked.

Kelty blinked, realizing she'd been grinning. "No. Sorry. Just thinking."

"About what?"

Hm, where to start. With how her little weekend fantasy was more fictional than the last novel she'd read about a dragon? How the dating scene in Calgary was like sitting in a too-warm plane on the tarmac while the pilot came on the intercom every fifteen minutes saying, "Looks like it will just be a little longer, folks" over and over again until you wanted to strangle yourself with the flotation device strapped to your foam booster seat?

She sighed, tucking her hair behind her ear. "I don't think you'd get it."

Sean rounded the table, beating her to the door. "Try me."

Kelty scanned the office floor through the glass. "Are we the last ones here?"

He shrugged. "Probably."

"And you feel fine about that."

His jaw ticked. "Why wouldn't I?"

"Like I thought." She waited for him to open the door, then strode to the aisle, cutting a path through the cubicles.

Sean hurried to catch up. "That's all I get?"

She nodded and picked up her pace. "Yep."

"I said I feel fine about it."

"I heard you the first—"

"Because I trust you."

Kelty's mouth opened and closed like a goldfish, and she slowed, turning to look at him. Alright. She was listening.

"A friend of mine at university went to a party and ended up in a girl's room. He said they only fell asleep, but two weeks later, she filed a police report." Sean shifted on his feet. "Since then, I don't stay anywhere alone with a woman I don't know," he finished.

Kelty stared at him. Not at all the response she'd expected.

After a moment, Sean asked again, "What was so funny?"

Whatever remained of her filter fizzled with her inhale. "That I'm going to drive home and probably not leave my apartment until Monday morning, but then I'll explain to my mom how it's impossible to meet anyone."

Sean grunted. "You could just be honest. Say you're afraid of commitment." He smirked, and the corner of Kelty's mouth lifted.

"Wow. Best compliment you ever gave me."

"You're welcome."

She wet her lips. "Well. When you mentioned trust, I

didn't think that was possible since we barely know each other, but clearly—

"It's the shoes."

Kelty's eyes flew wide. "What?"

"They look too uncomfortable for someone who wants to be in a relationship."

A laugh burst out of her, and she nearly dropped her bag. "These are the perfect blend of comfort and style." She held out her painted toes peeking through the cut out on her leather sling back.

"And you read and internalize sales copy. Another red flag." Sean waited for a reaction. If he was hoping for anger or shock, he wasn't going to get it. This was the most intriguing conversation she'd had in weeks.

Kelty's face split with her smile. "So what's wrong with you? Why aren't you with someone?"

"Who says I'm not?"

Her cheeks heated, her eyes blowing wide. "Oh, I'm so sorry, I didn't—"

"Kidding," he interjected. She froze mid-apology, and Sean laughed. "Sorry."

"Just wanted to make me feel like an asshole?"

"Don't pretend you didn't walk into that."

Kelty gave him another long look, then started toward the elevator bank.

"I might walk over to The Med for dinner," Sean said behind her.

She reached out and hit the down button. "And you're telling me this because . . ."

"You asked what's wrong with me. I like garlic in my food."

She snorted. "Oh. Instant pass."

"Right?"

"Although, if she likes garlic, too—"

"I should've specified. I require excessive amounts."

"Ah. So the overall stench—"

"Bleeds from my pores. A day and a half minimum."

"Mm."

The elevator dinged, and they both stared at the doors, waiting for them to slide open. When they did, Kelty stepped on.

"They do have other food there." Sean moved in next to her.

"Besides straight garlic cloves?"

"Right. And for anyone not sleeping with me, being present at the time of ingestion isn't harmful."

"Good to know."

The doors slid closed, and without intending to, Kelty breathed in, trying to catch his scent. What she got wasn't garlic. It wasn't off-putting in any way. It was subtle cologne and clean soap.

"You have to get closer," Sean murmured. "Even though this is a closed box—"

"I wasn't—I don't know what you're talking about."

The doors opened on the ground floor, and Sean stepped out, stretching his arm over the sensors. "There are usually two to four chairs at the table I sit at."

Kelty's feet were glued to the floor. "Seems reasonable."

"And again, totally safe."

"Right. Because I'm not sleeping with you."

He smirked. "Best compliment you ever gave me."

There it was. That flash of heat through her inner thighs. The elevator doors pushed against his arm, clunked, then slunk back into their casing.

"Well. Something to consider." Kelty's stomach growled. She was strapped in, locked into place by that stare. When he got like this—she didn't even know what *this* was—it was like his eyes turned into heat-seeking missiles.

"I can show you where it is. For future reference." Sean nodded toward the door to the street.

Kelty swallowed hard. This wasn't a date. He wasn't asking her to come in with him, he was simply showing her around. They still had a week of meetings, and she'd most likely end up working after hours again before wrapping everything up. It would be good to know what restaurants were available. "Okay."

CHAPTER
Seven

PRESENT DAY

SEAN SHOVED the door open harder than he needed to, and Emma breezed in behind him, dropping her shoes to the entryway tile with a thunk. The emptiness of the dark rooms sank into him. Kelty usually had the lights on. She usually texted him about dinner plans, or at least texted him, period. Checking his phone after the game and finding texts from his family instead of from her had knocked the wind out of him. Even before he'd realized what Carter was asking.

"Sean." Emma stalked into the living room, folding her arms and waiting for him to finish unpacking his gear. He needed to air it out in the garage overnight.

Sean took his time. He made sure his jersey and socks were right side out before tossing them in the wash pile. Then hung his pads with care on the hooks in the garage. When the door swung shut behind him and he had nothing else to unload from his bag, he forced himself to meet her glare.

"Are you going to tell me what happened?" Emma asked.

That was a stupid question. She wouldn't be there if Kelty hadn't already told her something, if not everything. "Cut the bullshit, Emma." He strode toward the kitchen.

"No, *you* cut the bullshit." She stormed after him. "You're seriously not going to participate in putting this together for Mom and Dad?"

Sean froze. Huh. That was not the issue he expected her to die on her hill for. "I didn't say that."

"Pretty much did." Emma held up her phone screen. "You know the Amazing Race has been her dream ever since the show launched."

Sean pulled the fridge door open and snatched a beer. "You know how much playoffs consume my life."

"Yeah, and this doesn't have to be a distraction. Most of the work is going to be in the next couple of weeks—"

"We start round one next weekend."

"It's round *one*, Sean. Who are you playing, Dr. Quinn? You'll win even if you don't show up and Tyler plays left handed."

"Maybe not. They're only sitting a few slots below us." Both of them had a bye first round because of their seeding.

Emma rolled her eyes. "Whatever, you know it's about match ups."

Sean opened his beer with the bottle opener attached to the underside of the island counter. Kelty had that installed a few years ago on his birthday.

"These are your parents. Your mom and dad who've been freezing their asses on metal bleachers for you since your boxers showed out the top of your pants. This would make mom's *life,* and you know it." Emma didn't give him a chance to respond. "Also, onto the next topic. You and Kelty have been together for *seven years.*"

Almost eight, but he wasn't going to correct her. "Well aware."

"Then you're also aware she's the best thing that ever happened to you."

Sean took a swig of beer, and Emma ground her teeth.

"Fine. I'll ask you straight up. Why don't you want to get married?"

"I'm not having this conversation with you."

"Right. Stuff it aaaaall down. That tactic has been ultra effective so far."

He took another long draw on the bottle, trying to hide the tightening of his jaw. That comment stung. Mostly because Kelty had hurled something similar at him before walking out the door.

Emma leaned on the counter. "I don't get it! She's done everything for you, Sean. What more could you want?"

It wasn't about what he wanted. Kelty had been very clear about that in Edmonton. She'd asked about going out to Penticton, and he hadn't understood what she was asking. He thought it was a theoretical, not a we-never-see-my-parents-and-I'm-pissed-about-it situation.

Could he have been more proactive? Definitely. But her parents didn't enjoy doing anything. Their idea of a visit was sitting around on comfortable chairs with mugs of tea, talking for hours. It made him antsy.

Sean swallowed slowly, willing his anger to settle. He couldn't drop mitts with his sister in the kitchen, as much as he wanted to. He was seconds away from spouting some bullshit about how he didn't get involved in her relationships, so she needed to stay out of his. Then he remembered his chats with Bowen when he first joined the team. He didn't have a leg to stand on.

Emma groaned and spun on her heel, pulling out a chair from the kitchen table and dropping into it. "*Sean.* You'd really rather ignore this and lose her?"

That was a bucket of ice water in his face. *Lose her?* The pinched nerve in his L4 started to throb. That's all he'd been trying to do for years. Not lose her. Not screw this up. He'd been working his ass off trying to hide that she was way out of his league in a thousand different ways. To hide that he was terrified of the moment when she looked around and realized she deserved better.

Now, here that moment was, and he was supposed to be surprised? Supposed to fight it or convince her to stay when he had zero leverage? "I'm tired. I need to—"

"Sean, for the love of all that's holy, talk about your damn feelings."

"Let's talk about feelings when I didn't just get home from a game."

"And when would that be, exactly? You're always coming home from a game or a practice."

"Not always."

Emma ignored him. "Is that the excuse you gave to Kelty?"

"That's not fair." Anger rolled through his middle like an unfurling flag, speeding up and snapping at the edges.

"Seems pretty fair considering you let her walk out of here with only—"

"What, I should've tackled her to the floor?" Heat seared the skin under his collar.

"This isn't hockey. You could've—"

"You don't think I wanted to stop her?" Sean slammed his glass down on the counter. "I had no idea what the hell to say! She thought I was going to propose. She wants me to propose, but I'm not—" He sucked in a breath at a flash of a memory.

Every Sunday when they were growing up, they sat in the family room and watched family videos his parents had recorded over the years. First on a handheld recorder with tapes, then later on a digital camera, before the advent of smartphones.

He hated it. Dreaded the whole tradition. Every week,

he'd try to find an excuse so he didn't have to sit there with his family and watch the same thing over and over again.

"Sean, do you want to try flipping a pancake?"

"Here, Sean, follow me, I'll carve a path."

"Sean, I'll teach you. Just jump."

No. The answer was always no. A tantrum when he was a toddler. A shake of the head when he was in elementary school. An excuse when he was in middle. Every shot brought back the feeling of his heart pounding out of his chest. His skin flushed hot pink under the scrutiny of his parents or siblings.

Then, when he'd finally gotten the courage to take the leap and fight for the things he wanted—to put his life and heart on the line—every fear he'd had came true. He'd failed. Over and over again.

It hadn't been worth it.

Sean looked up to find Emma watching him, her eyes shimmering with tears. "Don't—I can't take you crying right now." He scrubbed a hand over his jaw, his ribs too tight to draw a full breath. Guilt and shame washed over him. She wasn't even out of her first trimester yet. That meant she was vulnerable, and here he was stressing her out. Making her cry.

Emma swiped at her cheeks. "Well, I can't take you self-destructing right now, so I guess we're even."

He read everything in her expression. The worry. Disappointment. Fear. "I'm not in that place again, Ems."

"I don't believe you."

"I promise—"

"I don't believe you, Sean."

He twisted his glass on the counter, the pressure in his chest choking. "Well, you're going to have to." He turned and stalked to the bedroom, closing the door behind him.

The silence filled in like concrete. Heavy and cold. The bed looked exactly as it had when he'd left that morning. The bedspread was pulled tight the way Kelty made it last because he hadn't gotten in under the sheets.

Kelty's side of the dresser still held her jewelry dish and that stupid candle that was supposed to smell like a volcano, whatever the hell that meant. Her shirt was tossed over the low bench at the end of their bed.

He stripped, tossed his clothes in the hamper, and pulled on sweats. Every piece of the normally comforting nightly routine felt mechanical and empty. Brush teeth. Rinse. Use the toilet. Flush.

He returned to the bedroom and was about to turn out the lights when he thought better of it and instead walked into his closet. They each had one. A narrow walk-in with built-in organization. He always kept his door shut since Kelty didn't like to see the disorganization. It had almost gotten messy enough for him to feel the urge to clean. Almost.

Stepping over a pile of old gear he needed to sort through, Sean reached for a small tin sitting in the back corner of the shelf behind his folded sweaters. He pulled it out and wrestled off the top.

His heart picked up speed as he dipped his fingers in, rustling through its contents. This was something he used to look at all the time. The small metal spoon, the polished rock, the tiny, perfect shell. He moved a small swatch of fabric and picked up the item he'd been looking for. A miniature piece of sushi. Definitely factory made, but he wasn't ever going to tell Kelty that.

He flipped it in his fingers, then set it back in the tin and closed the lid. He probably wouldn't get to tell Kelty a lot of things.

Sean replaced the tin and lay down on the bed, pulling the blanket folded at the foot over himself. Thankfully, he'd never been one to struggle with sleeping. Even when his mind circled his issues like a vulture. Somehow, his brand of over-thinking worked like a sedative instead of adrenaline. Perfect for sleep. Not so great on the ice.

His phone buzzed, and he cursed under his breath. It was still on the washroom countertop. He bolted up and rushed out of the bedroom, reading the lock-screen notification as fast as possible.

Not Kelty.

"Siblings +" was the name of the group chat. The "+" entered the title when Alix married Carter. Tyler was added after Emma announced they were expecting, even though they technically weren't married yet. Ironic that she was lecturing him about it. He wasn't pissed he'd been wrong about Tyler, but it wasn't making him look any better. *If Bowen of all people could commit, why couldn't he?*

CARTER

> Nate and Naomi are in, so we're a go. Alix put together an initial plan. Look it over and tell us what you think

EMMA

> WOW. This is incredible. What can Tyler and I help with?

Over the top enthusiasm. Another dagger.

Sean tapped on the attached file and landed in a spreadsheet. Columns and rows with dates, notes, and assignments. Carter and Alix had gone full project manager. The race would span the middle two weekends in April with different "legs" scattered across Calgary and Canmore. Each stop was tied to a piece of his mom and dad's story—Douglas University, where they'd met, the rink where Rob had played in the first Elite League games, the concert hall where Sharla had performed her first solo. Challenges were designed around those memories with some daredevil shit he never in a million years would've chosen for his parents.

Tyler and Emma were handling logistics and permissions, while Sean and Kelty—

He blew out a breath. Carter wanted to task them with designing the physical clues and testing every challenge for timing and difficulty. On location.

What the hell kind of time commitment would that be? Emma's words came back to him. *These are your parents. This would make Mom's life.*

She wasn't wrong. Sharla Thompson loved The Amazing Race, but more than that, she loved her family. She loved seeing her children together, whether they were all sitting around the dinner table or talking on a video call. It didn't matter. Giving her two weekends of that without any extras would send her over the moon.

He couldn't do his assignments alone. But suggesting he work on tasks and locations with anyone else would set off warning bells. His parents loved Kelty. He couldn't throw a wet blanket over their celebration by airing their dirty laundry. And cutting her out felt like a shitty move. She was basically part of the family.

That thought sent a shock down his spine. Before he could process the irony of it, a text popped up on the screen.

Kelty

Anything for Rob and Shar

CHAPTER

Eight

IT WAS Sunday Supper at the Thompsons. Kelty had debated all morning whether she should go or not, but ultimately decided that showing up was better than not. She wasn't trying to pretend her relationship with Sean was hunky dory. She just didn't feel the need to make drama when she still wasn't sure what her staying at Penny's meant.

Had she left because she *wanted* it to be over? Had she left as an ultimatum? Had she left because of everything in Edmonton, or was it the past three years adding up and that had only been the final straw? Her insides felt like Christmas lights that had been tangled and left in storage. Every emotion and thought was twisted around another, and she couldn't find the ends.

Now she was staring the fact that her dad had another episode with his atrial fibrillation in the face. She'd talked through the medication changes and options with her mom that morning, not that she was any help. All the options sounded crappy to her.

She wasn't going to pretend that living next to her parents was a lifelong, burning desire. For most of her adult life, phone calls and once-a-year treks to BC had been enough.

Her family wasn't close-knit. Her older brother barely spoke to her or their parents, partially because he lived in Asia, fourteen hours ahead, and had for the last ten years. Mostly because she was convinced he had high-functioning autism and didn't know how to build relationships.

But she felt it now. The need to be home. To be with them while her dad was sick.

Yet here she was. Standing on the Thompsons' doormat.

The familiar scent of a home-cooked meal wafted over her before she knocked. A roast in the oven, butter glossing something on the stove, yeast from rolls browning behind glass.

Had Sean told his parents what happened? Had Emma? Would her being here cause more of a problem than staying away? She wilted at the thought, but Rob opened the door before she could chicken out and retreat.

"There she is," he said, his burly arms shooting out for a hug. He half-lifted her over the threshold.

"Hi," Kelty managed, toes catching on the runner. The entryway breathed family with a line of scuffed shoes under the bench and a row of framed school photos of each of their kids.

If she wondered why she showed up, this was why. Everything she'd wished her family was growing up existed between these walls. At the Ice Centre and One Place after the games. But, without realizing it, she'd given up handfuls of her own life to wrap her arms around this world, and it didn't feel quite right anymore.

Laughter swelled from the kitchen, and she looked up. Sean stood in the archway between rooms, a beer sweating in his hand. In less than a second, she took in everything about him. He hadn't shaved. Dark stubble shadowed his jaw, and there were thumbprints of fatigue beneath his eyes. He flicked a glance toward the door, blinked when he caught the shape of her, and looked away so fast, it snapped like an elastic band to her wrist.

"I was surprised when Sean showed up without you." Rob stepped back so she could remove her shoes.

Kelty smiled. "Yeah, I—"

"Oh, he said you had a few things to finish up. It's not a problem, we're just glad you're here."

Kelty nodded, pressure building at her temples. So. He hadn't told them. That was information.

Her heart thrummed as she followed Rob toward the kitchen. There was only one way in. Through the arch. Past Sean.

She held her breath and slid past him like they'd rehearsed it. Sean turned a little to the left, shifting the picture on the wall as if he'd noticed it was off-centre. As far as she knew, he'd never paid attention to frame symmetry in his life.

Kelty said a louder-than-necessary hello to Emma, scurrying past the island to jump into the conversation she was having with Rhonda and Jenna in the dining room. Penny and Brett had gone to a church service that morning and hadn't been available as emotional support friends. Emma promised she'd be there on time, and she'd come through.

"You made it." Emma's eyes glistened as she forced a smile and gave her a hug.

"Yep, as always." Kelty couldn't think about the emotion behind Emma's reaction. She was already teetering on the edge of tears at any given moment. For the next three hours she needed to disassociate, to embrace short-term memory loss, or she wouldn't be able to get through this.

"I can barely reach you past the boobs," Kelty said, pulling back and checking her out.

Rhonda snorted. "Don't get her started. She's offered to flash us twice already." Rhonda pulled her into a hug next. "Girl, I haven't seen you in weeks."

"Kay, the boobs are only going to be cool for another few weeks. Then my belly will be big and they'll look smaller."

Emma pulled her shoulders back, staring at her chest. "They're just so fun. I had no idea."

Jenna sighed. "Not all of us get to experience that particular benefit."

Rhonda smirked. "Well, for those of us who get to live with it full time, I can tell you, it's not all fun and games. Plus, your boobs will be perky in ten years when I have to roll mine up from my knees."

Jenna laughed, moving around Rhonda for her hug, then peeking through the arch to get eyes on Hope with Country in the living room.

Kelty followed her gaze. "She's getting so big."

Jenna nodded. "I know. It's diabolical."

Without warning, Sharla shrieked and threw her hot pad on the counter, rushing to the front door.

"Uh, she didn't respond like that when I arrived," Emma muttered, rushing past them to see what the hubbub was about. The three of them followed to see Sharla throwing her arms around a petite, brunette woman. She wore leopard print pants, a black sweater tank, and a camel-coloured leather jacket.

And the man beside her? He was a little shorter than Rob, but broad-shouldered and built like a linebacker. Rob clapped him on the back, both of them talking over each other.

"Is that—?" Country mouthed to Jenna from the living room.

She was already nodding. "How the hell do your parents know Logan Kemp?"

Emma turned, grinning. "They went to school together at Douglas. Did we not mention that? I feel like we would've mentioned that."

Jenna's jaw dropped. "No, you sure as shit didn't mention that, Emma Thompson."

Emma's grin widened as she ran to the entryway after her mom. Rhonda and Kelty devolved into laughter.

It hadn't been as obvious to Kelty at first as it was to Jenna, but yes, that was most definitely Logan Kemp. Blizzard legend.

"That man racked up 742 points over twelve seasons with an even split of goals and assists," Jenna hissed. "He wore the "A" for seven of those years, captained for two, and played in five All-Star games. Twice he finished top ten in the league for power-play goals."

"Thank you, personal hockey encyclopedia."

Jenna bit her lip, barely listening. The greetings and introductions were still unfolding in the front hall. Country already left his post with Hope, turning things over to André and Grace so he could be next in the queue.

"Why is he here?" Kelty asked.

"Oh, I don't know, probably because his jersey is being retired at the Saddledome in two weeks. Country and I talked about it on our stream yesterday." Jenna ground her teeth. "Emma could've said something then."

Rhonda nudged her. "Maybe she didn't know. Seems like they were all surprised by them showing up. Well, maybe not Rob."

Rob stood with his hands on his hips next to Logan, looking like a cat who'd just placed a dead vole on the mat as a gift. Kelty's eyes slid to Sean, now turned in the archway. Did he know this was happening?

"No, we have a hotel," the woman next to Logan was saying.

"But we have extra rooms here." Sharla pointed at the stairs.

"I think those will be occupied, won't they?" The woman turned to Rob. His eyes twinkled, and Sharla clapped her hands over her mouth.

"What did you do, Rob? Rob—"

"I'll tell you after dinner." He laughed and threw an arm over his wife's shoulders.

"You will tell me right now!" She spun to face him, then turned to Emma and Sean. "Are you two in on this? Is that why you came early, Sean? Did you—?"

Rob leaned in and whispered something in her ear.

Sharla slapped a hand on his chest. "You better not be shitting me."

The room erupted with laughter. Sharla Thompson rarely swore, but when she did, it was worth the wait. Rob took her face between his hands. "I would never." He kissed her lips. "Everyone will be here by next Friday night."

"What about—?"

"All of them."

"Even Nate?"

Rob nodded. "Nate, Carter, Liza, and Rachel." He paused a moment. "And Maddie and Chase."

That was when Sharla started to cry.

———

Kelty got the lowdown over dinner. All of Sean's siblings plus his parents' best friends from university were converging on Calgary over the next week.

It was a series of fortunate events. Logan's jersey being retired, the anniversary playoffs for the Elite league—apparently, Sharla's friend from Douglas started the league, which was intimidatingly badass. With the Thompsons' own anniversary in April, Rob along with Sean's oldest brother, Carter, had cooked up the biggest reunion they'd ever had.

"Are you really okay with all this?" Emma whispered as she reached past Kelty to snag the empty water pitcher.

Kelty placed another set of used utensils on her pile of dirty plates. "Of course. This is about your parents."

"Well, yeah, but they wouldn't expect you to—"

"I want to help." Kelty hoisted the whole stack of dishes from the table. "Sean and I can figure this all out in a few weeks after their anniversary." She said it with confidence, even though her stomach fluttered like a dragonfly was trapped inside. *Why had she said yes so quickly on the group chat?*

She was angry with Sean, and she couldn't see around this impasse. Sean didn't want to get married and start a family. He'd proven that repeatedly, and she was finally ready to admit that she did

So was this for her? Was she in this for Rob and Sharla or was she clinging to this last family experience because she knew it could be over?

The harder she pulled on those cords, the tighter the tangle.

She cleared the rest of the dining room table with Emma, then moved on to the fold-out tables in the living room. Rhonda and Penny were working on the kitchen table when they brought in the last load of dishes, and Kelty quickly slid into place at the sink to wash. Or dry. Whatever would keep her occupied and not sitting across from Sean with nothing to do. Or to look at besides his face.

Her miscalculation was obvious within seconds. Sean had been crouching, finding the dish soap under the sink to refill the dispenser, and she hadn't seen him until it was too late.

"Hi." He lifted the jug of soap and stood.

"Hi." Her heart felt like a medieval battering ram trying to break through her ribs. Before she could make some excuse and scurry away, Shar breezed into the kitchen.

"You two don't need to do the dishes, I can—"

"We've got it, Mom." Sean didn't break eye contact, and Kelty's cheeks began to burn.

Shit. If she walked away now, Sharla would know something was up. She mustered a "Mmhmm" as she turned her back to the island and spread the dish towel over the countertop.

"I'll wash, you dry?" Sean murmured.

Kelty nodded. The dishwasher was already running, and they only had a few pots and pans, bowls, and the place setting stragglers she'd just brought in with Emma. It wouldn't take long. Then she could escape back to Penny's, or better yet, stop by the house and switch out some clothes before Sean returned.

"I'm going to stay here," Sean said as he filled the sink.

Kelty's brow pinched. Had he just read her mind? Did he know she needed to grab a few things and was offering her time? "I don't need much. I'll stop by—"

"No, I'm going to stay here for the next couple of weeks. While my family's in town. So you can have the house."

Something twinged in her midsection. She didn't know it wasn't what she wanted him to say until the words were out of his mouth. Disappointment and a surprising flash of terror made her pulse speed. It was as if they'd both strapped in on a roller coaster car the other night and now all she could do was watch it plummet to the ground.

Tears stung the corners of her eyes. "Sounds good." It didn't sound good. None of this sounded good. She ached to reach out and hold him—be held by him—but instead she took the soapy plate from his hands and rinsed.

"I haven't told them but—"

"No." Kelty shook her head. "Don't. This is about them right now."

Sean nodded, using the scrub brush on a small frying pan. "Right."

Right? He said it with that tone he always used. Pandering with a hint of sarcasm. "What do you mean?" She kept her voice low. Pleasant.

"Uh . . ." he passed her the pan. "That you're right."

"About what?"

He flicked his eyes to hers. "Whatever you want, Kelt."

Pure, hot rage flashed across her bones. "Mm. Okay, so this is what we're doing. You're going to play the victim? Pretend this is all my fault?"

"That's not—"

"Don't," she hissed, her hands getting a little aggressive with the drying cloth. She glanced over her shoulder to make sure they were alone. "I may have misunderstood the charge on your credit card, but this?" She motioned between the two of them. "Is not only my fault."

She wanted to say it wasn't her fault at all, but she'd heard enough Bréné Brown snippets to know that wasn't true. It was her fault for not asking for what she wanted. It was her fault for not setting boundaries. It was her fault for second-guessing herself and being such a damn pacifist when it came to the subjects that actually mattered to her.

Sure, it was easy to tell Sean to apologize to Emma or his team. It was no problem to tell him she was going to cook vegetables and he sure as hell better eat them, or push him to get Christmas gifts for his parents.

But give her something? Apologize to her? Tell her all the things she wanted to hear? She may as well have been mute over the past two-thirds of a decade.

"Did I say I was blaming you?" Sean's voice was rough.

"You didn't have to say it. You're *acting* like it."

Sean scrubbed out a bowl, water and suds clinging to his hands and wrists. She loved his hands. There was something about them that always turned her on. He kept his nails short and clean, and the sheer size of them . . . the masculinity of his knuckles . . .

Kelty forced her eyes to the bottom of the stainless steel sink.

Sean cleared his throat. "I don't know how to act right now."

Kelty gritted her teeth. She didn't have anything to say to

that, especially since the lump in her throat was giving a good 'ol college try at choking her out.

She towelled off the bowl, then dried the plates and cups, stacking them like Jenga tiles until there was no more room on the countertop. Sean drained the sink and rinsed off his hands. All done.

Kelty hung the damp cotton towel on the handle of the oven, then turned to leave, but Sean's voice stopped her.

"What do you want to do? About this whole anniversary thing?"

Kelty swallowed hard. She didn't fully turn toward him. "We find a time to go and check them off. Maybe Tuesday or Thursday evenings when you don't have practice."

Sean leaned against the counter, folding his arms in front of him. His biceps flexed, his chest tight under his shirt, and those damn puppy-dog eyes . . . Kelty pretended to be entranced with the veins in the marble top of the island.

"That should work. We might have to do this weekend. To get through them all."

"I have a thing. On Saturday." She felt his frown before she looked up.

"A work thing?"

Kelty shook her head. She didn't have a thing. She didn't know why she'd said it except for the growing discomfort at being fully available to him. *No.* She wasn't going to cater to his perfect schedule like she had for years. Sean has practice, Sean has a game, Sean can't go because he has a tournament. Never mind the fact that she loved his hockey life and had never resented it in the past. Now it felt intolerable.

Sean ran a hand over the back of his neck. "Okay. How about Friday or Sunday? Wait, I think my sisters are coming into town Friday night."

"They'll be here that soon?" The belt around her ribs tightened another notch. Eliza and Rachel had become like little sisters to her over the years. They'd been around for holidays when they were younger, but now they both had their own lives. Rachel with her husband living in DC, and Eliza with her girlfriend and their wolf of a mountain dog in Montana. The last time they'd all been together was probably three years ago.

"Wait, sorry. My dad said next week on Friday. Rach is on her way to Montana end of this week, then they're driving up together."

Kelty pursed her lips. "Okay. We can just be in touch, I guess. Start with the first ones on the list."

Sean pushed off the counter and nodded for her to follow him. "There's something we should start with first."

Her heart kicked up like she'd just taken a shot of espresso. "Sean, I should go."

"I know, it'll be quick." His shoulders slumped as he walked. He didn't reach his hand up to slap the wall as he descended the stairs to the garage door. That was almost enough to make her walk a little faster, to wrap her arms around his waist and bury her cheek against his shoulder blades. Instead, she shoved her hands in her pockets.

Sean pulled the door open and flicked on the lights. When they were both inside the garage, he pointed to a banker's box sitting on Rob's organized workbench. "I came early to get this."

Kelty walked with him, peering inside as he lifted the lid. On top of what looked like a stack of papers and memorabilia sat a small framed picture. Her eyes widened. "Is that—?"

Sean picked it up and handed it to her. "Rob and Sharla Thompson. I think she was barely pregnant with Carter in this one."

Kelty ran her finger over the dusty glass. It looked like they were at a parade or something. Some kind of celebration. They stood on top of a small stage with Rob's teammates surrounding them as Rob pulled her into his chest so tight, her back bowed.

Kelty returned the picture to the pile. "What is this for?" She stepped back, folding her arms.

"Uh, sorry. I thought you'd looked at the challenge list."

"I looked at it. I didn't memorize it."

Sean's jaw twitched. They looked at each other a long moment, then Kelty blew out a breath. "I'm sorry. I didn't mean to snap."

He nodded once, then passed her the box. "Thought it would be easier to go through this at home—I mean, at the house. Not here—"

"No, yeah. I get it." Kelty reached for the box.

"I can take it to your car."

She shook her head. "No, it's okay. Just open the garage door."

Sean hesitated, but let her take it, then slid past her to get to the button. His hand grazed her hip, and tingles exploded across her skin. Damn it, her body had not received the message that Sean was off-limits at the moment.

She jumped at the sound of the mechanism springing to life, then strode onto the driveway, ducking to exit before the door had fully lifted.

CHAPTER
Nine

Seven and a half years earlier

THE CONFERENCE ROOM smelled like noodles and soy sauce. White cartons littered the table between laptops, little red dragons curling around grease stains. Kelty had chopsticks in one hand and an employee pension spreadsheet in the other. Anytime she could mix work with food, it was a good day.

Mason slurped up a noodle beside her, his elbow far too comfortable on the arm of her chair. "So you're telling me we've been overpaying into extended dental for a year and nobody noticed?"

She tapped the sheet with the end of her chopstick. "Not overpaying. Misallocating. Which means when the acquiring company runs this through due diligence, they'll ding you for being sloppy."

He grinned. "Sloppy isn't the worst thing."

Andrew chuckled, but across the table, Sean made a

sound somewhere between a grunt and a growl. "What do you recommend?"

Mason ignored his comment and leaned in. "You've caught more in two weeks than our accounting team has in two months."

She rolled her eyes, but her cheeks warmed. "Best compliment you ever gave me."

Sean's pen froze mid-scratch. His gaze lifted, and something in her chest tightened. Why had she said that? It had become an ice breaker she used over the years, but using it now . . . it felt like she'd betrayed him somehow. Which was ridiculous. All they'd done was flirt a little and talk about employee reports.

Andrew, oblivious to the tension in the room, reached for another dumpling. "Doesn't matter. None of this matters. We're circling the drain. Let the new guys deal with it."

Sean shook his head. "If we dump this on them, we lose leverage on the closing terms."

Andrew shrugged. "Like we have any leverage left."

Kelty cut in before Sean could bite. "Actually, you do. Cleaning up your benefits reporting shows good faith. It's not about leverage, it's about optics. You want them thinking you're professionals."

Ironic that she was giving that advice when she'd woken up the night before from a particularly vivid dream that involved this conference room table and the man sitting across from her. She dropped her hands to her lap.

Mason finished his noodles and pushed the container aside. "Professionals. Got it. Your wish is my command, Kelty." He stretched, muscles shifting under his dress shirt.

Sean's jaw tightened. It looked like he'd swallowed glass. She could've said something to put Mason in his place, but she was enjoying this a little too much.

"Your fortune cookie." Kelty held out an open palm, and

Mason grinned, handing it to her. She held it for a second, then set it back on the table in front of him. "Just making sure you were serious. Okay, on to—"

Mason's phone buzzed on the table. He glanced down, a frown etching his forehead. "Shit."

"Westbrook?" Andrew wiped his fingers on his napkin.

Mason nodded, already rising. "Their update patch glitched out during integration with the imaging software. Half the CT machines in their Toronto test site are frozen mid-scan."

Andrew swore under his breath, tossing his chopsticks into the carton. "That's going to kill our liability clause if they can prove downtime."

"Exactly why I need you on the call," Mason said, already striding for the door. He flashed Kelty an apologetic smile. "Sorry. Client fire. We'll circle back."

Andrew was right behind him. "Thompson, you good to finish up?"

Sean nodded. "Yep. See you tomorrow."

The door closed, and it was just the two of them. Sean's sleeves were rolled up, forearms dusted with dark hair, veins raised from the tight grip on his pen. He looked a little tired. Maybe sad? He was always so buttoned up, she had a hard time reading him.

"So. Misallocations." He leaned into his screen.

She nodded, focusing on the spreadsheets. "Line fourteen. You've been putting long-term disability contributions under the wrong GL code. It snowballs."

He huffed a laugh.

"What?"

Sean's eyes flicked up. "Oh. Sorry. That's . . . it's the name of my hockey team."

"GL code?"

His grin widened. "No. Snowballs."

Okay. He still played hockey? After he mentioned his accident, she thought he was done. Now she was imagining him on the ice and stripping off his gear at the end of a game, which was not helping with the whole professionalism thing.

"You kept it up?"

He shrugged. "I've played my whole life."

"What league?"

His brow raised. "You follow hockey?"

"A little." A lot was the correct answer, but she didn't want to come on too strong. Her dad was a massive Canucks fan. She'd gone to games with him since she was a kid. Now it was a part of her makeup and the way she still connected with her dad when they talked every Sunday.

He was the one who let her know there was a league available after players left the AHL or NHL. A team was starting up in BC. Was Sean a part of that? Or was this just beer league?

Kelty dragged her finger down the column of numbers, checking the totals for the third time. Across from her, Sean hunched over the acquiring firm's template. She cross-checked another figure, circled it, and slid the page an inch closer to him. "Off by twelve hundred."

Sean didn't look up, just scratched something out on his sheet and grunted. The way he concentrated—shoulders tight, jaw flexed—made her want to run her hands through his hair. Force him to take a breath and relax.

"What?"

Kelty blinked at the question. "Hm?"

"You're staring at me." Sean's eyes narrowed.

"Oh, no, I was just thinking."

He twisted his pen between his fingers, the movement disturbingly slow, almost sensual.

She straightened. "Finish this page and call it a night?"

Sean agreed. It took them another half hour, but then they

tidied up their dinner mess and packed up. Kelty looked for a cloth to clean the table, but Sean waved her off.

"Cleaners come in the morning."

They walked out together. Kelty expected to hear Mason or Andrew somewhere on the floor, but it was silent. "Well that's adorable." Kelty approached a desk, mostly cleared off except for a few pencils and a miniature piece of sushi perched near the unplugged keyboard. She picked it up. It was clay, not plastic. "This looks handmade."

"Part of our employee enrichment program. Arts and crafts."

Kelty rolled her eyes and set it back on the desk, continuing on down the aisle. The dim lighting and empty cubicles brought back memories of her first job after university, when she worked for a mid-sized consulting firm in downtown Calgary. Back then, she'd been the junior who always got stuck on the eleven p.m. runs or chasing down straggling invoices, reconciling numbers until her eyes blurred. Pretty much what she was doing now, only getting paid a tenth of the salary.

By the time she left that firm, she'd built a reputation for spotting gaps others missed—HR liabilities, pension obligations, benefit accruals. That skillset made her valuable. She didn't miss working fifty plus hours a week, but it was fun to revisit the late, cozy nights a few times a year when timelines were tight.

"You okay?" Sean's voice pulled her back to the present. They were already standing at the elevators.

She nodded. "It's just nice when it's quiet."

Sean's finger hovered over the buttons. He pressed.

Kelty frowned. "You hit the wrong one."

"Did I?" Sean stepped back, clasping his hands behind him. A smile played at the corner of his mouth.

Kelty's pulse kicked. She loved surprises. Ever since she was little, her mom would find little trinkets at thrift stores or garage sales and bring them home. Kind of like that piece of sushi. She'd set them up on the table, have them waiting for her when she returned home from school or sitting on her nightstand when she woke up.

Parenting magazines probably said that kind of behavior would spoil a kid, but it only gave Kelty a sense of wonder. Life could be beautiful at the most surprising moments for no reason at all.

The elevator opened. Sean motioned as if to say, "Please, after you." If he was going to murder her on the rooftop, at least he was chivalrous about it.

They didn't talk on the way up. It was like walking into a movie without watching the preview, hoping your friend wouldn't say a word about it so you could experience it blind.

Sean stepped off first at the top, and Kelty followed him down the hall to a solid door. He pushed it open and held it so she could walk through.

Cool air swept across her cheeks. She strode to the railing and set her bag on the ground. It wasn't a cutesy rooftop patio or garden. Just a basic concrete slab with a fan of some sort and other external manifestations of the internal guts of the building.

It was beautiful.

The city sprawled below, lights glittering like spilled jewels across a velvet blanket. The Bow River cut a silver line through downtown, and it made Kelty smile. She loved that river. For a high desert in the middle of a grassland, it felt like an impossible gift for a river to run through the city. Especially since it kind of looked like a moat around a castle. The Calgary Tower didn't really count as a spire or turret, but she could make it work.

"Wow."

Sean stepped to the edge, hands shoved in his pockets. "There's no restaurant, and it doesn't rotate."

"My hopes are crushed."

He grinned. "It's one of my favourite places in the city."

She hugged her arms around herself, the wind tangling her hair. Sean shrugged off his jacket.

"I'm fine."

He ignored her and looped it over her shoulders. Why was such a simple thing so comforting? She didn't need a guy to keep her warm on a rooftop, but hell if she didn't want him to.

"Thank you." She clutched it closer and leaned against the brick. She drew in a breath, her senses full of him. "I feel like you were lying."

"About?"

"The garlic. This jacket smells . . ." She wanted to say amazing, but opted for, "Smooth."

Sean cracked a smile. "Not a smell."

"Okay, olfactory expert."

He chuckled. "Fine. Explain."

"It's clean. Crisp. What cologne do you wear?"

"ck one"

She laughed. "I knew it."

"Okay, cologne expert."

Kelty grinned. He had a quick wit. She wished she could peer inside his head to see every smart-ass comment he wasn't saying when he sat across from her in the conference room. "A guy I dated at UBC wore that."

Sean grimaced, but she hurried on before he could take it the wrong way. "No, it's not a bad thing. I loved his cologne. To the point that I didn't give back one of his sweatshirts when we broke up."

"How long were you together?"

"Six weeks. His cologne was the best thing about him." She wasn't positive, but there was a good chance that sweatshirt was still in a storage bin in her parents' closet. "I get attached to scents. Not in a weird way, I don't think, but certain smells just make me happy."

She kept a box of barley tea bags in her apartment at all times, not because she liked it, but so she could feel a warm hug from her grandmother whenever she wanted.

Sean considered that. He leaned over the brick, staring at the cityscape. Kelty's pulse fluttered at her throat as she second-guessed everything she'd just said. Why had she talked about her ex? Why had she said anything about his cologne? She'd just revealed that she was constantly smelling him, which was embarrassing, to say the least.

As she was about to word-vomit something else to distract from her prior diatribe, Sean straightened and turned. His expression was unreadable, his eyes dark except for the reflection of the lights.

"I'm more of a touch person."

Kelty blinked. "As in . . . touch over smell?"

He nodded, running a hand slowly over the rough brick until it sat next to hers. "We touch a thousand things every day and barely notice."

Kelty's heart was a bass drum behind her ribs. Her lips were so hot, they felt swollen. His hand was so close. Before she could overthink it, she lifted her fingers and moved them barely on top of his.

This was the opposite of professional, but as she was being microdosed with aerosolized Calvin Klein, she could hardly be blamed. "How do you think we can notice *more*?"

Sean rotated his wrist, putting their hands fingertip to fingertip. He didn't answer right away, instead dragging his fingers down the inside of hers, centimetre by centimetre. "We take our time."

The entire rooftop shrank to the feel of his skin against hers. She wondered if she'd ever truly felt anything before in her life. This was electric. Like her battery had been drained, and she'd finally found an outlet.

Kelty's eyes fluttered closed. There was something about the dark combined with the warmth of his jacket that made her feel utterly safe. Like she was tucked in under her blankets at home. But unlike most nights of her life, this time she wasn't closed in alone.

Sean circled his fingers around her wrist and tugged her closer. She blinked her eyes open, her body moving through syrup.

He was taller, but not so much so that she had to crane her neck to meet his eyes. It was a comfortable gap.

Kelty dropped her eyes to his lips, hoping he got the hint. She didn't want him to talk about it or tell her he was going to kiss her. The wondering, the tension, was far more exciting.

Sean's jaw set, his brow pinching like he'd made a decision but wasn't sure if it was the right one. Kelty tightened her fingers at his waist, her heart beating at the speed of a hummingbird's wings.

That was all it took. Whatever he'd been grappling with disappeared as his hand lifted from her arm and landed against her cheek. His fingers threaded in her hair as he cradled her jaw, pulling her into him.

His nose grazed the tip of hers before he tilted his head and took her lips between his. It was as if the pins of an unseen combination lock tumbled into place. Everything Sean held back, everything he didn't say, poured out of him. Sentences of lips and tongue and teeth. Of chests and hands and hips.

Kelty melted into him like warm honey slipping from a spoon. Her hands climbed the back of his neck as he pressed her against the brick, and the sounds of traffic below faded behind the hiss of their combined breath.

She smiled against his mouth as the scruff on his jaw chafed against her cheek.

"What?" he asked before taking her bottom lip gently between his teeth.

"Shh. A few more minutes."

That made him grin. "Somewhere you need to be?"

She reeled him back in close and slid her tongue into his mouth. No more talking. Because it wouldn't take long for her to remember she was working for Sean's company. That making out with him on the rooftop of his building would be optically terrible for both of them. *And did she really know him?*

Shit.

It was already happening.

CHAPTER
Ten

SEAN PULLED into his driveway five minutes early, then sat in his truck. Like an idiot. This was his house, it wasn't like he couldn't go in, but being with Kelty alone after Sunday made him antsy. He'd rather lace up for a triple-overtime playoff game than ring his own doorbell because at least on the ice, he knew the rules.

He was about to sort through his parents' university memories with the one woman who had good reason not to want to see him. The one woman he couldn't stop thinking about.

She'd occupied his head since the moment he saw her in that conference room years ago. That had been dangerous territory. He'd gone all in once before with Claire. He was young and smitten. Positive she was his one and only. He looked past every red flag. Skipped extra practices when she wanted him to, drove three hours to catch her for fifteen minutes before she left on a trip. That's what love was, wasn't it? All-consuming? Unhinged?

Then she'd slept with Wheatfill. And he didn't find out after the fact. Sean walked in on it. His so-called best friend, his line-mate, the guy who felt like a brother to him. One night and it blew apart both halves of Sean's life. Friendship over. Relationship gutted. He spiralled. And while he'd never blame Claire or Jordan for his motorcycle accident, he wondered if he ever would've gotten on that bike had he not come home that night.

After losing his contract with the Blizzard, his walls were thick. Steel-reinforced and looped with barbed wire.

Then Kelty happened.

At first it was simple. She was a straight-up smoke show, and he wanted her. But that initial hard-on turned into curiosity. She was bold. Funny. She asked for what she wanted.

Being near her was a perpetual contact high. He let her in before he knew what he was doing. Sitting there in the truck felt nearly identical to those old feelings. Wanting her so bad he could barely breathe. Scared out of his damn mind. At least back then he didn't know what he was missing.

The front door swung open before his shoes hit the pavement. Kelty stood in the frame, hair tied up, wearing jeans and a worn Snowballs hoodie. His hoodie before she kept it one night and never gave it back. He wondered if she remembered that.

"You planning on coming inside? Or just sitting on the curb like a pervert until the neighbours phone the Mounties?"

Sean pushed the door closed and rounded the hood. "George would never phone the cops. He knows my truck."

Her mouth quirked. "If I told him to, he would."

Sean glanced over at their neighbour's house. Sure enough, George sat in the kitchen bay window drinking his tea. Sean waved and followed Kelty inside.

"Practice was good yesterday?"

Sean nodded, slipping off his shoes. "Yep."

"Feeling good for the first round?" Kelty straightened the throw blanket on the couch, and Sean stood awkwardly at the edge of the carpet. She looked up. "What?"

He pulled off his jacket and dropped it on the bench. Right where it always was. Kelty followed the movement, then met his eyes. "This is weird." She shoved her hands in the back pockets of her jeans.

"Yeah." He didn't know how to put words to it. He wanted her more than he wanted the Rose Cup, and that was saying something considering what had happened the year prior. But it didn't matter. "You're asking about hockey when we both know you already have the playoffs mapped out."

Kelty laughed, her smile finally reaching her eyes. Her skin looked almost golden in the sunlight pouring in through the window. That north-facing glass was partially why he'd purchased this house. Never in a million years did he think someone would live with him here.

How many times had he tried to push past the barriers in his own damn head? Moving in together had nearly sent him off the deep end, and Kelty had barely stayed then. He wouldn't have blamed her if she hadn't. He was an ass. Rude. Antisocial. Controlling. He hated himself for it, but he couldn't stop.

Every day he woke with his stomach in his throat, his heart racing. It was all he could do to get out of bed, eat, and go to work. Hockey kept him from going insane, but he'd been pushed to his limit. Years later, it had settled. But jumping into marriage? Kids? Sean balled his hands into fists to keep them from shaking.

"Have you opened it?" He nodded toward the box on the coffee table.

Kelty's shoulders dropped, like she'd been waiting for something but it hadn't come. "Um, no. I mean, yes, but only just to look at what was on top. I didn't want to go through it without you." Her voice dropped on the last two words. She forced a smile and motioned to the chair. "Shall we?"

It was fake enthusiasm, but he was grateful for it. He couldn't seem to form a simple sentence. Everything he wanted to say jumbled somewhere between his head and his tongue.

He walked in, the familiar creak of the hardwood floor under his feet seeming louder than usual. Kelty leaned over the table and removed the lid as he sat on the couch next to her. She took out the picture first. The frame was clear. No more dust. She'd cleaned it.

"Wow." Kelty removed an old, folded piece of paper. "I think this is . . . yep." She pointed at the top triumphantly. "A map of Douglas University."

Sean leaned in, trying not to notice how the evening light from the front window caught on the small hairs at her temple. Or how their knees were so close, he could feel her body heat. "Wonder how much it's changed."

Kelty nodded. "Your parents talk about it all the time, but I've never been on campus. Well, besides Ranchman's."

Sean set the map on the table and pointed out the sports bar. "Not technically on campus."

"Then I stand by my statement." She grabbed another stack of papers. On top was another folded piece. Rob Thompson's class schedule from 1994. "Your dad was a hockey player, right?"

Sean nodded. *Was.* He had the opportunity to play for a development squad, but when he found out his girlfriend was pregnant, he gave it all up. They'd heard the story a hundred times. How he'd gotten down on one knee in front of the entire student body.

Sean's brows pulled together as he reached for the picture.

"This is a pretty intense schedule," Kelty mused.

Sean gave her a look. "Because hockey players are stupid?"

Kelty snorted. "No, I just meant—"

"They should only take remedial classes."

She shoved his shoulder, laughing. "Stop. I'm not criticizing anyone's intelligence." She tapped the paper. "Look."

Sean's hand was frozen on the picture. Kelty's thigh pressed against his, and the contact shocked him speechless.

"Your dad was taking advanced physics and math."

"He was at Douglas because he didn't make the AHL. Probably didn't think he had another shot." After getting married before his senior year, Rob graduated and went into satellite communication and system design. He'd worked for a few companies over the years, but the physics and advanced math had done him good.

Kelty sobered. "Yeah. I didn't think about that." She sat straighter and glanced down at his hand. She sucked in a small breath before asking, "What were you looking for?"

Sean forced his fingers to move, to lift up the picture. He really didn't want to say this out loud, but he'd spotted the item he'd been curious about. A ring. On his mother's left hand. He hadn't noticed before how she'd been proudly fanning her fingers to display it. "Uh, you know the Thompson family lore. That my dad proposed in front of the whole campus after a hockey celebration." His lungs burned like he'd just done sprints around the ice.

Kelty stilled a moment, then reached out and took the photo from him. "You think this is when it happened?" She traced her finger over Sharla's hand.

"Maybe."

They stared at the picture, and Sean worked to ease the pressure in his chest. It felt like he was sucking oxygen through a coffee straw.

Of course Rob Thompson would throw caution to the wind, give up his life dreams and jump into love and family with both feet. That was who he was. The best husband and father in the world.

And Sean was a dick. What was his response when Kelty'd asked him to give up a weekend to go to BC? Not a speech and a proposal. He wasn't sure whether a grunt and "I think I have practice" was the exact opposite, but it was likely close.

Why hadn't he shut his damn mouth and thought about it? Taken a second to ask questions instead of assuming that, because she was putting on her bra and he was mildly distracted by her bare breasts, it was a casual ask?

Now it was too late. He'd done exactly what she expected for the thousandth time, and apologizing now wouldn't solve a damn thing.

"Ugh. Your dad's such an asshole." Kelty set the picture on the table. "Who does that? Asking in front of everyone so she couldn't say no even if she wanted to?"

Sean coughed a laugh, and Kelty grinned next to him. It didn't reach her eyes.

"He's been forcing her into things ever since," she snarked. "Six kids? Sounds a little controlling."

This had always been Kelty's superpower. Diffusing awkwardness. Making people laugh. He hated that she had to use that skill in this moment with him.

Kelty rifled through the box and pulled out a small book. "Ooh, this looks like Sharla's," she said as she flipped over the front cover.

"That's Crystal, Logan's wife who stopped by Sunday."

Kelty rolled her eyes. "You say that like you're not talking about Logan Kemp." She turned to look at him, flipping her hair out of her face. "Did you know him growing up?"

"My dad name-dropped him every chance he got."

She scoffed. "Then why is this the first I'm hearing of him?"

Sean shrugged. "He hasn't played in a long time." That was partially true, but the other piece was that all of the kids knew there were some things they talked about that didn't leave the walls of their home. Neither of his parents talked about Logan Kemp or other famous players they knew when it wasn't just the eight of them.

"Oh my hell, look at this." Kelty slipped a picture from the sleeve. "I thought this looked like a trivia night, and your mom labelled it. It's at 'the Den.' Does that mean anything to you?"

Sean shook his head. Kelty leaned to reach her phone, and he immediately missed the contact. When she sat back next to him, her thigh wasn't touching his.

"Sean, it's the student pub or bar or whatever on campus at U of C." Her head snapped up, her eyes bright.

"Okay."

"Okay? This is perfect! We're supposed to put together a trivia night, and your mom and her friends used to do trivia there." She gestured with her hand. "Pull up the spreadsheet. Does it have a location listed?"

Sean dug his phone out of his pocket and flipped to the screen. "Ah, yeah. Just says a study room at Douglas. Emma and Tyler—"

"Nope. We have to do this." Kelty checked the time, then tapped something on her phone and held it to her ear. She listened for a few moments, then dropped the phone. "They're not answering."

It was seven thirty. Prime student drinking time. "They're probably slammed."

Kelty nodded. "Right. Okay. Let's just drive over there."

Sean frowned. "We could wait and phone them tomorrow."

"The site doesn't list their hours, and we know they have to be open now." She stood. "It's okay if you don't want to go—"

"No, I'll go." Sean pushed off the couch to stand next to her. He might not be able to give her the yes she wanted, but he could give her this. "We can take my truck."

THE DRIVE DOWN Crowchild felt shorter than usual. Probably because Sean wanted to capture the moment and bottle it. Everything felt so normal, it ached. Calgary lights shimmered in the dark while Kelty hummed along to the radio. He tapped the wheel, pretending not to notice the way her hair brushed her cheek in the glow from the dash.

"So," she said, turning toward him, "we'll still have to come up with more clues. Is everyone playing? I'm assuming we aren't since we're making everything up."

Sean nodded. "Yeah. Carter thought this would be the best fit."

Kelty laughed. "For you? He didn't think you'd want to participate?"

Sean's grip tightened on the wheel. "You know me, Kelt."

She leaned back against the seat, running a hand through her hair. "I know. But it's not like you're a total stick in the mud."

"Mm. Thanks."

She grinned. "Best compliment I ever gave you."

The words tore through him like a tornado. "Kelt—"

"I'm sorry. I shouldn't have—" She turned toward the

window. "I just thought . . . if we had to do this. I didn't want it to be weird." Kelty spun back to face him as he pressed the brakes and stopped at a red light. "I did some thinking after Sunday, and I'm not mad, Sean. I mean, I was. I was really pissed, but then I realized I was mostly just sad."

His palms started to sweat. "And that's better?"

"I think so." The words came out on an exhale. "You were pretty clear when we started this whole thing that relationships were difficult for you. It was my fault for thinking that could or should change. That I—" Her voice caught.

"Kelt—"

"No, let me finish." She paused, swallowed a few times, then drew a deep breath and continued. "I love your family, Sean. I don't want to be harbouring this—" She gesticulated, swirling her hands in front of her midsection, "—toxic thing inside me while we're celebrating your parents and this incredible life they've created."

Sean pressed the gas. He followed the instructions on his phone as student parking signs started to appear.

Kelty pressed her hands into her knees. "I thought we could just have fun, but I get it. I won't say . . . you know. Our things."

Something inside him cracked. He didn't know if she could've said anything more soul-crushing than that.

As they pulled into the parking lot at the University of Calgary student center, Sean could only think of one thing. She wasn't angry. While this wasn't hockey, being on the ice had taught him plenty of life lessons. And if he wasn't fired up and a little angry before a game, it usually meant he'd given up hope.

He put the truck in park and killed the engine. He needed to respond. To say something, but as usual, the translation between his heart and head was offline. "I . . ." He gave the wheel a snake bite. "I didn't . . ."

She put a hand on his arm. "It's okay. We can just go in."

Kelty pulled on the handle and pushed the door out with her knee.

"I'm sad, too." The words slipped out, and a wave of nausea rolled through him.

Kelty turned back, her eyes shimmering in the light from the street lamp. "Yeah. I know."

———

Kelty walked ahead of him into the student center, and Sean was grateful. It gave him time to compose himself. He wasn't a crier, but moments like this seemed to be happening more frequently. Emma announced she was pregnant. When Hope was adopted. Country's wedding. Or even Fly aging out of the league.

The sensation of his eyes burning and his throat thickening, his chest turning into an overinflated balloon, had to rank close to torture. It wasn't about toxic masculinity or any of that bullshit—his dad cried at the drop of a hat and never made him feel like he couldn't. But something inside of him locked down like a crocodile anytime that emotion swelled, sinking its teeth into the meat of it and barrel rolling until it faded. He didn't know if he was capable of actually crying, of not fighting that tidal wave to the death.

Kelty turned and motioned for him to hurry up. The student center halls were empty, but as soon as they turned the corner, heavy bass and an amorphous voice over a loud speaker drifted into the atrium.

She waited until he was close, then ducked through the entrance. The Den had low ceilings, sticky floors, and neon signs advertising Molson and Labatt's. The place was packed, the sound deafening.

"This is a Tuesday night?" He called after Kelty.

She turned with a grin. "What?"

He shook his head and followed, touching his knuckles to her lower back so he wouldn't lose her in the crowd. No wonder they weren't answering the phones.

"I'm going to the bar!" Kelty pointed to the left side of the room.

As soon as she approached, a bartender who looked like an Eastern European EDM dancer made a beeline for her. He slung a towel over his shoulder and leaned over the bar. "Here for the contest?"

She blinked. "Uhhh—"

"They're all in the back. You just need to sign in—"

Kelty shook her head, cutting him off. "No, I'm not here for the contest. I wanted to talk to your manager, actually. I tried calling—"

"Yeah, not available tonight." He nodded as a student waved to get his attention for a drink order.

"Wait, it's important." Kelty put a hand on his arm.

Hm. Sean did not like that. The hairs rose on the back of his neck. He stepped in next to her, doing everything in his power not to slide his arm around her waist and pull her into him. "Can you take a message?"

The bartender looked up. His mouth quirked. He turned his attention back to Kelty. "Are you alum?"

She paused, then said, "Actually, yes. I took an online class years ago."

"Good enough for me." He pressed his hands into the bar, ignoring the cacophony of voices clamouring for his attention. "Listen, this is a fundraiser. We were supposed to have five guys and five girls, but one of the girls bailed. If you can step in as a special guest alum, you can meet with the manager."

Kelty laughed. "You have that kind of power?"

He grabbed a glass from under the bar and filled it with

beer on tap. "I do." He waited for the foam to slip over the lip of the glass, then handed it to a girl on their right. "I happen to be him."

Sean grunted, nudging her. This guy was an asshole, and he didn't like how he was looking at her. "We can come back later."

Kelty ignored him. "What would I be signing up for?"

The bartender pointed to a sign at the front. "90's throwback. Wet T-shirt contest for Bow River."

"You've got to be shitting me," Sean muttered.

The bartender somehow heard that comment through the fray. He held up his hands. "Hey, it's creative. And it's equal opportunity."

Kelty laughed. "That's hilarious."

Sean wasn't surprised in the least when Kelty started stripping off her sweatshirt. Of course she'd say yes to this. Not because she wanted the attention, but because someone issued her a challenge, and she loved the environment possibly more than David Suzuki. "Kelt, I'll come back tomorrow. You don't have to—"

"It's for the Bow River, Sean. And the good of the family." She handed him the sweatshirt and dug a hair elastic from her jeans pocket. She wore a thin tank top and no bra.

The bartender tossed her a white cotton tee. "Sign in at the back."

"Got it!" She pulled her hair up into a ponytail. "Aww!" Her eyes snagged on a small basket on the bar top. "Who makes matchbooks anymore? Those are adorable."

Sean followed her gaze. A collection of compact matchbooks sat next to the register. When was the last time he'd seen one of those? He turned his attention back to Kelty. "You're going to keep the tank top on, right?"

Kelty looked up at him through her lashes. "Depends."

"On what?" He set his jaw.

"How much money I want to raise." She bounced past him, and Sean grumbled something under his breath as he turned to watch her approach the guys at the back. Then he slipped a matchbook into his pocket.

WOULD Kelty normally jump on a bar in a university campus pub and allow someone to dump a bucket of water over her? Hell no. But with her dad dying, her family fractured, her forever relationship in shambles, the Thompsons' anniversary dreams on the line, and Sean so obviously disapproving? Yeah, she sure as shit did.

The student body erupted as the bartender/manager came on the microphone, announcing the contestants. Wrong word since they weren't competing for anything. Or were they? Not that she cared. Obviously, her mid-thirties body wouldn't stack up to the veritable teenagers around her, but still. She sent a silent prayer up to the feminist gods to spare her that humiliation.

"You used to go here?" A guy who looked like he could've been Nick Lachey's younger brother put his hat on backwards and grinned.

"Something like that."

"When did you graduate?"

She wasn't sure exactly how to answer that, but thankfully, didn't have to. The guy jumped up on the makeshift stage, collapsible platforms in a large rectangle next to one side of the bar, throwing his arms in the air as his name was called. Mike? Or Miles? Either way, it tracked.

Kelty scanned the packed room for Sean and found him close to where she'd left him. He stood scowling next to the computer monitor behind the bar on the other side of the horseshoe. His eyes were locked on hers.

She shrugged and gave a small wave. Sean barely moved his head, but she read the message loud and clear. *You don't have to do this.* If they were together, she would've blown him a kiss or made some kind of subtle sexual gesture that made him laugh. She didn't know what to do under these circumstances.

It was so easy to fall back into their patterns. To forget that there was a reason she'd walked out and stayed at Penny's and that Sean was staying with his parents. She couldn't do this again. She couldn't erase what happened the other night at the party or the truth of what she actually wanted. But what were the options when you loved someone, yet you hit a T-intersection?

There was no good answer for that.

So she controlled what she could control, which, at that moment, meant climbing up onto the platform and shaking her ass while the bartender hyped her up as a last-minute alumni participant.

The noise hit her square in the face as soon as she was standing above the crowd. It was like heat, collecting at the ceiling and swirling around her head, making her dizzy. The Tragically Hip was blasting, but it was buried under hoots and catcalls. Mostly for Mike/Miles, which was fair. He was doing a slow grind with his white T-shirt half pulled up his abs.

Then he pointed at the glass jars lining the bar. He teased a little more of his shirt, and when someone dropped a blue dollar bill through the mouth, he was like a music box ballerina that had just been wound up. He gyrated and thrusted, becoming a rock star in thirty seconds flat.

And then he turned to her with a question in his eyes. Well . . . It was for the Bow River. She nodded, then pointed at the jars. Hand after hand lifted to drop money through the glass, and Mike and Kelty put on a damn good show as the other contestants made their way to the stage. Her hands were in her hair as she turned and let him sway his hips with hers.

Bartender/Manager Guy didn't waste any time. He knew a good opportunity when he saw one. "Are you ready for water? Fill those jars!"

The rush of the crowd obscured the jars for a moment, but one of them must've been filled because before she could turn on the platform, water poured over their shoulders, soaking their shirts.

Mike/Miles laughed out loud, running his hands over his torso like he was kneading dough. Very hard, sculpted dough.

"Look at how important water is for this city!" The bartender laughed at his own joke, his huff of breath crackling in the microphone. "We need our river healthy, eh?"

Her shirt plastered to her skin and tank top. Kelty threw her hair back, not willing to go full Cardi B, but doing a few of her favourite club moves. She glanced up to find Sean, but he wasn't standing by the bar. Kelty's stomach sank. Had she pissed him off? Had he walked out and left her there?

He was so damn uptight. A little spontaneous fun never hurt anyone.

"You're good at this!" The girl next to her laughed, begging for more water so she could full-on flash-dance it with a folding chair someone pushed up from behind the bar.

The crowd went wild. Money rained into the big jugs. Kelty wasn't sure what she was supposed to do next since she and Mike had done everything but dry hump. Or . . . wet hump?

The song switched to a Britney Spears remix to screams of approval, and just as Kelty started to move, hands gripped her waist. She whirled, ready to push Mike/Miles off of her, but instead she froze.

"Sean?"

"C'mon. Let's—"

"What are you doing?" She held him at arm's length. He stood on the platform, his jaw locked, his eyes wild.

He shouted over the music. "We're leaving."

"I need to get that reservation—"

"I'll get the damn reservation."

The bartender called up to them. "Hey, bud, only contestants are—"

"We're getting off," Sean barked, tugging on Kelty's waist.

"Uh, no we're not." Kelty adjusted the wet fabric and shivered. "I'm finishing the competition."

His pupils blew wide. "No you're not." He looped a finger in her belt loop with a growl.

Okay. No. He was not going to pretend he had any claim on her right now after literally refusing to stake a claim.

What was his problem? If he wanted her, if he didn't enjoy watching her dance with another guy, then why wouldn't he do something about it? He acted like someone was pulling out a toenail every time he said "I love you" but then he pulled crap like this?

"Sean. *Sean.*" Kelty yanked on his arm, oblivious to the crowd hurling expletives in Sean's direction. He spun, his eyes blazing.

Oh shit. That was his *we're losing by two going into the third period* or *Wheatfill didn't get called for slashing* look. "Sean. We can talk about this after—"

"I'm not talking after." He turned, his hand now full of the waistband of her jeans. Kelty scanned the bar, trying to keep her balance.

Anger flared like a lit match. While it was the tiniest bit hot that he was pissed enough at her dancing in a wet shirt to lose his shit, he did not get to tell her what to do. He was out of his mind. Irrational. Luckily, she'd had nearly eight years of practice with his temper, and it was all bravado. On the outside he might look like a volcano erupting, but inside, he was all gooey magma.

Sean Thompson didn't scare her in the least.

As soon as she spotted the bucket, she lunged, snatched it up from the counter, and threw the water forward in a sloshing waterfall.

Directly onto the back of his head.

CHAPTER
Thirteen

KELTY HADN'T BEEN KISSED like that in a long time. Correction. She hadn't been kissed like *that* ever. And yet nothing. Not a text. Not an email. Well, besides work-related messages, but that was even worse.

Sean Thompson had kissed her on a rooftop, his hands in her hair, his breath against her mouth like he'd been starving. Then full radio silence?

Three days later, the silence had become a roar in her head. She checked her inbox compulsively, reread old messages as if she might've missed something tucked between meeting invites and accounting memos. Every vibration of her phone turned her into a Pavlovian idiot, heart leaping only to crash when it was just a shipping notice or weekend blow-out sale.

It was pathetic. She hated herself for it. And yet here she was, smoothing down her navy blouse as she pushed through the glass doors of the office building with an excuse that barely passed as rational.

She was just in the area and thought she'd grab a few files to take a look at over the weekend. Not necessary, especially since most information she needed was digital. But hopefully Sean wouldn't pick up on that.

He wasn't at his desk or in the conference room, from how dark it was behind the glass.

"Kelty." Mason rounded the corner and froze, his laptop under his arm.

"Oh. Hey." Her throat tightened. She wanted to turn around and escape, but Mason was already approaching.

She forced a smile. "I thought I'd pick up a few things to work on over the weekend."

"Music to my ears." Mason nodded toward the conference room. "I actually had something I wanted to look over with you. Do you have a minute?"

What was she supposed to say? This was her job. He was technically her boss at the moment. She nodded and followed him in.

Mason flicked on the lights and pulled out a chair for her, then sat in the one next to it. "I was just getting into benefit obligations."

"Riveting stuff."

Mason laughed. "I'd be happy to bribe you with lunch to split the work."

She dropped into the chair, her stomach betraying her with a grumble. "You don't need to bribe me. You're already paying me."

"Yeah, but this isn't technically your job." He raised an eyebrow, turning his screen toward her. "Do you have your computer?"

Kelty opened her bag. "Always."

They fell into easy conversation. When Mason wasn't trying to posture in front of Sean, he was easy to talk to.

They'd worked through at least half of the accounts on his list when Mason's assistant brought in Indian food. This wasn't her plan for the morning, but it was quickly turning up roses.

Mason reached out and threatened to close her laptop screen. "Time to eat."

"I know, just a sec."

He laughed, rising from his chair to open the tied plastic bag. He set out the containers of rice and curry, handing her a plate and set of utensils. "You're going to wither away."

Kelty rolled her eyes. "Trust me. I have plenty of fat stores."

Mason chuckled and started dishing up. It didn't take long for the warm spices to win her over. She closed her laptop and slid it to the side, then held out her plate. "Okay. Hit me."

"You want me to dish you up?" He smirked, holding up a plastic spoon.

"I'm too weak."

He laughed and set to work, giving her a generous portion of each dish. Saag paneer, lamb vindaloo, and chicken korma.

She thanked him, but as he set the last container down, the spoon caught his sleeve and flipped, splashing sauce the colour of turmeric on her shoulder.

He cursed and grabbed a napkin. "I'm so sorry."

"No, it's fine." Kelty shifted to see if it had gotten on her blouse.

Mason reached out to wipe it. "Shit. It stained your skin."

"It did not!"

He laughed, holding her arm up so she could see. "I fear it may be permanent. I don't know—" Mason's head lifted as the door to the conference room opened. "Oh, hey." He grinned, the look in his eyes turning wolfish.

Kelty spun in her chair.

Sean.

He froze in the doorway as if he'd walked into a crime

scene. His gaze took in the takeout boxes spread across the table, Mason standing above her, his hands on her arm.

The temperature dropped ten degrees.

"Well." Sean's voice was flat. "Looks like the party started without me."

Mason dropped his hands, wiping his fingers with the napkin. "Grab a plate, bud. Plenty to go around. I'll try not to turn you into a watercolour like I did Kelty." He winked, then sat back in his chair.

Kelty winced. She shouldn't feel guilty. Nothing happened between her and Mason, and even if it had, she and Sean weren't together. Yet . . . she had been glued to her phone most of the week for a reason.

There was something between them, obviously, and that filled her with a deeper sense of shame. Was it wrong for her to get involved with him? She'd had a rousing mental debate on that topic while revelling in her post-kiss stupor.

She wasn't technically working with him. She was hired as a consultant. And her contract, while with the owners in general, was executed through Mason. Technically, she and Sean were only taking tasks Mason assigned, which meant neither of them had any kind of power over the other. It probably wasn't ideal from an HR standpoint, but the company was dissolving. She already had a vested interest in making sure this acquisition was seamless, so how could this hurt?

Those were her justifications, at least. After she hadn't heard from him, she second-guessed herself a thousand times over.

Sean took a seat across from them at the table, and the air was so thick it could've been stabbed with one of their plastic forks. Maybe he wasn't even thinking about her and Mason. Maybe he was angry. Or hurt? She hated that she couldn't tell what he was thinking.

She focused on her food, which was delicious, listening to Mason and Sean talk shop. Then she worked—or pretended to—for another fifteen minutes, when all she wanted to do was crawl under the table.

She was just about to announce she had another meeting to get to when Mason's phone buzzed. He checked it, muttered something about a call he had to take, and slipped out the door.

Kelty's cheeks flamed. "Well, I actually have to get—"

"I didn't think you were Mason's biggest fan."

Kelty blinked. "Excuse me?"

Sean focused harder on his screen. "Just surprised to see you here without the rest of the team."

She wet her lips, drawing a deep breath and releasing it as she packed her laptop in her bag. He had no problem being with her on the roof without *the rest of the team*. A thousand responses flitted through her head, but this attitude of his was starting to piss her off. She went for the only thing that allowed her to pull back control. "Why didn't you text me?"

Sean's brow twitched. "I emailed."

"Mmm. Yes. The work emails were riveting."

He set his pen down and leaned back in the chair. "I thought we were being professionals?"

Nice. He was using her words against her. She slung her bag over her shoulder. "I told *Mason* to be professional."

"Hm." Sean rubbed a hand over his stubble.

"I was talking specifically about your numbers if you remember."

His eyes lifted from his screen and locked on hers. "I remember."

Kelty waited, not sure what was supposed to happen next. She wasn't going to slink out of there with her tail between her legs. He'd been the one to kiss her. Yes, she technically made the move to hold his hand, but he'd put his arm out and taken her up to the roof in the first place.

"Did you want me to text?" His voice was low.

Kelty swallowed hard. "Some form of communication is typically a good thing. After a meeting like that."

The corner of Sean's mouth quirked. "A meeting."

"What else would you call it?"

He let out a puff of air, pushing away from the table and leaning back in his chair. "Was this a meeting with Mason?"

Kelty rolled her eyes. "I came in to see—" She stopped herself. She didn't need to admit she'd come there for him. "I needed to get a few files."

Sean watched her. "You're working over the weekend?"

"Sometimes. Yes. This weekend, I might do a little cleanup." She stumbled over her words, and that wasn't like her. He made her so nervous. Why didn't he blink? His eyes were just always there. "I should probably . . ."

"Yeah." Sean stood and started clearing the lunch trash.

Kelty jumped in, stacking her and Mason's plates and walking them to the bin. "Okay. Well, I'll see you later then." She searched for any other reason to stall, to open up a conversation with a witty comment or ask a thoughtful question. Her mind was completely blank.

Sean reached for the door, but paused before pulling it open. "You prefer communication."

Her blood hummed. "I do."

"So there could be instances where non-professional behaviour would be tolerated."

She squeezed her thighs together. "Completely reasonable."

He nodded once, then yanked the door open. Kelty strode through to the hall, forcing herself not to look back as she walked to the elevator. She descended to the street, found her car, and got in, finally letting out a full exhale.

Her phone buzzed in her bag, and she pulled it out.

SEAN

Mason's going to text you. He wants to meet
end of the week

She stared at the message, frowning. Why was he telling her
this?

KELTY

Okay, I'll watch out for it

SEAN

Say no

She read the message three times, all her senses seeming to be
underwater. She couldn't stop thinking about that kiss on the
roof. The way he'd looked at her across the table in the
conference room. Something about him had her in a choke-
hold, and she couldn't tell if wanting to dive in deeper was
the best or worst idea she'd ever had.

There was something dangerous about him. Maybe just
intense? But none of her alarms were going off. She felt safe
being alone with him. Physically safe. Emotionally? Not so
much.

SEAN

Say you're only available Monday after three

Before she could figure out how to respond, another text came through.

MASON

Great to see you today. Sorry I missed you on the way out.

Would love to finish up next week. Friday okay?

I can bring in Thai food. Or burgers. Still not sure what you like but I'd love to know

Kelty felt like she'd just run a 5k. Her hands were sweating. This was the moment. She either decided to jump into whatever Sean was proposing or she opted out. Her thumbs hovered over the keypad.

KELTY

Hey! Thanks so much for lunch. I'm actually booked through next weekend.

Would Monday afternoon work? Maybe three-ish?

Three dots appeared, then disappeared.

· · ·

MASON

> I have to catch a flight at 4:30 on Monday,
> unfortunately

Her heart flip-flopped. Okay. Mason wasn't going to be there. She closed her eyes and pretended she wasn't thinking about Sean or his messages while channelling professional Kelty.

KELTY

> Could you leave the last reports?

> I could pop in and wrap it up so it's ready
> when you get back in town

MASON

> Sure

She dropped her phone in her lap and leaned her head back against the seat. What was she doing? What would happen if she showed up and met with Sean? What did she want to happen if—

Her phone buzzed, and her head snapped down like a mouse trap.

· · ·

Sean

See you soon

CHAPTER
Fourteen

SEAN SUCKED in a breath as water crashed over his head, soaking his shirt and jeans. The crowd gasped, close to silent for the first time all night. He was only aware of the bass pulsing through his chest, the ringing in his ears as he swiped the water out of his eyes and pushed his hair off his face.

He turned, wiping his cheeks with his hands, to find Kelty staring at him wide-eyed, holding a bucket.

Her eyes drifted to his chest, then snapped back to his face. He wanted to hoist her up, throw her over his shoulder, and . . . damn it. He was pissed. His hands were shaking. But there she was with her flushed cheeks and see-through T-shirt, and everything running through his head only involved peeling it off her.

Kelty pursed her lips, her face reddening.

"You think this is funny?" Sean's voice was a low growl. The asshole bartender said something over the mic, but nothing was getting through.

Kelty shook her head, her mouth still a thin line. Cheers and shouts rose around them, and she couldn't hold it in. A laugh burst out of her. She clapped a hand over her mouth, but it was no use. Once she started, she couldn't stop, and they both knew it. It was his personal mission to force her to the edge of no return as often as possible, but usually not at his expense.

She bent over, her ponytail swinging forward, her T-shirt stuck to every curve he'd spent years memorizing.

Sean's blood pressure skyrocketed. He told himself he was mad. Furious, actually. Because she hadn't told him she was signing up. Because she hadn't even glanced at him before bounding onto the stage like it was no big deal. Because some moron had immediately started feeling her up, like she'd forgotten that she belonged to him.

Except, she didn't. Not technically. Not anymore.

Kelty tossed her head back, eyes sparkling, a bubble of laughter escaping her throat as she swiped at the water dripping down her arms. Sean's gut twisted. She was so damn beautiful. She complained about her laugh lines or freckles on her cheekbones. She said her hair wasn't as thick as it was in her twenties. It was all bullshit. She'd never been more gorgeous, and the whole bar could see it.

Sean spun on the platform before the lump in his throat could choke him. He dropped to the floor and pushed through the crowd, miraculously ignoring the elbows in his ribs.

"Sean!" Kelty called from behind him, but he didn't turn.

Every step he took, the heat in his chest spread. She'd made an ass out of him. Or maybe he'd done that himself. But the root of why he'd gotten on stage was simpler. He couldn't stand the idea of anyone else seeing what he saw every night before he closed his eyes.

The last few nights had been hell, and she was rubbing his face in it.

"Sean, stop!" she called again.

It made his vision go white at the edges. He reached the bar in a handful of strides and smacked his wet palms onto the wood. The bartender had the mic tucked against his shoulder and a smirk that Sean wanted to sand off with a brick. Instead, he dug into his back pocket, pulled out his wallet, and slapped a stack of bills onto the bar hard enough to make the glasses hop.

"I want the second Saturday in April." He had to pitch his voice above the music. The DJ had turned on an old pop anthem that had the crowd screaming the words like they were scripture.

The bartender pretended to be busier than he was. "I said I'd meet with her, bud, not—"

Sean peeled off more bills. He didn't count. "All this for the Bow River!" he shouted, and the students erupted. Sean leaned in, not writing off the need to hand this bastard his ass. "For charity."

"We've got bands on Saturdays."

"Not at six o'clock, shithead."

Kelty pushed through the crowd, crushing into his side, her breath hitching. "I'm sorry, I—"

"Fine. Second Saturday." The bartender huffed a laugh like Sean was a toddler throwing a tantrum.

Kelty grabbed onto his arm. "Let's go, Sean."

He didn't want to go. He wanted to give that clown's testicles a root canal.

"Walk away." Kelty looped her arm through his and pressed her fingers against the inside of his elbow.

Instantly, the hold of his anger slipped. Heat rushed through him. What was it she'd said? That she wouldn't use their past against him? "That isn't fair," he muttered, turning from the bar.

"Do you want to end up in the back of a cop car tonight?" Kelty hissed, pulling him toward the exit.

She'd come up with that move early in their relationship after he got into a fight outside the locker rooms in Grande Prairie. She said it was their signal for him to shut up and leave a situation.

The image of Kelty walking out the door with her backpack flashed in his head, and his stomach dropped to his knees. Had he ever made her a signal? Could it have meant *stay?*

Sean pulled his arm from hers, navigated through the rest of the crowd, and pushed through the doors that led back into the atrium of the student center.

"That's how it's going to be?" Kelty stormed after him.

Sean walked faster. That was how it was going to be. He couldn't talk to her right now. His brain kept offering up images of her at the bar like happy-hour appetizers. "Have a good time?"

She was barely keeping stride. "Mm. There it is."

"What?" He snapped, knowing full well he was picking a fight. But he wanted it. He wanted to see how much he could get under her skin. Praying he still had that kind of power.

"Were you jealous or just protecting my honour?"

He made a sound of frustration that wasn't quite a laugh. "It was taking too long."

Kelty laughed out loud. "Is that seriously what you're saying right now? You got up on a bar in front of a crowd of people, which is your personal fiery hell, because you were bored? What, was I not putting on a good enough show for you?"

Sean descended the stairs, staying far enough ahead he wouldn't have to look at her. Oh, she put on a show. But it wasn't what he could see under her shirt. It was the full-blown smile across her face. That would haunt him. He already knew it. "I got the date for trivia."

"Well aware."

He broke through the front entrance like the doors were

beaded curtains. The late March air knifed clean through his wet clothes.

"You can't do real life like it's hockey, Sean." Kelty jogged to keep up.

"Worked pretty well in there." Her words bounced off him like marbles. How the hell was he supposed to sit there in the bar and watch her shake it for a bunch of boys whose balls hadn't even dropped? How was he supposed to act all buddy-buddy with the dipshit who got his jollies from asking her to climb up there in the first place instead of pulling out the calendar on his brand-new phone?

He stalked down the street to where they'd parked, only realizing halfway there that Kelty wasn't behind him. Of course she wasn't.

Sean stopped and scrubbed a hand over his face, water flicking from his hair. "We're both soaked and freezing—"

"Who's fault is that?"

He drew a deep breath, then turned fully to face her. "Can I drive you home? Please?"

"Wow. Asking nicely. What a treat."

Sean's jaw worked as she stood stock still on the sidewalk, considering. For half a second, he wondered if she might shake her head and phone a rideshare. But eventually, she walked over, her arms still folded tightly over her chest.

He turned and walked the rest of the way to the truck. It felt like he'd have better luck leaving breadcrumbs, but he opened the door and held it. Kelty took her time, but she eventually climbed in, shivering. He got in the driver's seat, cranked the heater, and drove.

They didn't talk for three stoplights. The wipers smeared water he hadn't noticed on the windshield. Calgary slid past. Dark storefronts, the old neon signs mixed in with gentrified, modern restaurant chains and office buildings. His hands tightened on the wheel until his knuckles paled.

"I don't get it." Kelty's head was fully turned, staring out her window. That meant she was close to crying. They'd been together long enough, he just knew.

She swallowed. "You say you don't want to commit—"

"I didn't say that."

Her shoulders tightened. "You don't usually use words, Sean, but it's pretty damn clear."

He stopped at a light, annoyed that he didn't have something to distract himself from this. She was always so blunt. His younger sisters, minus Emma, would dance around issues for days or weeks before finally getting around to what they wanted to say, but Kelty would lay it out straight to your face. He might've said Emma was having a bad influence on her, but that was what had drawn him to her in the conference room. In moments like this, though, it was more abrasive than a mosquito buzzing around his ears.

Sean grappled for anything that would make it stop. "I'm not the one who left."

Kelty turned to get both eyes on him, forcing him to see the shine there. The rosy tip of her nose. "If you want things all your way, then you don't want a relationship. You can say you want this or want me, whatever that means to you, but you don't, actually. You want what you want. You want it your way. You don't want to go to BC? Great, we won't go. You don't want me dancing on the bar? Perfect. Go ahead and pull me off. If I want this, I either have to get on board or . . ." She dropped back against the leather, sucking in a breath. "Yeah. Or."

Say something.

Say something, say something, say something.

It wasn't true. He thought about her all the damn time. He wanted to make her happy. He'd run barefoot to Penticton to prove it. But the idea of admitting that—the thought of saying it out loud or worse, signing a piece of paper—crushed his ribs until he couldn't breathe.

He struggled to pull air into his lungs as he turned onto

their street, a quiet curve of bungalows with big porches and stubborn hedges. Their house sat in the middle. White, tidy, a light on in the front room because Kelty hated coming home to darkness. He'd changed the bulb before going over to his parents.

You're right. I'm an ass. I want to change, but I don't know how, Kelt.

Say. Something.

Sean pulled up to the curb. Kelty tugged her damp shirt away from her skin. "At least this time I got you wet for a change," she muttered.

A strange, giddy ball of light lit up inside him. A joke. He wanted to laugh. He wanted to cry. Moments like this split him open, making him feel like he was hanging over the edge of a cliff by his fingertips. *I love you.* The words added to the list already streaming through his head.

"Kelt—"

"Thanks for the ride." She pulled on the handle, and the dam inside him broke. He put on the parking brake and stormed out of the truck.

Kelty froze with her legs slung over the seat. "What are you doing?"

He jogged to the side of the garage and punched in the code.

Kelty slammed the door and ran after him. "I can do it, Sean. You don't need to—"

He ducked under the rising door and pulled the trash bin from the wall. Kelty moved to the side as he wheeled it past her to the curb, dropping it clear of the driveway so she wouldn't have to round it to get out in the morning.

He wiped his hands on his jeans, then stood there, his breath heaving, staring at the plastic bin. It wasn't enough. It wouldn't ever be enough, but what else could he do?

The silence stretched. The ringing in his ears was slowly

replaced by the singing of crickets and voices from a back-yard at the end of the block.

"What's next?" Kelty still stood next to the garage.

That was a hell of a question.

She cleared her throat. "On the list. I could look at the spreadsheet, but . . . is it the stuff at Douglas?"

The anniversary race. Right. Sean nodded. "Yeah. I think so."

Kelty scuffed a shoe on the concrete. "Okay. I can get the clothes for the relay. That seems like a one-person job."

Those words rang in his head. Even though she hadn't moved, it felt like they were another three metres apart.

"Then we can do the hike on the weekend?"

Not Saturday. She had something on Saturday. That had been pressing on his sternum since she said it. *Why not give the specifics?* "Sure."

She turned to the walkway. "Just text."

"Yep."

"Goodnight."

"'Night." He watched until she got the door open and stepped into the square of light. She turned back, lifted a hand, and he lifted his in answer. Then he got into his truck and drove in the opposite direction of home.

SEAN HIT the ice hard enough that his skates sang. The rink air bit at his lungs as the puck leapt from the half wall and rolled against his tape. This was what he could count on. The consistency and predictability of it.

"Head up!" Tyler's voice ricocheted off the boards.

Sean toe-dragged around a cone and snapped a pass across to Brett. Brett one-touched to Country, who moved with a big man's miracle grace, then chipped it back onto Sean's tape at just the right angle. He didn't have to think. His hands knew. His lungs burned in the good way. Mental noise that had been swirling in his head all day dropped through his feet and froze there on the ice.

André called for it with a jut of the chin. The universal sign for, "Don't be selfish, bud." Sean floated a saucer over a stickblade by the width of a nickel and grinned when André caught, settled, and lasered bar-down. Ryan whooped, and Suraj hammered his stick against the ice in approval. Sean felt like Stoico on the victory semi-circle glide after that one.

"Don't look so smug, eh?" Country chirped. Sean saluted him for good measure.

"Bar downski, bud!" André crowed, and the guys guffawed.

Mike and Darcy worked a two-man weave along the boards with the precision of dudes who liked their socks ironed. That also did Sean's heart good. There wasn't a guy on the ice dinking around. They were locked in on playoffs, and he wouldn't have to slap them upside the head to get them focused.

50k. With everything happening over the last week, he'd momentarily forgotten that number, and it acted like lighter fluid on an open flame. It wasn't just the money. The Snowballs needed this. The Ice Centre needed this. *He needed this.*

They rotated through reps as a team until the edges in Sean's head sanded down. Neutral zone regroup, weakside support, strong side pressure.

"Get water, boys," Sean huffed. They drifted to the bench, helmets pushed back, breath clouding. After giving them all a few seconds to regroup, he continued. "Playoffs Saturday. We're tapping sticks with Dr. Quinn."

André snorted. "If she's tapping my stick, I'm not complaining."

"Just hope she warms her hands before the exam," Country quipped.

Curtis grinned. "Never gets old, bud."

Country pretended to tip his hat.

"Alright, alright. We know their goalie's glove eats pucks," Sean continued.

"Venus flytrap," Mike agreed.

"And Dr. Quinn's first line can skate," Sean went on. "We need pucks in deep. Make their D turn, put bodies where the stench is. No hero shit. We stack shifts. Stack periods."

André grinned. "Short shifts, hard shafts." Tyler shoved him, and he snorted. "Don't pretend you aren't putting that on a T-shirt."

After another forty-five minutes of work, they made it

back to the locker room and the realities of life settled over Sean in layers. Leaving the ice these days felt a little like grief, and he already had too much of that.

"Playoff mustache by Friday," Brett announced, peeling off his gear.

Ryan laughed. "You can't grow a mustache by Friday."

Brett grinned, stroking his upper lip. "Already coming in."

Country pointed. "Turn your head. So the light can glint off your angel hair."

Brett threw a glove.

André threw a sweaty arm over Sean's shoulder. "While we're sharing—"

"Not sharing," Sean grumbled.

"—Tyler said something interesting earlier. Hey, Ty. You want to repeat what you mentioned by the net?"

"Not especially."

André laughed dramatically. "He's being shy. Here. I can tell him—"

"Shut the hell up." Tyler laughed.

Sean pushed André's arm off, searching in his bag for his towel.

André pressed a hand to his chest. "I think it may have been a cry for help. He informed us that he has to drink electrolytes daily and leave the bedroom for a couple hours at a time or—"

Tyler threw Brett's glove, but André ducked, and it hit the locker. He danced out of his direct line of sight and continued in a rush. "Something like Emma being pregnant is the best thing that could've happened to him. The hormones are requiring constant bangi—I mean *finagling*—"

The groans and laughter swallowed the last part of that sentence. Sean kept his head down, not needing another excuse to erupt. He was glad Tyler had done right by his sister. That he took care of her and made her happy. But hearing about their sex life still made him want to throw Tyler into the boards like he had the first time.

Tyler held up his hands. "I love your sister respectfully, passionately, and with doctor-approved frequency."

Country snorted. Sean counted to ten in his head.

"Ty," Suraj piped up, "are you nesting yet? Do you own seventeen neutral-toned swaddles?"

"It isn't real until you own nipple cream." Curtis grinned.

Sean grabbed the circular tin holding the shampoo bar Kelty threw in his bag, saying some shit about how it was more sustainable, and bolted for the showers. He was normally a two-minute guy, for showers only obviously, but today, he took his time. He loved his team. He just didn't like them or anybody else right now.

He washed, then put up an arm to brace himself against the tile and let the scalding water sluice down his back. This tile could be updated or replaced if they won the Rose Cup and got the money for renovations. No more salmon-pink border or unintentionally grey grout.

Sean stared at the rivers of water flowing over his skin. He would just wait them out. Stand there until the voices dissipated. He couldn't do it right now. It was obvious as hell that he was a walking thundercloud. Even more than usual. But he couldn't begin to sort it out in his own head, let alone discuss it with anyone else.

When the only sound was his own shower, Sean turned off the water and grabbed his towel. He pushed back the curtain and dried off, then wrapped the towel around his waist and walked back to his locker.

He froze in the doorway. Four men, Tyler, Brett, Country, and André, leaned against the row of lockers, fully dressed, their bags next to them on the bench.

"Taking your sweet-ass time." Country glanced at his watch.

Sean looked between the four of them. "Not in the mood. For whatever this is."

André stepped forward and pointed at Sean's pile of things. "Clothe yourself, sir. We have destinations."

"No." Sean strode into the room and dropped his towel on the bench.

"Emotional wellness check," Tyler countered. "It's either this or group therapy."

Sean yanked on his boxer briefs and jeans. "I have plans."

"Right. With us." Brett slung his bag over his shoulder.

Sean pulled his shirt over his head. "I'm tired."

"Well." André leaned against the locker. "You're about to be exhausted."

———

There was no resisting. There were four of them and only one of him, and once he heard Emma was in on it, he knew Tyler wouldn't go home until he cried "Uncle."

So, he got in Country's truck. Within three minutes, he knew exactly where their destination was.

He groaned as they entered the parking lot.

André spun to grin over the seat. "Ladies' night."

It was the stupidest two words Sean'd ever heard in his life. "None of us is single." Brett raised a brow, and Sean scoffed. "I'm not—geez. You know what I'm saying."

Tyler opened the door when Country cut the engine. "Nope. Tonight we're your wingmen, bud." He gave a roll of his hand, motioning to the entrance.

Sean's eyes narrowed. This reeked of a trap, but he couldn't figure out why any of them would want him to dig himself further into a hole with Kelty. Was he supposed to refuse? Prove his loyalty? Hadn't he already been pretty clear he didn't want to be there?

He stepped out of the truck to the dirt parking lot, and they all walked into the bar. The Dusty Rose hit them square in the face with neon, perfume, and pounding bass. Clusters of women danced around high-tops in bright dresses and impractical boots.

Country inhaled like he was letting wine breathe. "Smells like possibilities."

André leaned in. "I'm thinking . . . her." He motioned with a nod to a woman with a black bob and a cropped black satin tank top.

Sean pushed past them and went straight to the bar. If he was going to get through this, he needed to be plastered. Not convenient considering work in the morning, but desperate times.

The boys wasted no time in their pursuits.

André followed him to the bar, giving up on Katherine Zeta Jones and instead turning to a woman in an eighties, off-the-shoulder T-shirt. The two of them were cackling in no time. Sean was downing his first shot when André angled a casual point in his direction.

Country somehow found a bachelorette party and, within moments, had three bridesmaids evaluating Sean with the intensity of mugshot analysts while he spouted something that was impossible to lip-read.

After Brett attempted to escort a woman in a red dress toward him—despite the alcohol loosening him up—Sean accepted reality. He was either going to have to drink until he passed out or confront them. Surprisingly, he chose the latter.

Sean turned his back to the bar. "Anyone want to tell me why we're doing this?"

Brett shrugged. "Playoffs are coming up."

Country nodded. "We thought a chance to relax—"

"Cut the crap," Sean barked. "Why the hell are we here?"

Tyler met Brett's gaze, then released a slow breath. "Uh, we—"

"Ghosts of Playoffs Present." André grinned. "I already coined it."

Sean stared at him. He was used to André's words not making sense, but this was a new low.

"This," André said, tipping his chin toward the dance floor, "is what single looks like. Beautiful, no?"

"Mm. And this." Brett pulled out his phone and swiped. "We already made you a dating profile on a few different apps. We'll send you the login info, but—"

Sean pushed his phone away, his face reddening. "This is what Emma put you up to? What, trying to scare me straight?"

André made a face. "If you're not straight, we can change the app—"

Sean slammed his glass onto the bar and stormed to the exit.

"Thompson, turn that pretty backside of yours around!" Country called. Sean didn't turn. He slammed the doors open, not caring that he made two girls yelp in surprise, and stomped in the direction of the truck.

"Thompson!" Country growled, and the sound of his boots slamming against the dirt moved closer.

Sean flew back as Country grabbed him, throwing him against an old Ford. "You didn't pay your tab, bud." Country jammed his shoulder into his stomach, pinning him.

Sean gave him a quick jab, but Country came back, twisting his arm until his shoulder screamed. He jerked his knee up, breaking his hold, then slammed a fist into Country's middle, but he was braced for it. Country hit a sharp kidney shot then pulled him tight, forcing his head into his chest.

"Sean, I love you like a brother, but you hear me. I won't

stop if you don't want me to. I'll beat the shit out of you if that's what you need right now, bud."

Sean gasped for breath, his lungs burning, his eyes stinging. His arms slackened as he leaned into Country. His shoulders shook, the dark bolus of emotion rolling over him in one typhoon-like wave.

Country clamped his arms around him, gripping his shoulders like he could pull the hurt from him with his bare hands.

Sean fought, trying to pull back, but the strength had sapped out of him. So he stood there and cried until his eyes ran dry. Until his legs could support him.

Country released him and gave him a moment. He turned his back and wiped the tears, blood, and snot from his face with his shirt. When he spun back, André, Tyler, and Brett stood next to Country.

"When are you going to learn your body can't handle shots?" André quipped, and Sean huffed a laugh.

Tyler nodded toward the truck, and they walked as a group to the back of the lot. Just as he was about to open the door, André handed him something. A card.

Sean peered closer. *Elodie Shaw.* André's sister. With a stupid number of letters after her name.

Sixteen

KELTY DIDN'T MEAN to spend an hour after work trolling through the thrift store, but the place was a time capsule. There were wedding dresses from the sixties, sports jerseys from teams that no longer existed or had been bought by some rich city in the States, which was even worse, and dance costumes from what had to be topless Cabarets. She couldn't stay focused on the task at hand, especially when she imagined Tyler having to put something like that on and skate.

At least the clothing was related to the goal. What she spotted next definitely wasn't. A taxidermied gopher wearing a tiny red Mountie hat.

She had to get that for the white elephant—

The thought stopped her cold. Would she be at the white elephant party?

Tears sprang to her eyes. She gritted her teeth and pulled out her phone, then snapped a picture and sent it to the girls' group.

New team mascot? He swears he's good luck

. . .

The text chain lit up immediately.

EMMA

> WHAT is that.

RHONDA

> WHY is that

PENNY

> So THAT's where that went

DELIA

> New album cover

Hearts and laugh-cry emojis littered her screen, and she instantly felt better. She set the gopher in the child seat of her cart and buckled him in with the strap. Safety first.

Next aisle over, she discovered a vintage curling sweater —cream-colored with red maple leaves knitted across the chest and "Lethbridge Bonspiel '88" embroidered proudly on the sleeve. She held it up. It was an extra-large and smelled like mothballs. Yeah. That was it. She threw it in the cart.

She wandered through the aisles, finding bowler hats, cat-eye glasses, beads, boas, cat sweaters, and polyester bell bottoms. The pièce de résistance, though, was on the far back wall. A vintage neon snow bib with the words "Banff 1989 Winter Games" hand-lettered along the sides in black marker. Whoever owned them had been an optimist. Or had a troubling personality disorder.

Kelty stood in the middle of the aisle, grinning like an idiot. The cart of champions. Her smile slipped at the first thought that came to her head. *It would be so much funnier if he were standing there too.*

———

Saturday morning came with a bright sky and a dump of spring snow. Of course that would happen today when she'd planned to tackle the rest of her spring clean-up. Kelty tugged on her hoodie and boots anyway and headed out back. Her task was simple but annoying. Rake up the thick mat of dead leaves and gravel that winter plows had scattered across her side lawn. It was south-facing, and from the window, it looked like the snow had already melted off half of it. If she had to wait until—

Kelty stalled at the side of the house, about to reach for the rake that was sitting there instead of inside the garage. She frowned, rounding the fence. The snow was in fact mostly melted, but the leaves were gone. The lawn was already spotless.

Uhhhh, what now?

She walked across the yard slowly, as if the culprit might

leap out from behind the compost bin. Nothing. Just bright green shoots of grass poking up through the brown in her perfect yard. She hadn't hired anyone. She definitely hadn't done it last weekend. Which left—

No. Absolutely not. Sean hadn't been over here. She would've noticed it. And he'd balked when she asked him to do it a few weeks ago.

But . . .

He had taken out the trash bins.

Something pinched in her chest, and she tightened her grip on the rake. Had he come that morning? Was he still there?

She scanned the street for his truck. Nothing. It was Saturday, and she'd told him she had plans today. Which meant if he saw her at home, he'd know she lied. Which meant she needed to *actually* have plans.

Kelty hurried back to the house and put the rake in the garage. All she wanted to do was curl back up in bed, but she could take a quick trip to the store or something. Or! She smiled to herself. No yardwork. She could make it to the bakery before they sold out of pain au chocolat.

She quickly dressed, put on a little concealer, and pulled her hair up. Then she hopped in the car.

The sun was bright, reflecting off the patches of snow and making the whole world light up like it had a flash. She cranked up her car stereo on the drive and sang along, drumming the steering wheel with the beat to drown out the thoughts fighting for attention in her mind.

Had Sean come over? It had to have been him. But why? Why was he doing things for her when anytime they talked he sat there brooding?

None of it made any sense. His actions said he loved her. Sometimes in a weird, possessive way, but still. So why couldn't he just spit out what he was thinking? It was beyond maddening. And confusing. And all the things.

She finally drove into the parking lot, pulling out of her Sean spiral. The bakery smelled like heaven the second she walked in. Sugar, butter, coffee, and the faint tang of yeast rolls fresh from the oven. She ordered at the counter—one London Fog, a chocolate croissant, and a piece of quiche, because why the hell not?

She turned, scanning for a table and stutter-stepped at the sound of her name. Kelty whirled.

"Hey." Mason stood from a corner booth, giving a small wave.

What. The. Since when did he come here? She scanned her memory, wondering if she or Sean had ever mentioned the bakery, which was ridiculous because the entire city knew about it. It wasn't like it was *theirs*.

Mason motioned to the table with an invitation in his expression.

No. She did not want to walk over. But what was she supposed to do? She'd obviously come in alone, and her food wasn't wrapped up for takeaway.

"Hey." She forced a smile to her face and strode over.

Mason looked pleased. "What are the odds?" He slid past the table and took her drink and plate, set it down, then gave her a hug.

He smelled different. Like money.

"Are you on your way out?" She pulled back and glanced at the table. His coffee was nearly empty.

Mason shook his head. "No, I was about to order another. Just getting some work done."

"Working on a Saturday?"

He shrugged. "Sit, I'll be right back."

She cursed under her breath as she dropped into the chair. So much for her celebratory breakfast. Now she was going to have to make small talk and somehow not let her negativity slip about the party. Or the whole cutting Sean out of his venture thing. Or anything about Sean in general.

Mason returned a moment later and, thankfully, wanted to do much of the talking. He told her about meetings that weekend, about his latest ski trip to Jasper, about dating horror stories, slipping in the occasional probing question. "Probably been a while since you had to deal with that, eh?" Or her personal favourite, "Any life changes on your end I missed?"

Kelty deflected, sipping her tea and focusing very hard on her quiche.

She wouldn't have noticed the jingle of the bakery bell had Mason not stopped mid-sentence.

"Were you—?" Mason frowned, looking down at her plate.

Kelty turned, and her heart jumped into her throat. Sharla and Rob walked toward the counter, followed by Emma, Logan and Crystal, two people she'd never met, and—

There was Sean. Standing just inside the door. His eyes locked on both of them.

CHAPTER
Seventeen

KELTY PULLED into the underground lot already sweating. The clock on her dashboard read 4:41. So much for punctual. To her credit, the only reason she was late was to avoid arriving two hours early.

She'd booked a pedicure and manicure. Waxing had been on the table until she realized she would've looked like a plucked chicken. You know, if anyone were to see her down there, which she wasn't expecting but also *maybe hoping*, since her lady parts had been intermittently on fire since receiving such blatant instructions from Sean.

He'd told her what to do. No questions, no please or thank you. That kind of confidence from him made her list of the hottest thing she'd experienced thus far in her life, no questions asked.

So. She'd cleaned her apartment. Menu planned and shopped. Done anything and everything to make a torturously slow week move a little faster. *See you soon.* It may as well have been a month since he'd sent that text.

She parked, smoothed her wind-tangled hair, slipped on a blazer she'd abandoned in the passenger seat, and took the elevator up. The mirrored doors slid shut on a glimpse of herself with bright eyes and flushed cheeks. She looked like she was trying to sell Korean skincare.

She blew out a breath and tried to calm her nerves. This was just work. Maybe. *Probably not.* And there went her labia again.

When the elevator opened on their floor, the open office looked as if it were in a pre-five o'clock haze. Coats hung on chair backs, screensaver constellations drifted across monitors, and a few stragglers were packing up with the unhurried thirty-minute ritual of *it's almost time to go but not quite.* Sean stood at the end of the aisle by the glassed-in conference room, sleeves pushed to his elbows, tie crooked in that way that made her knees wobble.

He watched as she approached, something like a smile tugging at one corner of his mouth. Not a greeting. Just a *there you are.* He didn't offer a handshake or a hug. He just held the door to the room open and let her pass, his hand grazing her lower back and igniting every nerve beneath her skin.

"You good to dive in?" he asked. A professional question.

"Absolutely." Her response was made awkward by the fact that she couldn't catch her breath. *What was he doing to her?* Either this was the most masterful foreplay or he was an idiot. If he didn't kiss her again after all this, there was a high probablity she was going to slash his tires.

Kelty set her bag down. They'd gone over employee benefits already. They'd mapped payroll and vacation carryovers and the dental plans. They only had a few tasks left. Final asset verification, signage transition, keycard audit, and walkthrough of the storage rooms so nothing weird got lost in the handover.

Sean stopped next to her, and the air shifted. A subtle waft of his cologne filled Kelty's senses. Her eyes fluttered.

"Water?" He held out a glass. His fingers grazed hers as she took it, the barest brush, and heat skated down her spine. Sean didn't seem to notice. He turned and picked up a tablet from the table.

"I've got the list of assets here. Walk with me?" Sean didn't turn to face her. Was that purposeful? Kelty wanted to crane her neck and glance down to determine if there was a reason, but she couldn't get away with it.

"Sure."

Sean nodded once and walked to the door. They did a slow circuit of the floor, confirming that the larger monitors going to the design team were tagged for transfer, and tested a handful of doors to verify keycard permissions. Sean stood close when she scanned, his shoulder almost touching hers as she watched the little lights flick from red to green.

For the love. She was going to spontaneously combust.

In the storage room behind reception, boxes towered in neat columns labelled with Mason's handwriting. She tapped information on each item into the tablet. It was boring work, but at least it didn't take any of her focus.

Sean reached up to check the top shelf when she couldn't quite see the labels. The small of her back burned where his palm landed for a steadying second as she stood on her tiptoes to count a row of docking stations. She couldn't get enough of the accidental touches or peeks of his skin.

They drifted to Facilities to confirm the sign-off on access changes, and by the time they finished the final pass by the mailroom and the little kitchenette, the lights were low and most desks sat empty. Sean double-checked one last thing at the print station, then nodded toward the conference room.

They stepped inside, and the empty space felt cavernous, their reflections ghosting the glass. What came next? Kelty's pulse slammed in her throat. She walked toward her chair, then turned back to hand Sean the iPad, but he still stood next to the door.

"I just found out what this switch does." Sean lifted a hand, hesitating.

"It's not the lights?"

A muscle in his jaw twitched. He shook his head. "Privacy glaze." He flicked it, and the transparent glass fogged at once, the outside office dissolving into a milky blur. "If the lights are on, you can still see shadows, but if they're off . . ." He shifted his hand and flicked the second switch.

Kelty gripped the iPad as her eyes adjusted. Some light filtered in from the west side of the office. Just enough for her to catch Sean's silhouette moving toward her.

She sucked in a breath as his fingers grazed her hip, her hands beginning to tremble. Sean took the iPad from her and nudged, pushing her back until the backs of her thighs hit the edge of the table.

"I've been thinking about this table." He set the iPad down, sliding it away from them.

"Oh yeah?"

He nodded, pressing closer. *Yeah.* There was one very big reason he'd been keeping his back to her most of the evening.

"Every time you're in here."

Her mouth went dry. "It's a nice table."

Sean tugged at her blouse, untucking it from her slacks. Her skin prickled as his hand slid beneath the fabric.

"You're sure nobody's here?" she whispered.

He lowered his head, scraping his stubble against her cheek. "Door's locked."

His other hand slid to the back of her neck, fingers threading into her hair, and then his mouth brushed hers. It wasn't ravenous. It was a slow lean into gravity, the gathering of a tide. He tasted clean, just like he smelled. Masculine and something that reminded her of a day at the lake.

The kiss deepened out of inevitability, and they tumbled

the only place they could, closer together. Her hands climbed his shirt of their own accord, learning the path of buttons, the give of fabric over muscle.

"Can you be quiet?" he whispered against her mouth. Her blazer fell open and his fingers slipped beneath it, over the thin fabric of her blouse.

"It's hard."

"Correct. But can you be quiet?"

She laughed, accidentally clipping his front teeth with hers. "Sorry, I—"

Sean breathed in her words, slipping his tongue between her lips, tasting her. Whatever she'd meant to say melted through her and into the floor.

"Is this okay?" His hands found the button of her slacks.

Heat licked low in her belly. She nodded, her hands growing more frantic. *Why were they still wearing so many clothes?* "I never do this."

"What? Sit on a conference room table?"

A laugh rasped out of her. "Never."

He kissed the corner of her mouth, the line of her jaw, slowly, as if he had hours. Her heart stalled. They probably *did* have hours. All night if they wanted. Did anyone track what time people came and went?

She grinned at that verbiage.

"What?" His mouth paused at the hollow under her ear, smiling against her skin.

"Nothing."

He kissed her neck. "Something funny?"

"Just—" She sighed as his hand slid under her waistband. Her spine liquified as he covered her hip with his palm then followed the curve, his wrist forcing her pants tight. It was intolerable. After imagining every "what if" all weekend, she had absolutely zero need for foreplay.

She worked at his tie, trying not to seem desperate. It was useless. Sean's laugh rumbled in his chest.

"Stop. I'm bad at this." She worked it loose, then fumbled with the buttons until she got his shirt open. She yanked it free of his pants, and his breath hitched when her fingers found the warm skin above his waistband.

Undressing in a public place, an office she worked in, was both hot and terrifying. She'd gone over potential ramifications of getting involved with Sean, but had she thought through what would happen if someone walked in on them? Mason left that afternoon, but what about Andrew?

She could barely latch onto the worries because Sean's knuckles brushed over her stomach. The room shrank, narrowing to the feel of him. Sean tugged her pants down, then hoisted her up. She gasped at the cool glass on the backs of her thighs.

He shimmied her slacks passed her knees, then over her ankles, and dropped them on the floor. She gripped his hips, pulling him into the space between her legs, revelling in the warmth of him.

"Off." Kelty brushed his waistband. Sean chuckled, then leaned down to comply. Kelty pulled the shirt off his shoulders, too impatient for him to resurface.

Which he didn't. As soon as he stepped free of his pants, he gripped her knees and his stubble grazed her inner thigh. She sucked in a breath.

"Hm." Sean kissed her. "Good information."

"You're killing me." She spread her palms over his back, learning the planes and ridges of his muscles.

His breath warmed her skin. "That's the goal."

Kelty huffed in frustration and dragged him up to her level. "Sean. I'm never going to expect you to read my mind."

"That works well for me."

She worked to catch her breath, pressing a hand to his cheek. "Good. So. I need this to happen. Right now."

Sean kissed the inside of her palm. "I think I can accommodate." He pulled her to the edge of the table. "Any requests?"

Requests? She could think of a hundred things she wanted him to do to her right now, which meant literally anything was on the table. "Whatever you want."

He raised an eyebrow, then dropped his gaze to the chair next to them. After considering a moment, he pushed it out of the way, still gripping her hand, and pulled the one next to it closer. No armrests.

Kelty grinned. "I think I can accommodate."

PRESENT DAY

KELTY DROPPED her fork to her plate, her brain still trying to process what was happening. Sean's jaw worked as he tore his eyes away from her and Mason to join his parents and their friends at the counter. Emma craned her neck, her eyes wide. Kelty shot her a panicked look, then whipped out her cell.

"Everything okay?" Mason asked.

"Mmhmm. Just didn't know they were heading over so soon." Kelty tapped out a text to Emma.

> I swear I didn't meet Mason on purpose. He was just here!

She dropped her phone to the bench next to her, and gave Mason a bright smile. "Must've miscommunicated."

Mason looked skeptical. "Are you and Sean—"

"Fine. We're fine. It's just that his family has a bunch of friends in town, so he's been showing up for all the events. You know how it is."

"Kelty!" Emma strode toward them, and Kelty jumped up from the bench so fast that the table shifted.

"Hey!" She rushed forward and wrapped her in a hug. "So crazy that you're all here. What inspired this?"

Emma sighed. "You know my mom. She always wants to make things special for out-of-town guests."

Kelty did know that. She should've considered that when coming to the bakery they all loved.

"Is that Logan Kemp?" A man next to them peered over his morning paper.

Emma winced. "He wore a hat. I don't think it's helping."

Kelty scanned the restaurant. Everyone was staring. "Yeah. I agree with that assessment." She couldn't blame them. She'd basically done the same thing when he walked into the Thompson home.

Logan smiled and took a selfie with a kid who materialized from thin air in a Blizzard hoodie. She felt bad for him but was secretly grateful for the distraction.

Mason leaned forward on the table. "Sean never mentioned he knew Kemp."

Emma shrugged. "Old family friend." She slipped past Kelty and leaned down to give Mason a hug. "Long time, no see."

"I'd say."

Emma gave a polite smile just as Sean arrived next to Kelty. He'd probably done the same mental math she did. His parents would expect them to be excited to see each other.

"Hey." Kelty pitched her voice up, going for light and airy. "You made it!"

Sean's gaze flicked from her to Mason and back. "Looks that way."

The silence between them ballooned, and Kelty quickly reached for him. The hug was stiff. She wanted to rip up the floor tiles and disappear under the foundation.

"Should we—?" Kelty gestured vaguely toward him, then panicked when Sean didn't move.

"Good to see you again, Mason."

Mason stood and clapped him on the back. "Yeah, didn't know you were coming."

Kelty groaned internally. *What the hell? Why was he making it sound like she'd planned this?* She'd told Sean she had a meeting. Anything she said would sound like an excuse.

She turned, searching for anything to pull her away from this soul-deadening thirty seconds.

Logan had become a one-man photo booth. Kelty nudged Emma. "Should someone save him?"

She sighed. "Pretty sure he's used to it."

Mason stood, pushing his mug to the middle of the table. "I should let you all . . ." He gesticulated with his hands, swirling the air between them. "Great running into you."

Kelty nodded. Better. At least that didn't sound like they'd agreed to meet.

Sean nodded. "Good to see you."

Mason smiled. "I'll reach out." He tossed it off like a casual thing, but his eyes lingered on Kelty just long enough to make her throat lock.

She plastered on her most diplomatic smile. "Safe drive."

He was gone a moment later, and Kelty bolted to the coffee caddy under the guise of filling a glass of water. She made a stop at the Thompson table, said hello to everyone, then made her exit.

What kind of cruel joke was this? The literal worst thing that could happen in this situation was Sean finding her meeting up with Mason. How? It was like walking down a street with no traffic and then crossing paths with another pedestrian, two cars, and a bicycle all in the same ten seconds. *Was there a scientific law that demanded the attraction of chaos?*

She retreated to her car outside the bakery, heart still thudding like she'd sprinted a mile in heels. She opened the girls' chat with shaking hands. They all knew what was happening at this point. Once she'd stayed at Penny's, there was no point in trying to hide it.

KELTY

> Soooo went to Éclaire de Lune and found Mason there

> BUT WAIT. It gets better

> I couldn't avoid him, so I was sitting there chatting with him when Sean and his entire family walked in five minutes later

> I want to swerve into traffic

The dots popped up immediately. She breathed a sigh of relief.

JENNA

> Oooohhhhhh noooo

PENNY

It looked so bad

GRACE

Did you explain???

What do I say?? You know Sean . . .

JENNA

Yeah. Ask Emma??

She's still in there with her family

PENNY

Maybe she can do damage control!?

Kelty dropped her head back against the headrest and closed her eyes. Hopefully Emma would say something, but Grace was right. She needed to clear the air.

She blew out a breath and lifted her phone, scrolling to Sean's contact. Her thumbs hovered. She started typing, deleting, retyping, until she finally settled on something that felt right and pressed send.

CHAPTER
Nineteen

IT WAS ONLY ONE DAY, but Sean already missed his Sunday mornings. Sleeping in. Waking up next to Kelty. Coffee and toast with eggs on the porch. *Waking up next to Kelty.*

Sunday mornings were not for watching four women turn his mom's kitchen into an episode of *Iron Chef.* He leaned in the doorway, mug in hand, hoping his coffee was enough to protect him from the chaos or the ache building in his chest.

It wasn't.

Kelty had walked in five minutes before, cheeks flushed from the early spring chill, wearing hiking pants, trail runners, and a hoodie with the strings pulled tight. Before he could even process the sight of her, Sharla had yanked her inside with a squeal and announced, *"You're just in time!"*

She kicked off her shoes and now stood at the island beside Sharla, apron tied over her hoodie, peeling carrots next to Crystal, Logan's wife, while she chopped onions. Madelyn Wilson, a celebrity of her own right in the Thompson household, measured flour into a mixing bowl, laughing and dancing along with the nineties music his mom was pumping.

Sean hated it.

No. He hated how much he liked it. How much he loved the sight of Kelty sliding into his family like she belonged there.

He scowled into his mug.

Crystal noticed him first. "Someone woke up on the wrong side of the bed."

Sean took a sip of coffee. "I'm good. Thanks."

Madelyn smirked. "You had that same look on your face when you were two."

Kelty glanced up at that, her eyes flicking to his. Sean felt a stupid lurch in his stomach. He turned away, pretending to study the family pictures on the wall that he'd memorized years ago.

"I'm surprised you're awake." Sharla glanced at the clock while she stirred a pot on the stove.

"We're going on a hike," Kelty said, setting the now-naked carrot on the cutting board.

The faces of all three women lit up.

"Ooh, where at?" Sharla asked.

Kelty shrugged. "Not sure. Sean planned it."

This inspired even brighter smiles. Sharla beamed at him. "Is it a surprise?"

Sean took a long sip of coffee, wishing he could drown in it. "You know me, Mom. Big on surprises." He felt like he was seventeen again, his mom praising him for asking a girl to Grad with chocolate bars taped to a poster board. Which he never did, by the way. That was Jordan Wheatfill.

Sharla swatted him as he took his mug to the sink. He hadn't talked with Jordan much since he and Rhonda became a thing. There wasn't a need to do more than tap gloves after the games, but all signs pointed to them meeting in the finals again this year. Kelty had mentioned more than once that it would be nice to have a real conversation. Make things less awkward when Rhonda brought him out. But of all the conversations he should be having to make things less awkward, that didn't make the top ten.

"Well I didn't realize you were leaving now. Get going. We can take care of all this." Sharla shooed Kelty out of the kitchen. "You'll be back for supper, right?"

Sean nodded. "That's the plan." His head felt fuzzy. His body was so antsy, his hands shook.

"Want me to drive?" Kelty asked, leaning over to put her shoes back on.

"We should take the truck. Might hit some water on the road."

She nodded and straightened. "Okay, then." She twisted her hoodie in her hands. "I can contribute gas money or—"

"No." Sean herded her out the front door.

"I'm just saying—"

"No." Why the hell would she think he wanted gas money? Never once in all the time they'd been together had he asked her for that. The fact that she thought of it—that she offered—made his head throb.

This was a task for his family. They were heading out to Norquay to test the course. Make sure it wasn't going to kill Sean's parents and their septuagenarian friends. Kelty was giving up her time on a Saturday to be there and she was offering to pay him?

The pounding at his temples only got worse once they were in the truck. Kelty was dead silent. Sean kept his eyes on the road, but every nerve was aware of her beside him. Her knees drawn up, fingers fiddling with the string on her hood.

They left Calgary behind, trading gas stations and big box stores for prairie fields dusted with morning frost. The horizon shifted as the Rockies rose ahead, jagged and majestic, snow still clinging to the ridges. The Bow River snaked alongside the highway, swollen with snow melt, turquoise and glittering in the morning sun.

Sean loved this drive. Today it felt like sitting in a pressure cooker.

Kelty finally broke the silence. "It's ridiculously beautiful."

He glanced over. "Yeah."

"Have you ever done Norquay?" She swivelled to face him. "I know we've never done it together, but did you do it before?"

Sean nodded. His family had done it when he was in high school. His dad had decided it was some kind of rite of passage. That every kid in their family needed to know they could make it through a course like that. He heard horror stories about the trip with just Nate, Eliza, and Rachel.

"You didn't believe me about Mason."

Sean's grip on the steering wheel tightened. What was he supposed to say to that? That he wasn't skeptical that they'd both randomly shown up at the bakery at the same time on a Saturday morning after neither of them had seen Mason in three years even though he'd been living in Calgary the whole time?

"Do you really think I'd do that?"

He wet his lips. "Meeting up with an old friend isn't a crime."

"He's not my friend," she snapped. "I would hope you'd trust me more than some stupid moment like that. And I get it. It probably looked suspicious. When you showed up, I panicked because I felt like an idiot." Kelty pressed her knee up against the dashboard. "I didn't have a 'thing' yesterday. I was annoyed that my whole life is basically your life. It felt pathetic to say 'Sure! I can come whenever because I have no plans outside of the Thompsons and Snowballs.'"

Sean slowed, the car in front of him going ten kilometers per hour below the speed limit. He wanted to honk, but at the moment it was convenient to have a few extra minutes in the car. "You're not pathetic."

"Thanks," she quipped.

Sean took a moment, trying to remember how they talked to each other before. What he would've said if they didn't have an entire rink's worth of ice between them. "I had no plans outside of Snowballs and you, so I think we're even."

Yes, they both had work, but that was a mutually agreed upon means to an end. Their jobs weren't terrible. There were even parts of work that they both enjoyed and were motivated by. But ten out of ten times they'd choose to pull up with friends or family instead of logging in or going to the office.

"And I believe you about Mason," he added when Kelty didn't respond.

She pursed her lips. "Did that—are you okay? Do you need to swallow the puke that just worked its way up your throat?"

Sean huffed a laugh. "I'm serious."

"You're a terrible liar."

"If you say you didn't plan it, I believe you."

She paused. He heard the words in his head even if she didn't say them. *Best compliment you ever gave me.* "Well that's what I say."

He twisted his hands on the wheel. "Okay, then."

"Okay."

———

At the Norquay base, guides handed out helmets, harnesses, and carabiners. Sean buckled his on easily, muscle memory from years of scouting activities with his brother and dad. Watching Kelty, however, was like watching someone wrestle a particularly stubborn octopus.

"You're stepping into it, not strangling it," he said.

She tugged at a strap, scowling. "This thing has more loops than a damn pretzel."

"Want me to help?"

"No," she snapped, then grabbed onto his arm when her foot got stuck and she stumbled. "Okay, maybe. But don't gloat."

He gloated. But only to hide the flush crawling up his neck at the feel of her skin and the sound of little puffs of air catching in her throat as he tightened the waist strap. He stepped back quickly, peering up at the towering rock face.

Rocks weren't soft. Rocks didn't smell like vanilla. Rocks were hard— Nope, that wasn't helping.

"C'mon." Kelty nudged him as she started up the path. The straps on her harness accentuated her curves, framing her backside smack dab in the centre of his view. That wasn't helping either.

The first section lulled them into false confidence. Wide rungs bolted into limestone, a steady upward zigzag. The view stretched out behind them, Banff shimmering in the valley like a fantasy world.

Kelty climbed steadily, but her breathing was laboured. She shook out a hand after gripping the steel cable.

"Doing okay?" he asked.

"Peachy." Her voice was tight.

"Cool. If you could speed up, then?"

Kelty flipped him the bird and almost lost her grip.

Sean laughed. "Flipping me off isn't worth falling for."

"At least I'd die doing what I love." He raised an eyebrow, and she grimaced. "That's not what I meant."

"Sounded like an invitation."

She snorted, and for a moment, everything felt normal between them. It sent his heart slamming to his knees. He needed to fix this. He needed her to know that she had nothing to do with his inability to say yes to everything she wanted.

But did it matter? In the end, if he couldn't give it to her, wasn't she better off finding someone who could? Regardless of his sob story?

"Sean." Kelty stopped at the top, bracing herself against the wall. Two cables stretched across a slot canyon. One for feet, one for hands. Nothing beneath but air, rock, and pine treetops. "I can't do this."

"We're clipped in."

"This thing?" She flicked the carabiner. "It's made of tin foil."

Sean chuckled. "If it can hold me, it can hold you."

"Circular reasoning." Kelty shuffled her feet.

He moved behind her. "Eyes straight ahead. I'll be right—"

Kelty reached back and grabbed his hand. "Can the cables hold both of us?"

"Yeah." He didn't know if that was true, but she was asking for his help. He would've told a bigger lie than that to keep her fingers gripped around his.

She took a step forward and wobbled, promptly overreacted, and jumped back. Her hand smacked against his chest, fingers curling into his jacket for balance. The touch shot through him like lightning.

He held her to his chest, ignoring the thrill of heat at feeling her body fit there. "Okay. This is what we're going to do."

"Mmhmm."

Sean pushed the hair from her cheek. "You're going to use both hands on the cable."

"But—"

"I'm going to stabilize you. My hand on your hip. The whole way."

She looked up, her eyes wide. "But you need both hands." The morning sun hit her cheeks, edging them with gold.

Sean sucked in a breath. "I'm good. Promise."

Kelty's lips twitched. She blinked, then stepped back and nodded once. "Okay. Thank you."

And just like that the moment was gone. He was a hiking guide instead of her boyfriend. They inched across together, breath syncing in ragged bursts, until finally their boots hit solid rock. Kelty sagged against the wall with a groan of relief.

"See?" he said. "Piece of cake."

She glared at him, yanking at her hoodie and pulling it over her head. Her tank top rode up just enough to reveal the strip of stomach above her pants. He tried and failed to ignore it.

"Okay," she muttered, peering upward, "who decided humans should be part mountain goat?"

"Uh, Alberta Parks."

"Alberta Parks can bite me."

He smirked. "Doing more of what you love?" Kelty laughed at that, and he felt like he just hit a wrister top-shelf.

They reached a wider section and paused to drink water. The valley stretched below them in dazzling Technicolor. The turquoise river winding through a quilt of forest and meadow, mountain peaks jagged against a cobalt sky.

"Okay," Kelty said, exhaling, "so what if this whole 'Amazing Race' idea is completely insane."

He took a swig of water. "You think Sharla can't handle it?"

"I think Sharla will murder you if you make her cross that suspension bridge."

"She's tougher than you think."

Kelty raised a brow. "It's your inheritance." She set her water bottle down and walked off the trail. "I'll be back. Just going to pee."

Sean frowned. "Hey, Kelt? I don't think—"

His whole body seized when he heard the sound. The scrape of rubber, the gasp of surprise.

He jumped up just in time to see Kelty's foot skid out from under her in the loose scree beside the path. She flailed, arms pinwheeling, before she dropped and slid out of view.

CHAPTER

Twenty

THE PAIN WAS sharp and white-hot, radiating up from her ankle into her knee and hip. Kelty sat on the rock, clutching her leg, trying to swallow the hiss that escaped through her teeth.

Sean was there instantly. "Don't move," he barked, dropping to his knees beside her. He cradled her ankle like it was made of glass, his fingers gently pulling down her sock.

"It's just twisted." She grimaced as he touched the skin that was already swelling. "I can walk."

"The hell you can." His jaw was tight, his eyes blazing. "You scared the shit out of me." Something in his tone silenced her. He moved his hands up her legs. "What else hurts?"

"Nothing. It's—"

"I saw you go down. What else, Kelt?"

Her stomach flipped. She straightened and showed him her palms. Scraped up. Bright red, but only a little blood. "My ass probably looks like that, too."

He nodded. "Let me see."

"Sean—"

"I'm not joking. If you're bleeding, we need to bandage it."

Kelty allowed him to help her up, balancing on one foot. "Right side."

Sean nodded, holding her against him while he slipped her pants down and checked her skin. At least she'd worn good underwear.

"Just scraped," he said, but didn't move.

"You need a few more minutes back there?"

He carefully slid the waistband up into place. "I was being thorough."

"Uh-huh." She rolled her eyes at his smirk.

Sean lowered her back to the rock and pulled out the First-Aid kit from his pack.

She stared at her scratched up hands. "Nothing's going to stick there."

"Wow. Not much faith in me as a medic."

"You're not a medic."

He scoffed. "I patch up my guys every night on the ice."

"André does that and you know it."

Sean grinned. "Who do you think taught him?"

He pulled a package of gauze and a roll of bright pink something out of a plastic bag and motioned for her to put her palms up. With his head lowered, concentrating, Kelty could observe everything without notice. His hat turned around backward, his hair curling around his ears, the dust smudged on his cheek, probably from her.

He spread antibiotic ointment over the gauze, and she winced as he layered the squares on her cuts. "Sorry," he murmured. When he pulled a strip from the pink roll, she balked.

"What is that?"

He tore a piece off with his teeth. "Horse tape."

"What?"

Sean started wrapping her hand. "Country brings it in. It's

stretchy, doesn't have any adhesive, sticks to itself." He circled it around and affixed the end. "Too tight?"

She shook her head. "Feels good."

Sean nodded and started on the second hand. When he was finished, he shoved the supplies back in his pack and offered her water.

She grimaced. "I still have to pee."

Sean did a commendable job of not looking excited. They both knew she wouldn't be able to hold onto a tree branch with her hands like that. "Go ahead. You can laugh."

"Do you want me to crouch so you can sit on me like a toilet or just—"

"Shut the hell up." Kelty tried to get up from the rock, but struggled to balance. Sean assisted her, and she couldn't help but laugh. It was funny. Straight out of a romantic comedy if real-life, non-sexy comedy was allowed to be a thing. "Just . . . hold my wrists."

His brows pinched, his hands still holding her waist. "What do you mean?"

She sighed. "I'm going to pull down my pants—"

"I'm listening."

She smacked him and winced.

"Be nice. You don't want to hurt yourself."

Kelty ground her teeth. "I'm going to pull down my pants and crouch. You're going to hold my wrists so I can lean back and not pee on myself or fall on my already scratched ass."

His lips twitched. "Perfect."

"Get it out." She waited as Sean's face split into a smile. He loved accidental comedy, especially if it was at someone else's expense. His Instagram feed was almost entirely people wiping out on skis or tripping in public.

"I'm sorry you're hurt."

"Mm. Thank you. Very sincere." Kelty motioned to the trees. "Can we just get this over with?"

Sean nodded, helping her hobble over. "How do you want me?"

"Can you not make this sound sexual?"

"It's a simple question."

"Just turn around."

He winked. "From the back. Good choice."

Kelty growled in frustration. "Just stand there until I'm ready."

"I'm so hot right now."

"Sean!"

He laughed, holding his hands out behind him.

"Just a second, I need—"

"I can help."

"No!" Kelty worked at her pants, trying not to dislodge the horse tape. It didn't matter if he saw her naked. He'd seen every part of her body a thousand times, but it was the principle of it.

Finally, she got her underwear over her thighs. "Okay, just don't let go."

"Got it."

"I'm serious, Sean." She held out her hands so he could grab her wrists, then lowered to a crouch.

"Is it happening?"

"No it's not happening!" She hissed. This was worse than trying to pee in a lake. Her body didn't know how to let go under these circumstances.

"Do you—"

"Just shut up, Sean!"

His shoulders shook, and she had to close her eyes to keep the red hot rage at bay so her urethra had any chance of opening.

It took a few seconds, but her body finally released. She sat there and dripped dry for a minute, then slowly rose, careful not to put too much weight on her ankle. "Okay."

Sean let go of her wrists when she tugged. She pulled her pants up and blew out a breath. "Thanks."

Sean turned to face her. "My pleasure."

Kelty rolled her eyes. She tried to take a step back to their packs, but her ankle wasn't having it. Before she could ask him to lend a hand, he moved. One second she was standing, the next she was in his arms, swept up like she was a stuffed animal.

"Sean!" she squeaked, grabbing at his shoulders.

"Don't even start." His grip only tightened, muscles flexing beneath her taped palms as he maneuvered back to their packs. He set her down. "Put it on."

"Sean—"

"We're over the hard parts."

"You're not carrying me down this mountain!" She slung her pack over her shoulders.

Sean did the same, affixing his pack to his front, then leaned in. "Do you like it when I tell you what you can't do?" She gave him a look. "Exactly."

Sean turned and crouched, waiting for her to climb on. Seeing him there, waiting for her, doing everything in his power to make sure she was safe and taken care of, made a lump lodge in her throat.

Why was it so easy for him to pack horse tape and antibiotic ointment, to carry her down a damn mountain, but when it came to saying the words she wanted to hear or making plans for their lives together? The way he acted then was the equivalent of him never following her down the rocks.

Sean grunted. "You need a few more minutes back there?"

She scoffed. "Just being thorough."

CHAPTER
Twenty-One

SEVEN AND A HALF YEARS EARLIER

THE BOTTLE of seltzer on the conference table hissed as Kelty scrolled through the projection charts. Across from her, Sean rested his hands on the glass table, and that was why she'd stared at the same screen for the past five minutes. She couldn't stop glancing at them. His broad, scarred knuckles, a nicked thumbnail. *Why were they so hot?*

Mason leaned back in his chair. "Run me through the earn-out triggers again. I want it airtight before they start poking holes. Less wiggle, more backbone."

"We've already tied it to gross margin, not top-line," Andrew said. He tapped his trackpad, highlighting a chart. "Quarterly reviews. If they miss twice, it freezes."

"They won't miss," Sean said. His tone was calm, but Kelty caught the flex in his jaw. "Supply chain's clean. Contracts are sticky. We can stand on this."

The AC coughed on. Kelty angled a page on her legal pad

so only Sean could see the margin. In block letters she wrote, *You good?*

His gaze slid down, brows softening for a heartbeat. Under the table, his shoe brushed her ankle. Over the past week and a half, her gravity had shifted. All in Sean Thompson's direction.

"We should extend the indemnity tail before they ask for it," Mason said. "Better to offer it than get pushed."

"For reps tied to tax and IP, sure," Kelty said. "But general reps? Eighteen months is standard. If they want longer, they'll have to give something back."

Mason squinted at her. "You say 'standard' like it's gospel."

"It's not gospel," she replied, uncapping her pen, "but it is the only thing a judge will recognize when you ask them to enforce a clause you pulled out of your ass."

Andrew almost smiled. "So, twenty-four months for tax and IP, eighteen on the rest. We'll be ready if they push."

"Escrow?" Mason asked.

"Ten percent," Andrew said firmly.

"They'll try for twelve," Mason muttered.

"Then we make it clear anything north of ten cuts into price." Sean wasn't looking at his screen, instead frowning at the phone sitting in his lap.

Kelty tapped her pen to her lips. "Ten and a half isn't a number most men reach."

Sean's eyes flicked up. *There he is.*

Mason laughed out loud. "Why aren't you coming to the negotiations again?"

They moved on, covering reps, warranties, schedules upon schedules, HR rollover narratives, and risk-sharing strategies.

Kelty scribbled notes, translating legal and financial jargon into plain language, building a bridge between Mason's aggression, Andrew's precision, and Sean's steady pragmatism so they could all be on the same page after the weekend.

By evening, the sky outside soaked the windows navy. Someone ordered Thai that congealed on the credenza. Sean hadn't touched it yet, which was strange. She didn't know much about him outside of this office, but the fact that he liked to eat was probably the first things she'd stored away.

"Nice work," Mason said, closing his screen. "I'm happy with how this all looks going into Monday."

Kelty smiled. "That's the goal."

Mason cocked his head to the side. "What are you doing tonight? We all deserve to go out and celebrate."

Kelty's heart galloped. "Oh, no, I actually have some projects to finish up at home."

"That's what the weekend is for."

She laughed. "They're big projects."

"Ten and a half big?" Mason watched for a reaction, but Kelty didn't get a chance to respond.

"He'll be prepped for the harassment case you file tomorrow." Sean brushed past them on the way to the food.

"What?" Mason threw out his hands. "She's the one who brought it up."

"She brought up a fact. She didn't ask how long your dick was."

Andrew snorted, and Mason shifted his weight. "Got it. Well, I'm sorry. Just making a joke."

"It's fine." Kelty stepped back. "Sorry I can't come celebrate."

Mason nodded. "If you change your mind, you have my number." He touched her elbow, then stalked out of the room.

Andrew whistled. "Nice."

Sean filled his plate with rice and basil pork. "Someone's got to save us from lawsuits." He looked up and winked at her, which made it quite difficult not to think about what he'd done while she sat on that table.

She turned to grab her things, trying to hide her blush from Andrew, and saw a message on her phone.

Stagger. Meet at the truck. Ten minutes?

She worked to keep the grin off her face. That's why he got his food late. "Alright, well, good luck on Monday. I don't think we'll have much more to work on as long as all goes well."

Andrew nodded. "Fingers crossed."

Kelty threw out her trash and paused at the door. "It's been great working with you."

Sean nodded, walking back to his seat. "Thanks for everything."

She exited the room and stopped at the washroom first. She killed a few minutes there, then pretended she was on a phone call and paced to the far end of the floor, looking out the windows at the city below. It wasn't the rooftop view, but it gave a perfect snapshot of the restaurant strip.

Sean and Andrew's voices drifted across the room, then disappeared. A few people still worked at their desks, but in another fifteen minutes, this place would be empty. Kelty counted to ten, then walked back to the elevator bank.

The ride took forever. On the ground floor she paused near the revolving door to chat with the night security guard who loved showing her the crossword clues from the morning paper, and the realization hit her. She was going to miss this job.

Her palms started to sweat. After Monday, there was no guarantee she would see Sean again. They'd have no reason to get together, and they hadn't talked about what came next.

She stepped onto the sidewalk, cool air pressing her

cheeks. Their building sat where the river pulled the wind straight up the avenue. She let it strip her thoughts until she reached the far corner, where Sean's truck crouched under a streetlamp.

He leaned against the driver's side, watching her as she crossed to him.

"Hey. What happened in there?"

Sean nodded for her to get in the truck. They'd been doing this for a few days now. Meeting up and talking before she got in her car to head home. This time, when she closed the door, all he did was hand her his phone.

It was a screen shot. Texts to a girl named Emma.

"She's my sister. Those texts are from her ex."

Kelty read over the message chain. "Holy shit."

"Yeah."

Kelty looked up. "When did this happen?"

Sean ran a hand over his face. "She just sent them."

Kelty re-read the first few texts. "He cheated on her."

"Yep."

"And he's trying to tell her it's her fault."

"Right."

Kelty handed Sean the phone. "She knows that's BS, right?"

Sean blew out a breath. "She broke up with him."

"Good. And this is him, what, trying to convince her to come back?"

He nodded. "He's done it once before."

Kelty reached for her seatbelt. "Well, we have to go over there." Sean looked up, and Kelty clicked in. "She's out, which is amazing, but she's vulnerable because breaking a pattern hurts more than keeping it. It doesn't mean she wants the pattern back, but my guess is she's lonely. Especially if they've been together for a while."

He studied her face. "What about your car?"

"Where does she live?"

"About fifteen minutes from here."

Kelty settled into the seat. "You can drive me back. Ooh! And we have to stop for chocolate. That's—"

The words stuck in her throat as her seat belt released and Sean yanked her across the bench, tipping her head back and kissing her. The residual oil from the Thai chilis made her lips tingle.

Sean pulled back, resting his forehead against hers. "I want to see you. After this is over, I want to see you."

Kelty kissed the corner of his mouth. "You should have some time on your hands."

He chuckled, threading his hands in her hair. "Come over for supper on Sunday."

"At your place?"

He smiled against her cheek. "Something like that."

CHAPTER
Twenty~Two

KELTY STARED up at the front entrance to The Ice Centre.

She could leave.

The thought flashed through her head like a dare. She could skip the entire playoffs, throw all her crap into her car, and drive to Penticton tonight. Well, she'd have to stay overnight in Revelstoke or something, but she'd be there midday tomorrow.

It was tempting.

She sighed, locked the doors of the car, and hobbled across the parking lot with the rest of the fans who showed up early to get good seats. With how popular the Elite League games were, someday soon they were going to have to come up with a better seating system. Though bench warming with friends was part of the fun.

She showed her ticket on her phone and moved with the crowd through the atrium. The entrance to the gold rink spat her into white and blue glare, the sound of sticks clapping the boards echoing through the cavernous space.

Kelty drew a deep breath. Cool, clean rink air. There wasn't much better.

She scanned the stands for the Thompson herd. Their group had commandeered a full section near centre ice, easy to spot by the unruly garden of toques and blankets. Sharla and Rob were flanked by Sean's sisters, Eliza and Rachel, who'd arrived in town that morning. Then there was Maddie and Chase and Crystal and Logan. He had chunky, fake glasses along with a toque. Smart.

Carter and Nate sat with their wives, Alix and Naomi, and there was Suraj's wife Rashi, Curtis' family, and what looked like the Snowballs' entire extended friend ecosystem. Emma, Penny, Rhonda, Lindsay and Vaughn, Anne and Tina. The whole gang was here. And—holy shit. That was Jack Harrison and Delia Melise. *How did they get in without a media blitz?*

"Kelty!" Sharla waved her down, and Kelty's heart softened like melting butter.

She wove through knees and blankets to sit in the middle of their entourage.

"You made it," Maddie scooted over so Kelty could drop into the gap between her and Sharla.

"I was about to start a betting pool!" Penny called out.

"I would have won," Emma noted. "I said you'd be thirty minutes early, just because of the limp, and I was only two minutes off." She held up her phone screen as proof.

"Your accuracy is commendable." Kelty grinned and set her water bottle on the concrete floor under the bench. She could've called when Emma would arrive, too. She hadn't been attending games as long as Kelty, but they'd settled into a rhythm.

Her whole life with Sean was a rhythm. Maybe that was part of the problem. Maybe it wasn't just about marriage and kids, maybe she just felt . . . stuck. He had goals and finish lines he was working toward, but her? Kelty scanned the benches, taking in the cowbells and blankets, the mitts and snacks. She was only a spectator.

Rob leaned around Sharla to squeeze Kelty's shoulder. "How's the ankle?"

"So much better," Kelty said. "Sharla's Epsom advice helped."

Sharla patted her knee. "Of course it did. Hydration, too. I brought vitamin waters." She always brought something. She had a Mary Poppins tote full of snacks, tissues, and emergency meds. The bag rustled as she passed Kelty a bottle of dragonfruit flavoured water.

Down on the ice, the Snowballs lined up by their bench, a sea of baby blue. Boyd squatted and shuffled in the goal, stretching while girls filmed him for TikTok. The opposing team clustered near the far faceoff dot. Dr. Quinn Medicine Hattrick wore oxblood jerseys with a silhouetted stethoscope on the crest. They had serious beard game this season.

It was almost too easy to sink into the typical chatter before the game, to pretend these playoffs were just like any other in the past eight years. They delved deep into Emma's hormonal changes, Penny's PT office she just opened with Brett, Jenna's new sister YouTube channel. Kelty was so happy for them. And each new, exciting thing was another knife to her ribs.

She was grateful when the DJ cut the music and they stood for the national anthem. When it was finished, the guys circled on the ice.

"If they win, I want lights installed," Jenna said, unfolding the blanket for her daughter, Hope, sitting next to her.

"You think they'd do that?" Rhonda asked.

Jenna nodded. "We could only approve blue and white."

Penny snorted. "Forced Snowball propaganda."

The puck dropped. Tyler won the draw clean, a confident

pull back to Darcy, who wasted zero time, flinging it up the boards to Curtis. Curtis saw the forecheck bite and threaded a needle up the middle to Suraj. Suraj took it on his backhand, pivoted, and tipped it to Sean, streaking over the blue line.

Kelty's ribs squeezed. She loved watching him play. Years ago, when she attended her very first Snowballs game, it felt like a switch had been flipped inside her. The strength and speed, the decisiveness of his body on the ice, altered her brain chemistry. She wasn't attracted to men with perfectly manicured hands or a nice sweater anymore. She wanted this. Brute force. Grit and determination.

She crossed her legs and swallowed hard.

Sean dragged the puck through his skates to shake a defenceman—he still practiced shit like that in the garage on the weekends—and cut wide. The angle looked rough. He held. Waiting for the trailer.

"Tyler," Emma breathed, and there he came, like clock-work. Sean's pass kissed air and fell to Tyler's tape. He hammered a shot. It thunked square on the goalie's chest and died, but the speed sent a ripple through their section.

"Shoot corner, bud!" Rob yelled, his hands cupped around his mouth.

Sharla nudged him. "He probably tried."

"He's got to get up over that pad."

Sharla rolled her eyes.

The Snowballs forechecked like the puck owed them rent. Brett pinned a defenceman against the glass. Curtis stepped up at the blue line to hold a clearing attempt, chipped it deep, and Sean won a race around the back of the net. He went for broke on a wraparound that the goalie smothered with his left pad. Whistle. Pile of bodies.

"Punch him in the stethoscope!" a small voice sounded, and Kelty turned to see Ryan's daughter, Amaya, standing with her fist in the air.

"Parenting these days," Crystal murmured with a grin.

Logan was crying, he was laughing so hard.

Sean's sister Rachel leaned down from the bench above. "How's work? You still doing the line-item wizardry?"

Kelty sighed. "You know me. Vendor compliance queen."

"Hot," Eliza said.

"Is Sean favouring his left side a little?" Rob asked, leaning over to Chase.

"I didn't notice, but—"

Their conversation was cut off as the Snowballs drew a penalty. Darcy took a stick to the hands on a breakout. Power play. The baby blue gathered at the faceoff dot, the puck dropped, lost, won back, and then everything clicked. The puck skated like they attached it to string. Point to half-wall to low bumper to slot. Country waited, held the goalie's eyes, and then no-looked it to Brett, who was creeping back door. Brett smashed it top shelf.

"Over the pad, that's it!" Rob crowed.

Their entire group stood to hug and fist-bump anyone they could reach.

The game sped forward, most of it being played in Dr. Quinn's zone as expected. The Snowballs were strong, and this wasn't going to be much of a fight.

A whistle blew. Icing. Faceoff back in the Snowballs' zone. Dr. Quinn rolled a line with a winger whose shot could break glass. He fired low, snagged by Boyd's left pad with a thud that reverberated to rafters. Rebound kicked straight to a waiting stick. Boyd exploded across the crease and stacked his pads like it was 1987. The arena roared. The winger fell over Boyd's stick and slid into the post.

The Snowballs bench hollered, sticks banging the boards.

"Buy that man a beer!" Jack called with Delia hooting right next to him.

The period ticked toward zero. Sean backchecked through the neutral zone with a beautiful hesi to buy some space, lifted a stick at the blue line, shovelled the puck to Tyler, and created a two-on-one. Tyler held, looked shot, then slid it across. Sean tapped it in with a lazy grace that made Kelty's blood heat. He glided past the crease, stick up, receiving a swarm of hugs against the glass.

Two nothing.

Between periods the DJ played a mix of classic rock and K-pop. The Zamboni carved clean arcs across the ice.

The second period built like a storm. Dr. Quinn pinched harder at the points, threw pucks from bad angles, hunted rebounds. Boyd turned his blocker and glove into a metronome. Darcy swallowed minutes on the back end with patient footwork and no-nonsense clears. Country, who lived for chaos, tried a breakout through the middle that led to a two-on-one for Dr. Quinn, then redeemed himself by busting his ass back to defence and laying out to block the shot.

He scored late in the second, and then it was all Tyler in the third. The man was everywhere, on top of every puck. Dr. Quinn scored once, and he answered twice with a goal and assist.

"Geez, he's on tonight." Emma watched in awe.

Rob laughed. "I thought the puck was the only thing that would earn his devotion."

It was a joke, but it punched the bruise inside Kelty's chest. Tyler changed. He committed. What did Emma have that she didn't?

"I'm going to get air," she told Sharla, and stood before anyone could argue. Her ankle twinged, but after a few days of rest it was nearly back to normal.

The atrium was busier than expected mid-period. People heading to the washrooms, getting last minute snacks, and a kid's birthday party spilled out of a community room with paper crowns and frosting faces.

Kelty walked past the stairs to the far end of the hall, turned the corner, and leaned against the wall, letting the cool cinderblocks press through her Snowballs jersey. Playoff noise seeped under the door in waves—the scrape, the roar, the whistle shriek. She inhaled. Held. Exhaled.

"Escaping?"

Kelty jumped. She looked up to find Mason standing in front of her. Black jacket, jeans, and hair mussed in that perfect just-woke-up style.

She straightened. "Hey. What are you doing here?" Stupid question. It was obvious. The only reason he'd be there was to support Sean. Kind of surprising and . . . a little bit sweet.

"Came to see Sean. He's playing out of his mind."

He wasn't wrong. "Yeah. Easy win tonight."

He watched her for a beat. "So I'm going to cut to the chase. I saw you walk out and I followed."

"Obviously." Kelty drew another breath, working to keep her nerves in check as her brain auto-generated a hundred reasons why Mason would follow her into the hall. None of them predicted his next words.

"I saw you leave the launch party, Kelt. I went down to get something from my car and saw you storm out without Sean. I probably should've left—I wasn't trying to spy—but I didn't want you to see me and . . . I don't know. Then Sean came out, and . . . anyway. I saw you at the bakery the other day, and it's pretty obvious things aren't great between you two."

Kelty wanted to cut in and argue, tell him he was wrong, but she didn't have anything to rebut his observations.

"I've thought about you ever since I moved back to Calgary. I actually looked you up." He dropped his eyes, laughing to himself. "I couldn't believe you two were still together."

"It's so unrealistic that I'd be in a long-term relationship?" She wrapped her arms tighter around herself.

Mason quirked an eyebrow. "Ah, no. That *he* would be." He stepped closer and leaned against the wall. "I've known Sean a long time."

"So have I."

"Fair." He nodded, considering his next words. "He doesn't seem like the kind of guy who puts down roots. No, it's more like he can't put down new roots, if that makes sense? Ever since that thing—you know, with that girl and his friend Jordan—"

"Yeah, I know the thing," Kelty snapped, her chest cinching like a corset.

"Right, so ever since then, it's like he can't let anyone else in, you know?"

Kelty straightened. "He let you in."

Mason scoffed. "I mean, kind of."

"No, Mason. He let you and Andrew in. Fully. Do you know how hard it was for him to ditch his safe job and jump into that startup with you? Right after everything with hockey fell through?"

Mason's neck reddened. "I know. It was difficult."

"Yeah. Difficult. And then what happened, *Mace?*" Words and understanding bubbled up in her like hot magma, boiling over until she couldn't keep them from spilling out. "The company went belly up, he lost most of his savings because of that acquisition, and then you come back to town and don't even tell him about your new gig? Don't even give him the chance to apply for a—"

"I didn't think he'd be interested! I know how much that crushed him, and I had no idea if this venture was going to be any different. I didn't want to—"

"Mason, you didn't even call. You had your fancy friends and you knew exactly what you were doing when you kept things close to the chest. So, gee. I wonder why Sean has trust issues. I wonder why he won't put down new roots." Kelty shoved past him, annoyed that she couldn't make a more dramatic exit because her damn ankle could only go the speed of a sloth.

"So that's it?" Mason called.

Kelty slowed and spun. "What do you mean that's it? Yes,

Sean and I aren't exactly together right now, but there isn't anything here, Mason. There never was."

She turned the corner, swiping at her eyes, and jolted, pulling up short. Because Sharla Thompson blocked her path back to the atrium.

CHAPTER
Twenty~Three

Seven years earlier

SEAN LAY on his back while the ceiling fan ticked the room into slow motion. Sheets tangled around his shins, Kelty sprawled across his chest, knee snug between his thighs, cheek under his collarbone. Her shampoo left a citrus trail on him, lemon layered over clean skin.

He traced the ridge of her spine with a knuckle, gooseflesh rising under his hand. She hummed into his sternum, smug and sleepy.

"You're so pleased with yourself," he said.

"I did strenuous work. You should tip me."

"I paid in advance."

She grinned against his pec. "That's salary. Tips are separate. Also, I'm charging you for hazard pay."

He angled his head. "What hazard?"

"You ate jalapeños."

He laughed out loud. "You couldn't feel that."

"The hell I couldn't!"

Sean stroked her hair, tugging a little. "An elite athlete needs jalapeño nachos after a game."

Kelty pushed up onto an elbow to grin at him, her lips still swollen. The sight knocked something loose in his chest.

"You came to watch at ten p.m. on a Tuesday. That's dedication."

"I came to watch you miss two almost empty nets—"

"Okay." He rolled, dropping her onto her back with a shriek. "I don't need your criticism."

"It's constructive!" She laughed as he tickled her ribs, throwing her legs around his hips and dragging him down to her level.

He kissed her, catching her hand and pressing it to the mattress. She relaxed, stroking her hand over his back.

She released an exhale, blinking slow as he lifted his lips from hers. Her free hand floated up to his cheek. "At least you shaved for me."

He smirked. "Less of a hazard."

Her fingers stilled on his throat, her heart picking up speed against his ribs. "I love you."

Sean stopped breathing. The fan clicked above them.

He saw the moment fear flashed across her face, and he wanted to grab the last five seconds and force them to replay.

"I know it's been, what, barely six months?" she said in a rush. "I know that's not a lot. I didn't mean to blindside you—"

"No, stop." He pressed a finger to her lips.

He squeezed his eyes shut, the image of his university apartment forcing itself into his head. A closed door. Shoes he knew in the front entryway.

He cleared his throat. "It's not that I don't—"

"It's okay. You don't owe me the sentence tonight. I didn't say it to hear it back. I said it because it's true, and I didn't want to keep that from you."

He stared at the headboard. Her dark hair splayed across

the pillow. "The last time I—" He stopped, then forced the words out before they choked him. "The last time I said that, it sounded like begging."

Kelty nodded, running her hand over his neck, his shoulders. "It's okay. I get it."

She didn't because he didn't even understand it himself. How hard was it to say what he felt? He did love her, he knew he loved her, but even admitting it internally felt like swallowing motor oil.

He swallowed. The sound felt like it went through a microphone. "I need time."

"Of course. Take all the time you need."

CHAPTER
Twenty~Four

PRESENT DAY

SHARLA MOVED FIRST. She hurried Kelty into the alcove leading to the office doorways and held perfectly still until Mason passed in the hall, then held out the extra hot chocolate in her hands.

"How much of that did you hear?" Kelty took the cup, grimacing.

"Enough." Sharla gave a sad smile.

Kelty's mouth opened to explain, but what was there to apologize for? Everything she'd said was the truth. "I'm sorry we didn't tell you. We didn't want to throw a wet blanket on the family time and the anniversary celebration, and—"

"I don't care about any of that." Sharla's eyes were fixed, intense. "I care about you and Sean. What's going on?"

The first tear hit her wrist, a hot bullet. The second found the hollow above her collarbone. By the third, she couldn't see the inspiring posters taped to the wall anymore. *Courage Is a Habit,* my ass.

She hunched against the wall, clutching her cup like a comfort blanket. "I can't keep doing this. I love your family. I love this." She flung the hand not glued to the chocolate in the direction of the rink. "I look at Rob's stupid proud grins and you holding his hand and One Place and Sunday Supper—" She choked back a sob. "I can't lose it. I can't lose you. But I think Sean doesn't want the same thing I want and I . . . I can't build a life out of waiting for him to wake up and decide he wants to take the next step."

Sharla bent over, set her cup on the floor, and pulled Kelty into a hug. That's when she broke. The sobs yanked up from somewhere behind her ribs and ripped a path out. "I want the box you have in your closet. And the photo albums."

"Shh, I know. I know."

"I want to have kids who come home and make up games to play together to celebrate our undying love—and I just realized you don't know about the games." Kelty pulled back. "I'm sorry, I didn't mean—"

Sharla clapped her hands to her cheeks. "I know you all have been planning something, I'm not an idiot."

Kelty nodded, sniffing back a laugh. "I love Sean."

"I know."

"I love you and your family—"

"I know. And you won't lose me. You won't lose us. No matter what happens with him, you won't lose us."

How she wanted to believe that. "You can't make that promise. If Sean moves on—"

Sharla pulled back enough to look at Kelty's face. Her eyes were steady. "Do you really think he will?"

It felt like a block of granite landed on her chest. Kelty blinked. No. She didn't think he would. Not with anyone who was serious, anyway. Because she wasn't the problem. It wasn't that she wasn't good enough or he didn't care about her enough. The problem was, "He's scared."

Sharla nodded. "Sean's always been scared. Ever since he was little. Why do you think he fights so hard on the ice?"

Kelty wiped her nose with the back of her hand. "But what do I do?"

Sharla sighed and dropped her hands, then picked her cup up off the floor and took a sip. "Did you know I dated Logan once?"

Kelty's eyes flew wide. "What?"

A small smile played at the corner of her mouth. "I don't talk about it anymore because it was so long ago and all of us are over it, but I was living with him when I met Rob."

"No."

Her eyes danced. "Yes. Rob was Logan's best friend."

Kelty coughed a laugh. "Did you—?"

"No, I didn't cheat on him!" Sharla slapped Kelty's arm playfully. "I thought Logan was perfect, but then I woke up one day and realized I was the only thing holding us together. Logan loved hockey. He ate, slept, and breathed it, and he didn't know how to love anything else."

Sharla took a sip of her hot chocolate. "Sean's not quite the same. He's not obsessed with the sport like Logan was." She pondered a moment, then continued, "Rob, on the other hand, was ready. He loved me, he made it clear—"

"He told you?"

She scoffed. "Oh, no. He never said it out loud, but he showed me. Every day. Did you know he used to wash out my water bottles at night?"

"Wait, he was living there too?"

"Quite the situation we were in." She laughed, then sighed with reverie. "But here's the thing. Walking away from Logan was the first grown-up thing I did. I could love him and still see that he didn't love the version of life I wanted. If I'd stayed, that would've taught him my needs were optional. Women like us don't do optional, Kelty."

Kelty swallowed, the lump growing again in her throat.

Sharla's eyes grew glassy. "I adore you. I adore my son. But if he isn't ready or capable of giving you the things you deserve, if he can't be the person who meets you in the middle with arms open, you let him go, do you understand me?"

Tears spilled over onto her cheeks. "I do love him."

Sharla smiled, her own tears tracing paths over her skin. "Oh, honey. Don't I know it."

THE HORN HAD CUT the air clean ten minutes ago, but Sean was still out on the ice. Jerseys vanished through the gate. The ref scooped up the puck, thought better of it, and tossed it toward Sean with a nod that said, *Have at it.* So far the Zamboni doors stayed shut, and he was going to take every second he could get.

It was an easy win, first playoff game in the bag. The boys had whooped and hammered Boyd's pads with their sticks. He was a brick wall. The celly's would be in full swing in a few minutes, but Sean couldn't bring himself to jump in.

Every time he left the ice it was the same. Didn't matter if they won or lost, if the practice was good or terrible, all of it felt empty. As long as he was locked in, focused on the game or the drill or whatever the hell they were doing on the ice, he could ignore the constant pit in his stomach. But once he walked down that tunnel . . .

Sean cut a tight loop at the blue line, letting his inside edge bite, his weight low, hips loose. He took the puck onto his stick, drew a slow figure eight around the faceoff dot, the same lazy pattern he'd traced since he was nine. In, out. Heel, toe.

The stands emptied to metal skeletons.

He leaned into a C-cut and sprinted a blue-red-blue, stick out front, eyes up. At the far end he loaded and snapped, far post, bar down. The ping echoed, then the carom clattered along the dasher like applause.

Movement by the box pulled his head around. Not the bench, his team would've yelled at him if they wanted to yank him. The penalty box door opened like magic. Then his dad stepped out in his jeans, gloves, a helmet, and skates, followed by Logan Kemp and Chase, also laced and grinning like they'd snuck past the security guards with sticks in hand.

"What the hell is this?" Sean called.

"Need to knock you down a peg after that win, bud," Rob chirped, tightening the strap under his chin.

Sean chuckled. "You're going to break a kneecap, old man."

Chase laughed. "Rob, I think your son's pissing his pants."

Sean angled toward them, glancing back toward the metal doors.

Logan skated next to him, clapping him on the back. "Don't worry. We asked them for twenty. The ice is all ours." He scuffed a skate over the pock-marked surface. "Though you boys did a number on it."

He zipped back to Rob who motioned for the puck. As soon as it hit the tape, his dad grinned. "Sean and Wilson against me and Kemp. Puck drops now, sweethearts."

Chase barked a laugh. "Is that what he calls you?"

Sean set his jaw. "Better than your wife calling me Daddy last night."

"Ohhh, damn." Logan dragged out the syllables, already going for broke. Sean hustled to catch up.

The puck clacked against the ice, and he lunged, but his dad cut him off with a hip. Sean's breath punched out of him, and the puck was gone, zipped up to Logan.

Logan dangled once, twice, then tucked it behind his back. "Little tired, Seany? You need a nap? Juice box?"

Sean charged, stick down, shoulders squared. He no longer cared that these boys weren't suited up. He wanted the puck. Instead he got the heel of Rob's stick across his shin pads.

"Shit, Dad!" He yelped, staggering.

"Keep your head up," Rob growled, grinning wide, sweat already dripping down the bridge of his nose.

Chase stole the puck back and flipped it toward Sean. He caught it, adrenaline roaring through his chest. He cut wide, his legs burning, and drove straight at Rob. He let the puck slide, snapped it hard, and it pinged iron.

"Almost," Logan scooped up the rebound and spun out. "Participation ribbon, eh?"

Sean thought about barreling into him, but didn't want to kill Logan Kemp before his jersey was retired. He tapped him into the boards instead.

Logan smirked. "You raised a good boy, Thompson."

Sean tapped harder, earning a grunt and the puck. The victory didn't last long. Rob plowed into him and laughed as he staggered, then grabbed Sean's jersey and yanked him forehead to helmet. "Loved watching you play tonight." Then he shoved, sprinting back toward the net.

How the hell was he still that fast?

Sean pulled himself together and got in position for Chase. His dad slipped up, and Chase took advantage, snapping a pass behind the net. Sean snagged it, flipped right and went left, then tapped it to Chase as he screamed in from neutral.

He ripped it, bar down, clang and net, perfect. Chase whooped, Rob smacked Sean's helmet, and that's when Jem laid on the horn like he was calling cows in from the hills. The four of them snapped their heads up as the Zamboni nosed out from the back.

"Out!" Jem jabbed a thumb, his orange toque crooked.

Sean cupped a mitt to his ear. "What's that, Jem? One more shift?" Two short blasts of the horn answered. He laughed and went to retrieve one net while Jem hopped down and did the other.

They exited the ice before he ran them over.

"Puberty give you that mustache?" Logan pointed at the blond whiskers clinging to Chase's lip.

"I'm bringing it back."

Rob chortled. "You're not my coach anymore. I can tell you what I really think."

"Get changed, eh?" Logan nudged Sean. "I'm telling your mom you're the reason we're all late to the pub."

Sean took off his gloves and helmet as they clomped down the rubber. "You're going to One Place?"

"Why the hell not?"

He thought that question was obvious.

Rob leaned in. "His disguise is over by the stairs."

"Good playin'." Chase nodded in approval.

Sean lifted his stick in salute and warmth pushed up through his chest.

"Miss it?" Rob asked.

Logan dropped his eyes. "Every day and twice on Saturdays."

Chase rolled his shoulders and winced. "Miss the locker room most. Not the same when you're coaching."

Rob nodded. "Takes you a while to figure out who you are again, eh?"

His friends grunted in agreement, the whole group slowing as they approached the turn to the stairs.

Rob turned to Sean. "But you do find it."

Sean's jaw worked. He gave a sharp nod, not trusting himself to speak.

"See you up there," Rob said, and the three of them turned

to the stairs. *The ghosts of playoffs future.* Damn it, he was going to kill André for planting that in his head.

Rob laughed as Logan jostled him before racing up the stairs first, and Sean's heart started to pound. Those weren't his ghosts. That wasn't his future. By the time his dad was his age, he'd been married for fifteen years and had a gaggle of kids.

What was he doing with his life? What did he want his future to look like?

Kelty. Anytime he thought about his future, it was Kelty. But realizing that didn't fill him with warmth and love like everyone else described. He didn't feel safer knowing that he wanted her until death do them part. Wasn't true love supposed to feel warm? Like you would throw caution to the wind? Not like he needed to find the nearest escape route?

The locker room door banged open, music and laughter spilling out into the hall.

"Oh, hey, cap." Brett grinned, waiting for Tyler. "Waiting for someone?" That hopeful look in his eye twisted a knife in Sean's ribs.

He shook his head. "Nope. Just . . ."

Brett clapped him on the shoulder. "See you up there?"

"Yep. See you there." Sean hurried into the locker room, ignoring the voices trying to get his attention and rifled through his bag to find his phone. He swiped it open and tapped on his contacts, searching for the name that André handed him in the parking lot of the Dusty Rose.

Elodie Shaw. Therapist.

GAME TWO against Dr. Quinn was a victory lap. The Snowballs ate them for breakfast, at their home rink in Medicine Hat no less. It was just under three hours away, so most of the group made it out to watch.

Tyler pinballed a shot off two defenders and into the net. Country got a deflection with his thigh and then did a dance that made Jenna blush. Boyd saw twelve solid minutes of nothing and still pulled a glove save that drew a gasp out of everyone's lungs.

But Kelty couldn't stop watching Sean. Whether he was on the bench or on the ice, it didn't matter. Every second felt like the last. The last time she'd see him jump over the boards. The last time she'd watch him check a guy into the boards.

They still had another best-out-of-three series to play and then hopefully the finals, but it didn't matter. She was going to move to Penticton. Not forever, probably, but at least for a little while. She could work remotely and navigate through whatever this was, helping her parents in the process. Now that there was an expiration date, every second felt like a period. A punctuation mark. And yet trying to soak it in seemed to only make it go faster.

Monday, the Stiff Sticks arrived with sharp elbows and a goalie who liked to chirp. It pissed Sean and Darcy right off. Despite too many penalties, the Snowballs squeaked out a 3–2 win.

Wednesday was in southern Alberta. Another few hours drive. Stiff Sticks nicked them 2–1, and the whole team stood in the parking lot afterward, blinking like birds who'd run into a window.

But then there was Friday. The deciding game. Nail-biter didn't begin to cover it. The Snowballs were higher seeded, and the thought of them getting knocked out before the finals made everyone antsy. Their section stood during the third period because none of them could sit still.

Suraj roofed one on a bad angle, but Curtis finally threaded end-to-end and slid it to Tyler for a tip that made the crowd erupt. There was one minute left, and it was a tie game. Sean took a faceoff in their zone and won. Brett hacked it toward the net, and Sean chipped it over the goalie's pads. He got a glove on it, but then Tyler was there giving it just enough of a kiss that it flipped up and over the line. Everyone lost their damn minds. 4-3.

They held hands, linked arms, and prayed to the hockey gods that the Snowballs could hold on for the dying seconds. When the horn blew, the celebration felt like the ball drop on New Year's Eve.

"One more team." Rob was glowing. "Beat them and we've got the cup!"

One more team. Emma, Penny, Jenna, Aelin, and Rhonda watched their phones like hawks, waiting to see who won the other series, but the guys arrived before any text messages. They took over three tables at One Place. Kelty stayed for a bit, not forcing any pretense. The whole team knew she and Sean weren't staying together. Now that Sharla knew, was there really any reason to pretend? Carter and his wife seemed oblivious, but they also weren't paying attention to their seating arrangements at the pub.

It was later that night when the party started to wind down that Carter made the announcement. He stood on a chair and banged a butter knife against his pint glass until the chatter died down.

"Ladies, gents," he said, his eyes glittering as he gestured toward Rob and Sharla. "As you know, these two lovely people are celebrating another year of marriage."

Cheers went up around the table. Carter waited for it to die down. "My lovely assistants will be handing out some information that will be needed for the next two weekends."

Eliza and Rachel rounded the table, handing out cards to anyone in the Thompson family, Logan and Crystal, and Madelyn and Chase. The whole Snowballs team was well aware this was happening, so there was no concern about them feeling left out.

Sharla opened the envelope and devoured the words on the card. She looked up at Carter with wide eyes, back to the card, then up at him. She slapped Rob's knee and squealed.

Carter laughed. "That's right. You have won a slot on the Amazing Race—"

"Don't call it that! We don't have the licensing rights!" Rachel called out.

"The Amazing-ish Race," Carter corrected.

"Did you all plan this?" Sharla looked around the table in complete disbelief.

Kelty grinned. So, she thought they were planning something, but this wasn't on her radar. There was something so satisfying about pulling off an actual surprise. She didn't think she'd ever been a part of one before.

Carter began his explanation. "Teams of two, listed on your card. You'll receive route info, detours, the odd road-block—" He paused for effect. "—and yes, there will be a U-turn."

Rob thumped his pint. "Pit stops?"

"Multiple." Carter flipped through his stack. "Greeters. Photos. Check-in mat. Departures the next day based on arrival order. Time credits and penalties."

Sharla's hands were cupped over her face. She might've been hyperventilating.

Carter called out names like a draft. Thankfully, Kelty and Sean didn't have to be a team. They'd already vetted the challenges. Now they got to relax and time the rest of them. She'd have to thank Carter later. While the earlier tasks weren't ideal, this was exactly where she needed to be at the moment to preserve her sanity.

When Carter finished, his wife Alix handed out lanyards with team names. He then moved onto the rules. "You'll receive timestamps at each task. Some are races you complete as fast as you can and check in. Some are single activities with a mutual time window. Self-drive only. Walk, run, bike, skate. We're not paying your Uber. Obey all traffic laws. You get a speeding ticket, you take a thirty-minute penalty at the next pit stop and get a lecture from Dad."

The Thompson kids groaned.

Carter continued, "Phones stay pocketed for trivia. And you may ask strangers for directions or help, but you cannot bribe anyone. A U-turn will exist on one leg. If you choose to U-turn a team, they must complete both detour options. Choose wisely so we don't break up the family."

Alix handed Tyler, Emma, Sean, and Kelty referee bands.

"Don't mess with these four. They can assess penalties, no questions asked." He clapped his hands together. "Okay, if you haven't already, flip your card to see your first challenge."

Kelty peeked over Eliza's shoulder. On the card, there was a bright route info strip in block letters.

. . .

REPORT TO: The Den
   ARRIVAL WINDOW: 6:00-6:15 PM
   TASK WINDOW: 6:30–8:00PM
   RULE: Phones in basket.
   BONUS: Win the night = 10-MINUTE
   CREDIT. Second = 5-MINUTE CREDIT. Third = 2-MINUTE
CREDIT.
   PIT STOP: Check in with Rob and Sharla on the red mat by the
jukebox

Underneath, in smaller text read:

ROADBLOCK: One team member completes the lightning round solo, no outside input.

Kelty was in awe. She and Sean had done some work, but looking at everything they'd set up, it felt like next to nothing.

Carter pointed at the jukebox, where a piece of red fabric had been duct-taped into a rectangle on the floor. "That is your mat. When you finish tomorrow, you run—don't walk, don't saunter—run to Rob and Sharla. You hug them, you present your finished task, and you take your check-in photo. Then you get your departure time for the following leg. All starts tomorrow. Sleep. Hydrate."

"What is the trivia on?" Eliza asked.

Carter grinned. "If I told you, I'd have to kill you."

"It's about Mom, it has to be," Nate said. "They're going to be at the mat."

Speculations and chatter ensued. Kelty wanted to join in, to pretend not to drop hints while dropping different ones to every team or regale them with the tale of the wet T-shirt contest at the Den.

But she'd already planned a task for herself that night before the envelopes came out. And as Sean approached the bar, she knew it was time to make good on it.

"Carter was right." Sean leaned on the polished wood next to her.

"About what? That they love it?"

He nodded, asking Pat, the owner and bartender, for another pitcher of beer for the table. Kelty drummed her fingers on the bar top. She could make small talk about all of this. Or she could rip off the Band-Aid.

"Hey, I'm not sure how long you were planning to stay with your parents, but—"

"As long as you need." Sean kept his voice low, suddenly serious.

Kelty's stomach flipped. That made it sound like he thought this was temporary. That she only needed some time to get over this, and then she'd be ready to have him move back in and they could start up where they left off.

She steeled herself. "Actually, after playoffs, I'm going to move to Penticton for a while. So I wanted to let you know the house would be empty."

It was Sean's house. She paid half the mortgage, but it wasn't in her name. They'd thought about getting her added at one point. Now it felt like a glaring neon sign.

"Oh." His breath left in a rush.

Kelty couldn't stand there and watch the news wash over him in waves. She straightened, not even bothering to ask for her drink. "I'll see you tomorrow, Sean," she murmured as she escaped to the front doors.

"Hey! Looks like we're playing Pucks Deep!" Someone called to resounding cheers.

Kelty kept walking. Courage was definitely not a habit.

Twenty-Seven

SEAN SAT on a stool at the Den with his eyes drooping. He hadn't slept. Not really. Two hours on Wednesday, maybe four Thursday, barely one and a half last night after what Kelty said at One Place. His hands hummed, a low-voltage buzz radiating from his elbows to his fingertips. He told himself it was playoff nerves, but the truth sat heavy and depressingly simple. He was losing Kelty, and there wasn't a game strategy for that.

But there were drills.

He'd gone to his first therapy appointment in-person. Elodie's office had a plant big enough to remember dinosaurs and one of those cat hand clocks. He didn't remember anything else about the room because he'd been either too cold or burning up the entire time he sat on her couch. The whole thing felt like a fever dream, but as he stared at the question Nate and Naomi worked on in their trivia packet, he couldn't get one moment out of his head.

Question four. Who said 'I love you' first and where?

. . .

A muscle in Sean's jaw tensed. He couldn't remember when it happened for him. Elodie had asked him the same question, and he remembered every detail of when Kelty said it. The tangle of the sheets, the scent of her skin. But when had he said it? The question itched under his skin, panic rising like the tide.

Carter and Alix scrambled from their seats, slapping cash for their tab onto the table and running toward the door.

"How are they finished? We're only on question six?" Eliza complained.

"Suckers!" Logan and Crystal laughed as they ran out second.

"Not fair," Rachel huffed. "They knew each other in university!"

Sean shrugged. "Maybe you should know your parents better."

She rolled her eyes. "Maybe you should bite me."

When everyone finished, they rushed over to One Place to see who had made it first. Logan and Crystal apparently used their U-turn straight out of the gates, and Carter was still fuming.

Rob and Sharla were on cloud nine.

"Okay. Time to go." Eliza tugged on Sean's arm.

"I'm driving you?"

She nodded. "Mom suddenly turned into a party queen. I don't want to wait for her."

"Me either," Rachel added. "Ooh, but we should see if Kelty's ready to go, too. I think she drove over with Penny, but Penny and Brett already left."

Sean felt like he'd just downed a Red Bull. "Why'd she drive over with them?"

"Her car's in the shop."

That was a gut punch. She was dealing with her car without him? He'd never felt more impotent.

He cleared his throat. "She probably got another ride."

Eliza was already striding away from him. His sister leaned in close to Kelty so she could be heard over the music. Kelty's eyes flicked to his. He immediately looked down at his hands.

"Alright! Let's go!" Eliza announced, stringing Kelty along behind her.

Sean forced air into his lungs. He'd texted once last night after she told him about the potential move, but hadn't heard back. That had been enough of a sign for him.

She was really leaving.

"I can't believe you're letting him stay at our house," Rachel said, linking her arm in Kelty's.

Sean's hands curled into fists. Right. They still thought everything was fine between the two of them. Not sure how they hadn't picked up on the ice fields of tension, but they still had a few people to pretend for.

"I don't let your brother do anything, you know that." Kelty grinned, but her words struck a chord.

"I don't do whatever I want," he said.

Rachel laughed. "Oh c'mon, Sean. We all remember how you ate Cheerios for dinner every night in grade seven."

He scoffed, pushing through the doors to the sidewalk. "That was a bedtime snack."

"You ate two bowls!" Eliza crowed. "One was for dinner, definitely."

Sean normally would've laughed, but tonight he wasn't in the mood to be reminded of his unwillingness to compromise, even as a kid.

"Shotgun!" Eliza raced toward the truck.

"How old is she," Rachel muttered, and Kelty grinned. The first real smile he'd seen all night.

"We can make out in the back seat if you want. Make her jealous." Kelty winked, and Rachel laughed out loud.

"If it's in the family, doesn't count as cheating?"

"Exactly!"

The two of them climbed in the back, and Sean already wanted to break something. This was bullshit. All of it. It was like watching your vehicle rolling down a hill and not being able to stop it.

Every feeling from his hospital bed after the motorcycle crash, his dorm room after he found Jordan Wheatfill and his girlfriend in his bedroom, then the conference room after finalizing the decision to shut down the company way back when, lit up like a wildfire.

So he drove. He locked his jaw closed and drove, tuning out the chatter between the three of them. His tire pressure light went on a few minutes later, but it was cooling off for the night. He figured he could add more air in the morning if necessary, but then they were only a block from the house when the truck pulled left. A low growl started under his foot.

"Shit," he hissed under his breath. Hadn't he just replaced these tires?

The truck flopped. He eased it over to the curb.

"What's wrong with it?" Eliza asked.

Sean got out of the truck. There it was. The tire looked like a man melting into a couch. He popped the tailgate and yanked the panel where the spare lived. Empty.

He stared at the hollow. There was no way. He always kept a spare here.

"No spare?" Eliza peered over his shoulder.

"I always have a spare."

"Hm. Doesn't look—"

"Don't finish that damn sentence." Sean stalked back to the driver's seat. It was fine. He'd phone his dad or Brett. Someone could pop over and give him a hand.

"Are you trying to call Mom and Dad? They're not answering." Rachel held up her screen.

Okay. Snowballs group chat it was. Sean tapped out a

quick message and waited. All of them had to be up. Possibly a little hammered, but awake.

Eliza shivered, scrolling on her phone now, looking for options.

"Here. We can walk," Kelty said. "It's two blocks. A little more comfy to make calls there."

Eliza slumped. "Yes. I'm freezing and need water."

The three women started walking.

"Sean, c'mon." Rachel waved him over.

"I'm good."

Eliza shot him a look. "Please come inside so I'm not worried you got murdered on the way."

"Yeah. We wouldn't know for hours," Rachel deadpanned.

Sean didn't have the energy to argue. They walked down the block. It was easy to see the house since the light was on inside.

They entered and took off their shoes. Sean stayed glued to his phone, not wanting to look around the house. Especially at night.

Nobody had responded in the group chat. The last time that happened was when André sent a picture of a mole he'd removed. Fine. He'd start hitting people one by one. Country. Tyler. Brett. Curtis. He went down the list one at a time, sending emergency texts.

Kelty flicked on a lamp in the living room. She hung her jacket on the bannister and headed for the kitchen. "Water. Tea?"

"Herbal," Rachel called, already folding onto the couch like it belonged to her.

"Mint or sleepy bear?" Kelty's voice floated into the room.

"Yes," Rachel groaned.

Eliza dropped into the chair and tucked her feet under her, phone finally abandoned on the arm. Her eyes were shut in seconds.

Sean stayed by the door, his thumbs moving, messaging again on the group chat.

Hey. Anyone up?

It was too late for Canadian Tire. Kelty's car was in the shop. What other options were there if nobody was answering their damn phone?

The kettle clicked on. Water hissed. Kelty fetched mugs. Their mugs.

Sean jammed his phone in his pocket. He was going to have words. With all of them.

Rachel patted the cushion beside her without looking up. "You going to lurk by the door all night like a bouncer at a church dance? Sit."

Sean ground his teeth, but a few minutes later, he gave in to her taunt. Just as he sank into the cushion, his phone vibrated. He scrambled for it, then held himself back from chucking the device across the room when he saw it was from 7-Eleven.

Eliza's yawn exploded into a laugh halfway through. "I'm gone, man. Dead."

"Why don't we just crash here?" Rachel's eyes were half-lidded as Kelty brought in the tea.

Kelty handed Rachel a mug, then Eliza one, before setting one down by the chair for Sean without asking. She'd made him peppermint. His usual.

"Of course you can stay here." Kelty's eyes lifted to his. He saw the gears working. His sisters didn't know they weren't together. His sisters had always felt like they were her little sisters, and she didn't want to disappoint them.

"I haven't heard back from anyone. That might be best."

Sean frowned into his mug. He could take the floor in the bedroom. Find blankets or something. They wouldn't have to announce to everyone that they weren't sleeping together, and floor sleep couldn't be worse than what he was getting at his parent's.

"You sure that will work, Sean?" Rachel asked. "I know you've gotten zero sleep this week."

Kelty's brow twitched.

"It's fine." His voice was clipped.

Kelty nodded. "I have extra toothbrushes. I'll put them in the hall washroom."

The girls nodded appreciatively, and Sean offered to help. He found the blankets in the hall and by the time he returned, she'd already made a cushion bed for Eliza on the floor.

Watching her care for his sisters twisted something low in his gut. Love and grief braided into one.

Rachel was already horizontal, tea abandoned on the table, socks still on. "Love you, Kelt," she mumbled into the pillow.

"Love you back." She met his eyes with a placid face firmly intact. "Okay. Looks like we're set." She spun on her heel and speed-walked into the bedroom.

Sean stood, stunned. Was he supposed to follow her? If he did follow her and she didn't want him to, she would be pissed. But was he supposed to raw dog it on the floor?

Maybe she was coming back. Bringing a mattress topper or something. He thought they still had one rolled up some-where. Probably in the garage?

"Sean?"

He flinched.

Kelty leaned back into the hall. "If you haven't been sleep-ing, you should probably take the bed."

His heart raced. "I'm not going to make you—"

"I'll build a pillow wall."

He blinked. "A what?"

"A pillow wall. Just—" She sighed. "Just come in." She kept talking even though he wasn't following yet. "You have Pucks Deep next week, and they're going to be assholes. I know you're not convinced Jordan's a good guy off the ice, but you've seen him with Rhonda. He's a total softie." She blew out a breath. "But I agree with you that he's a dick out there sometimes."

The last topic he wanted brought up right then was Jordan frigging Wheatfill. He didn't care how many times Rhonda brought him to the bar. He still didn't enjoy sharing beers with him.

It took him a minute to take a step toward the bedroom. When he did, his heart felt like it had soaked up twice its volume in water.

Every night. This used to be his life every night, and he'd taken it for granted. He'd settled into his routine, never wondering if it was enough for her. Or straight up ignoring it when she said it wasn't.

Sean didn't know endings had a sound.

It was the soft rustle of Kelty in the bedroom. The thump of his feet moving like they were encased in concrete. The tick of the damn fan.

"I put a toothbrush in the washroom." Kelty didn't turn toward him. She was already in her cotton tank top and shorts. He should've walked in sooner. What he would've given to see her put them on.

He walked into the washroom and peed, then brushed his teeth and splashed water on his face. When he returned to the room, Kelty was under the covers, writing in her notebook.

He paused in the doorway. "Want me to put on a shirt or something?"

Kelty shook her head, not looking up. "It's fine. Just wear what you normally would."

"Just my boxers."

"Mmhmm. That's fine." She patted the pillows stacked next to her. Ah. The infamous pillow wall.

Sean stalked to his side of the bed and stripped. He'd be lying if he said he didn't take his time, wondering if she stole a glance. By the way she still stared at the paper when he turned, he doubted it.

He slid under the sheets, and they smelled like home. The mattress held his shape the way an old glove remembers a palm.

Kelty turned out the light. He lay on his back and let it hit like a check to the boards. His breath shook. He pressed it down, the way you smother a cough at a funeral. He could cry. Easy as turning on a tap. He stared at the ceiling instead, eyes burning.

These were the dying seconds that mattered. But this time he didn't have his team with him. He had to watch the clock tick down all alone.

———

Sean was in the conference room, seated in his chair. Kelty perched on the edge of the table in front of him in a tight pencil skirt and that blouse he'd only seen once. It was open down to her bra, her dark hair swooped over her shoulder, curling under the collar.

She kicked one heel off, then the other, letting them thud on the carpet. "Professionalism," she said, the word crooked in her mouth.

"Not a huge fan." His voice came out rough. His tie was loose.

She reached out and hooked a finger through his belt loop, reeling him closer. "Shut the blinds."

He stood, his pants so tight it was difficult to move. Were there blinds in the conference room? He found a cord and pulled. The room dropped into shadow. He walked back to the table, and she dragged her hands down his chest.

"Perfect." She stepped back and sat on the table, pulling him between her knees. When had she taken her skirt off?

Fabric rasped when she pulled at his shirt, the cuff buttons catching. Her hand slid up his back, her nails on his skin. "I thought about this at the rink. You look so hot on the ice."

His eyes rolled back in his head as her hand reached past his waistband. "I saw you in the stands." Her thigh lifted, hooking his hip. "But you left."

"I didn't leave."

"I saw you —"

Kelty kissed him, tugging at his lips with her teeth. "I want you, Sean. Now."

His heart wanted to beat out of his chest. "Okay."

She sighed against his mouth, and then something nudged him from the side. He blinked. What the hell was that? Another nudge, and his hold on Kelty's waist started to slip.

He grabbed onto her tighter, but the room tilted sideways. "Hey, don't." She didn't answer. "Kelty —"

He surfaced slow, unwilling. The pillow and mattress beneath him coming into sensory focus. His breathing was short and stilted. His bed. His house.

No. He wanted to go back. He wanted that dream—all of it. He lay stock still, realizing it wasn't just the sheets he was touching.

Something—someone—lay sprawled across him, cheek pressed under his collarbone. Hair tickling his throat. A palm splayed low on his stomach.

His body answered before his brain caught up—tight, insistent, the kind of arousal that bordered on pain. He couldn't lie here. If she moved, if she shifted against him, he was going to make a mess all over both of them.

He shifted to the side, and she made a soft sound, her fingertips pressing into his stomach. *Shit.* How was he going to extricate himself without waking her? More importantly, how did she get there over the pillow wall?

Sean tried again, and again, her hands tightened against his skin. He squeezed his eyes shut, trying to convince any of his blood to flow north.

But it was a losing battle. Because Kelty's hand was moving.

Twenty-Eight

KELTY WOKE to the feel of his skin, her body aching, desperate to press against him. *Sean.* He was in her bed. Why was that a problem?

"Hey. You awake?" His thumb was at her wrist, holding her hand in place.

Heat from his chest gathered along her spine. His breath skimmed her shoulder, and she nearly moaned. Yes. This was exactly what she wanted. What she needed.

Him. All of him.

Moving against him was muscle memory. More natural than breathing.

"Hey, Kelt—"

"Stop." She pulled her hand away, pressing it back against his stomach.

He hissed air through his teeth, and she knew exactly what that meant.

She tilted her head until his mouth was close. His jaw felt like sanded wood against her cheek.

A far away alarm bell rang in her head, but she pushed it away and touched her mouth to his. Holy hell, she'd missed this. He kissed her back, tentative. His fingers trembled as he cradled the back of her neck.

A small sound broke from her, and he answered with pressure, with breath. His resolve broke, and he set his hands free. His fingers mapped her. Her ribs, hips, stomach. This while his lips found the hollow at the base of her throat where he always slowed.

She dragged her hand into his hair and pulled, hungry. He swore against her skin, his breathing ragged. It was the most potent aphrodisiac.

He fumbled with the hem of her shirt, then peeled it over her head. It was seamless, practiced. Sean groaned when he found only skin, and the shiver that passed through her, nearly sent her over the edge.

Kelty was frantic, uncoordinated, as she tugged at his boxers.

"You sure?" he rasped.

She kissed him hard in answer.

Yeah. She was sure.

CHAPTER
Twenty~Nine

KELTY WASN'T sure about a damn thing.

Morning split the room with light, and Kelty blinked her eyes open to see Sean lying naked next to her. The pillow wall desecrated. She rolled onto her back, clutching the sheets to her bare chest as middle-of-the-night memories flooded her system. *Damn it.* What had she done? She'd woken up *on* him, and then . . .

Kelty groaned internally. *Oh, it was good.* So good, her body was already humming, begging for a repeat.

She slid out of bed, praying the floorboards wouldn't creak and wake him. Her feet hit the floor and her ankle didn't complain. How was that possible? Two orgasms and her tendons were healed? How come nobody mentioned *that* on WebMD?

Kelty waited a moment, and when Sean didn't move, she snatched her clothes from the end of the bed, padded to the washroom, and inched the door shut.

In the mirror, a stranger blinked back. Her hair was wild, her mouth swollen, her neck the same shade of red it would be after running a mile in July. She pressed a cool towel to the mark blooming on her neck in plain view for all to see.

What. The. Hell had she been thinking?!

Last night, she convinced herself it was fine. They'd slept next to each other thousands of times. He needed sleep. She was dead on her feet. Never in a million years did she expect her traitorous subconscious to throw her over his chest. *She made a pillow wall!*

Kelty scrubbed her face and used the toilet. She used her concealer to hide the hickey he'd given her as best she could. Then there was nothing left to do but walk back into the bedroom and hope beyond hope that he was still passed out. She could salvage this. Just avoid him. Forever. Easy.

But when she stepped back into the bedroom, Sean was sitting up. Their sheets balled up and held over his crotch. Heat flashed down her inner thighs. He looked so good. She hadn't been able to see him last night, though the feel of him was more than enough.

Sean's eyes were wide. He looked like she'd roofie'd him and dragged him to her bedroom. "Morning." The word ground in his mouth.

Her back stuck to the door frame like she was being interrogated. "Morning."

"Hey, Kelty? Do you have face wash?" Rachel's voice called from the living room. Salvation by sibling.

Kelty took the escape. She plucked her bottle of Neutrogena from the counter and swept from the room. *Shit, shit, shit!* What was she going to do about this? What was she going to say?

In the kitchen, the world reset to eggs and coffee.

Eliza sat at the counter, motioning to the coffee maker and the pan on the stove. "Hoped you wouldn't mind."

Kelty shook her head. "No, thank you so much." When was the last time someone made her breakfast? She threw an English muffin in the toaster and grabbed a mug for coffee. The girls had already loaded their mugs into the dishwasher from last night. "I think you two should sleep over more often."

Eliza grinned. "Your setup is actually pretty comfy."

Sean appeared from the bedroom, and Eliza grinned. "Well. You look . . . relaxed."

Kelty almost dropped the plate she was pulling from the cupboard.

Sean ran a hand over his hair and made a choking noise in the back of his throat. "Slept well, I guess."

Wow. Way to play it cool.

Eliza raised an eyebrow, lifting her mug to her lips. "Uh-huh."

"Thank you so much for this." Rachel reappeared, setting the bottle of face wash on the counter.

Eliza snagged it next. "My turn." She left her mug and disappeared to the washroom.

Kelty grabbed a cloth and started wiping down any surface she could find to avoid turning around and looking at Sean. All the work she'd done to shut things down, to convince herself that she was saying goodbye, was undone in a very spontaneous, very hot ten minutes. And possibly a second episode when neither of them were asleep a half hour after that. *Because what was there to lose when they'd already done it once?*

It was a very convincing argument at two in the morning.

"So. Today is a challenge at Douglas? I'm so pissed. Eliza and I have to give fricking Carter a twenty-minute head start." Rachel read the message they'd all received that morning about meeting at the Douglas Dome.

Sean hovered on the other side of the island. When his stomach grumbled, Kelty took pity on him. "Do you want some eggs?" The pan was cool enough now, she lifted it from the burner and set it on the granite countertop, then reached into the cupboard and got him a plate.

"Thanks." He stepped closer to open the cutlery drawer

and get a fork, and Kelty's body lifted toward him like he was a magnet and she was made only of iron filings. She spun to find something else to clean.

"What about the truck?" Rachel asked, picking pieces of egg directly from the pan and popping them in her mouth.

"Ryan's got a spare and a jack," he said. "He's coming by in a few."

Thank the heavens. She'd text Penny and let her know she had a ride. As long as she didn't have to be alone with Sean, it would be fine. She could ride in the back with Rachel and claim it was because Eliza got carsick.

Kelty set the rag next to the sink and started on her eggs when Rachel said, "Wait is that—? Sean, did you seriously give her a hickey? How old are you?!"

Sean dropped his eyes to his plate, but—was that a smile playing at the corner of his mouth? *Had he done that on purpose?*

Kelty's face burned. "Well. I'm going to go get ready." She picked up her plate and coffee mug and breezed past him into the bedroom.

She chose to ignore the heated, whispered conversation happening on the other side of the door, set her dishes on the dresser, and focused on getting dressed. Sean's closet door hung ajar. Strange. He always closed it. She pushed the door shut.

Focus. They didn't really have to do anything today besides load the costumes into his truck and time people in the challenge, but she wanted to look good. Hot even? She mentally berated herself.

She would just choose a shirt with a high neck.

AFTERNOON LIGHT SLANTED through the maple at the Thompson house as Sean pulled the deflated tire from the back of his truck. His dad had a friend who towed it over while they were at the challenges that morning. Sean didn't think he'd be able to focus on anything after last night, but watching Carter skate in a feather boa had been enough to take his mind off things for a minute.

The front door banged open, and Chase emerged in what looked like a hiking shirt and cargo pants. "Ready to find this leak?" He grinned, walking down the drive. Chase had offered to take a look at the tire, and while Sean was perfectly capable of diagnosing issues on his own, he agreed to let him help. Chase had apparently worked as a mechanic when he was younger. Couldn't hurt.

"You said it happened slowly?" Chase toed the tire with the tip of his boot.

"It didn't blow out."

Chase nodded. "You slept at home last night?"

Sean pursed his lips. His mom had asked him the same thing. He was starting to get the feeling that all of them were catching on. "Yep."

The garage door opened, and Rob appeared with an air compressor. Perfect. The whole gang was here.

Chase grinned. "Okay, Sean. Let's find your hole."

Sean huffed a laugh. "Waiting to say that all day?"

"Possibly." He squatted, eyes scanning the tread. He rotated it once, then pointed. "There."

Sean frowned. He crouched and squinted. At the crown of the tread, dead center was a tiny silver glint. A screwhead sat flush. "Huh. How'd you spot that?"

"Experience. These things love the crown. Worst puncture, best patch. If you're going to get poked, pray it's there." He laughed at his own joke.

"Found it?" Rob set the compressor down on the drive.

Chase nodded. "We'll get this fixed in no time."

Sean's eyes narrowed as the two of them walked back to the garage to get supplies. That had all seemed too easy, and both of them seemed too eager to help.

Chase stalked back out and dropped a handful of knickknacks on the concrete. "You want the honours?"

Rob gave him a look, and Sean knew in a split second what he was thinking. As a kid, he said no to this every time. He didn't want to mess it up. Didn't want to be bad at it.

Sean swallowed the tension rising in his chest and nodded. "Teach me."

Chase grinned. "Okay, step one. Yank the offender." He handed Sean a pair of pliers. "Step two, we ream the hole bigger so the plug seats right. Step three, the sticky worm goes in."

Sean grunted, gripping the screw with the pliers. "Never want to hear you say that again."

Chase ignored him. "And step four, we inflate and baptize in soapy water. Check for bubbles." He paused, waiting for Sean to pull. "Yep, just straight out."

The screw resisted like a tooth, then slid free with a

squeal. It was short and gleaming. Too clean to have been sitting on the road.

Chase took the reamer, a rasp on a T-handle, and speared the hole. "You want a snug seat. Plug's got adhesive, so heat and friction will cure it. It'll outlast the truck."

Sean put his hands on his hips. "Since when do you have plugs in your garage, Dad?"

Rob grunted. "I always keep a few things around."

Sean would bet a hundred bucks that if he walked in and inspected the tool bench, he'd find nails to hang pictures and that's about it.

Chase threaded a goo-coiled plug into the eye of the insertion tool and drove it in until only two whiskers stuck out of the tire. He yanked the tool free.

"We trim the whiskers," Chase said, snipping with a box cutter. "Then air."

Rob was ready. He clipped the compressor to the valve, flipped the switch, and the machine whined to life. The tire plumped.

"Give me a second." Rob turned off the compressor and hurried inside, returning with a spray bottle of dish soap and water. He handed it to Sean.

He misted the patch. No bubbles. Clean.

"All set." Chase wiped his palms on his shorts. "Need help getting the tire switched out?"

Sean shook his head. He'd barely put the spare on with Ryan. It would be easy to take off.

"You look well rested, son. Good night?" Rob clapped him on the shoulder, not meeting his eyes.

That was when he was certain they were up to something. If they set this up, forced him to spend the night with Kelty, well, he didn't know whether to cuss them out or thank them. It had been the best night of sleep he'd had in a long time. And that was saying something considering how much physical activity he'd had in the middle of it.

He couldn't stop thinking about her. It was bad before, but now he still had her scent on his skin. It was like he'd needed to consume her, and it wasn't just him. She'd been just as desperate.

But was that a surprise? Kelty loved him. She wanted to be with him. She thought he was going to propose on that rooftop, and she'd been ready to say yes.

He was such an idiot.

Sean pulled out his phone and texted Elodie. It was a Sunday night. She didn't owe him special treatment, but he prayed she'd offer it anyway.

> Can we meet tonight for a session?

He stared at the phone, his heart racing. He needed to know how to fix this.

When the three dots appeared, he held his breath.

> I've got time at 7:30 p.m.

———

By seven o'clock, the Thompson kitchen counter was dusted with lemon zest, flour, and sugar like confetti. Ricotta tubs were stacked in the sink, and plates of fluffy, blueberry-dotted pancakes sat on clean plates in a line on the table.

"Contestants," Sharla called, banging a wooden spoon against a pot. "Present your offerings."

Crystal and Logan's looked like a magazine layout. Powdered sugar veil, curls of lemon peel, little basil leaves kissing the top. Madelyn and Chase's edges were crisp and browned from the cast-iron pan. It was hard not to be in a good mood, especially when Rachel and Eliza had obviously used ChatGPT to make their speech. The metaphors were unhinged.

This was a challenge Kelty, Sean, Emma, and Tyler participated in. Knowing it was coming didn't give them a particular advantage. He certainly hadn't done any prep, and Tyler and Emma had purchased all the ingredients.

After the presentation portion was complete, they all grabbed forks and tasted each of the dishes. Each team had to submit a score sheet, which meant he had to talk with Kelty again. The baking had been easy. They were good when they had a problem to solve.

"What do you think?" Kelty held the pen over the paper.

"Number one is us. Obviously."

"Obviously." She scrawled the number down. They both knew their pancakes weren't even in the top three, and seeing Kelty trying to keep a straight face made Sean's mouth quirk.

"Number two?"

"Crystal and Logan," they both said at the same time. They went down the list with no arguments.

"Hmm." Kelty set the pen down. "Well, that was easy."

Sean's heart twinged. He leaned back against the counter, watching the rest of his family argue over their rankings. Everything with Kelty was easy, that's why they'd gotten together in the first place.

But now he wondered. How much of that was purely because of her? Sure, she put him in his place plenty of times, but how often did she bend? How often had she been giving him what he wanted and not saying a word about her own needs?

He cleared his throat and pointed at the page. "If you have a different idea for one of those, you can change it."

Kelty shook her head. "No, I think this is good."

"Are you sure? You were thinking fourth place for—"

"Sean, it's fine. I'm sure."

She looked up at him, opened her mouth, then closed it. With a glance over her shoulder, she angled her body between him and the rest of the group and leaned in. "What happened last night? That—I know it was my fault, and I'm sorry. I don't think it's a good idea."

Sean's pulse drummed in his ears. "Yeah. Right. But it wasn't your fault."

She scoffed. "It was."

"Kelty—"

"No, it was. I shouldn't have put you in that position. I'm sorry." Her eyes glazed, and she blinked quickly.

"Yeah, I would've chosen cowgirl."

Kelty's eyes widened. Her mouth pursed, and then she burst out laughing. She laughed so hard, he could see her starting to tip into tears, so he turned and grabbed her a glass of water.

"Sorry." He grinned. He wasn't that sorry.

Kelty gulped down a drink, wiping her eyes. "No. Thank you."

"Is he being a dick again?" Emma threw an arm around Kelty's shoulder.

She shook her head. "No, just made me laugh."

Emma gave him an impressed look, and he sent one back that said, "Don't act so surprised." They collected the forms and started the tally. Emma cry-laughed when she saw the note "#1 because of the slutty crust." There was no name on the form, but that was one hundred percent Rachel.

He pulled out his phone to open his calculator app and

saw the time. *Shit.* Two minutes to seven thirty. "Hey, I have to run." Kelty and Emma both frowned. "Sorry. I have a thing." It was not lost on him that Kelty had given him the same excuse, but he wasn't going to announce his therapy session in front of the entire family. He turned and strode to the stairs before they could ask questions.

Nobody bothered him on the way up to the second floor. He locked the door to his childhood bedroom and opened his laptop, hoping his video chat app wouldn't require an update or reject his login information.

He pressed the link Elodie had provided him the first time they'd met, and it opened seamlessly. Elodie's face popped up in a tiny square, then bloomed into the full hotel-room reality. Bad art on the wall, blackout curtains drawn.

"You're travelling?"

"I am."

"Sorry. You didn't have to do this."

She scoffed. "What else am I going to do at nine o'clock in Ottawa on a Sunday night? I'm not my brother."

Sean chuckled. "Okay. Well, thank you."

She leaned in, all business, and opened her notebook. "Check-in. Give me a number for your balloon—zero, no air, ten, ready to pop."

"Seven," he said. "Maybe eight."

"What's in the balloon?"

He could've said playoffs or the family challenge. But none of that was the real issue. The idea of being honest made his limbs feel weak.

He choked out an answer. "Kelty."

Elodie nodded. "Okay, that's good. Give me thought bubbles. What's the ticker tape in your head?"

Sean stared at the abstract squiggles framed on her wall. Just say it. The thoughts were all right there. He just needed to let them out.

He drew a breath and released. "If I don't fix this now, I'll lose her forever. But I'm the problem. I'm the thing I have to fix and I—" His voice caught. "I don't think I can fix that."

How many times had he tried to put himself out there? To go for what he wanted? It never ended well. Even if he did tell Kelty the truth—even if he had proposed on that rooftop . . .

"I think it will all fail again. No matter what I do," he finished.

"Hm. That's a pretty rough diagnosis."

Sean nodded, running a hand over his face.

"The good news is, it's just a story. Your brain is making horror films and then charging you admission."

But was it just a story if he'd seen the ending before? "It's all the info I have to go on."

She smiled. "Absolutely. You're not crazy, Sean. Your brain and body are trying to protect you. But here's a question. Do you feel protected?"

He blinked. "What do you mean?"

Elodie leaned back in her chair. "Well, if these strategies are keeping you safe, then you should feel safe, right? Protected, happy, comfortable. You should be exactly where you want to be. Is that true?"

He laughed once, harshly. "No." It was the easiest answer he'd ever given.

"Okay." She gave it a minute to settle in. "We talked last time about behaviour as a strategy. Perfectionism keeps you safe from shame by making forward motion impossible. No risk, no failure. And spoiler alert, relationships are risky. The most risky, actually."

Sean shifted in his chair. "Yeah. I remember."

"So let's go back to that story. Your emotions seem split based on what you've told me. Part of you wants to dive in, part of you wants to run. But your reasonable mind is presenting all this data and discounting the connection you feel with Kelty. So what does your wise mind say? Is that data correct? Should it pull all the weight in this decision?"

Sean sat with that. He didn't have a clue how to break it down.

"Let's put it this way," Elodie said. "You have playoffs right now, right?"

He nodded.

"So your emotion says . . ."

"I want to win."

"Right, but what's the data on the Snowballs winning the Rose Cup in, say, the last three years?"

Sean bristled. "It doesn't matter. The teams are different, we've implemented new training strategies, and—" He stopped, catching onto the metaphor. "Oh shit."

Elodie grinned. "Oh shit is right. If you were playing hockey the way you're living life—"

"I'd never show up to the playoffs."

Her smile widened. "These are the playoffs in your damn life, Sean. The teams are different. You've implemented new training strategies. Are you going to show up or assume that outdated data knows best?"

SEAN'S GROIN was tight before warmups, and it took everything in him not to shout from the rooftops why. Sure, Kelty said it couldn't happen again, but the fact that it happened not once, but twice, and that he'd made her laugh until she cried had given him a shred of hope he was clinging to.

Maybe he wasn't too late.

They just needed to get through this first game against Pucks Deep. Then he could figure out what his next move had to be.

The Snowballs' dressing room buzzed with rituals as much as nerves. Country laced his skates inside out, muttering the same three lines of a Garth Brooks song under his breath. Brett sat with his stick across his knees, retaping the knob for the third time, peeling and wrapping until it looked like a white beehive. Tyler refused to put his jersey on until exactly seven minutes before puck drop, strutting around in shoulder pads.

Sean had never been especially superstitious, but after staying at the house, he couldn't help himself. He opened his locker and picked up the miniature clay piece of sushi. When

Kelty left for the kitchen, he pulled the tin from the back of his closet. It took some maneuvering, but he got it into the truck without her noticing. Back at his parents' house, he added the matchbook he'd picked up at the Den.

It was risky to start up a new tradition during playoffs. But the last few years hadn't gone especially well for them. And he was practicing with risk. He pressed a kiss to the clay, then put it back on the shelf in his locker for safekeeping.

He slammed the door closed. "Listen up!" Sean motioned for the guys to move in close before they headed to the tunnel. The looks on their faces said they weren't expecting a speech. He was more than happy to surprise them.

Sean held out his stick. "Everybody falls in love with the part where the puck kisses your tape. The celly. The screen-shot. But here's the truth. You don't own that puck. You borrow it. Each touch is about a heartbeat long, one to one-and-a-half seconds on your stick before it's gone again. In the offensive zone it's even shorter. You blink and it's off to the next guy.

"Even the monsters live with the puck maybe a minute total in a game. One minute. There's a hell of a lot of game-play outside of that. So what matters tonight, boys?

"You. Shoulder-checking twice before the rim. It's F3 high so our D can pinch. It's a good line change at forty-two seconds so the next wave hits fresh. It's you tying up on a draw so the weak-side winger walks out with a free puck and we're gone to the races.

"It's F1 through the hands, F2 on the body, F3 reading the bounce and killing the reverse. It's a net drive that drags a defenceman to church so the late guy can pray in the slot. It's talking loud, do you hear me? You are the maps app for your linemates. I want to hear that shit in the rafters.

"You want the puck more? Earn it. We don't reach. We don't hook because we were lazy for two strides. We don't gift their power play a stage. We suffocate and make them beg for a whistle!"

The Snowballs roared around him, banging their sticks on the floor.

Sean raised his voice above the din. "I don't give a flying *shit* what our stats are against Pucks Deep, do you hear me? We're a different team this year. We're stronger. We're grittier. And I heard Wheatfill's a little distracted lately."

The boys laughed, and he closed in. "This pot is ours, boys! Let's get out there and take it!"

They stormed into the tunnel, and when they stepped on the ice, the connection he felt with his team, with himself as a player, was stronger than it had been in weeks.

Sean Thompson was back.

After a strong warm-up, they lined up near the box. Sean tugged at the cuff of his glove, flexing his hand inside the leather as the announcer's mic squealed once, then cleared.

It was Madelyn Wilson's voice that filled the arena. "Good evening, Calgary!" The crowd roared in response. "Before we start, I wanted to tell you a little bit about what you're watching. When I started the Elite League at Douglas University, people told me I was wasting my time. They said players who didn't make Juniors or the AHL or NHL didn't need another place to play.

"But I watched the players I knew around me, the tough choices they had to make, the sacrifices, and that wasn't good enough. Because talent doesn't disappear just because you turn eighteen, or because one scout doesn't see you on the right night. Players deserve opportunities, and Alberta deserves hockey."

The crowd erupted a second time, and Sean breathed against the pinch in his chest.

"There are now ten Elite League teams in Alberta," Madelyn continued. "Ten. And every season, they're drawing bigger crowds, playing at higher levels, and proving what we all know—Alberta hockey runs deep."

André laughed. "She's going to incite a riot."

"Saskatchewan and Manitoba have both added teams, B.C. is close behind. And with our new partnerships with Hockey Canada, we're building pathways for younger players to develop alongside veterans, and older players to keep competing when the usual doors shut."

A stick jabbed Sean in the ribs. "Hear that?" Country leaned over, helmet tipped back just enough to show his shit-eating grin. "Older players. That one's for you, Thompson."

Madelyn wasn't done. "Sport isn't only about making the big leagues. It's about who we become by playing. The mental and physical toughness. The strength in our friendships and communities. Tonight, as a special celebration for the thirtieth anniversary of this league, I want to honour the players who were there at the start. The ones who took a chance on me and made this possible. Ladies and gentlemen, they've travelled from all over the country. Put your hands together for our original Elite League roster!"

Sean peered up into the stands as a ripple moved through the crowd. Men in worn jerseys, some of them bald, some greying at the temples, pushed to their feet, waving their hands. The sound swelled with cheers and whistles.

There, halfway up the section, was his dad. Rob Thompson. Standing tall next to Chase. Sean's breath snagged.

"Shit, to have a dad like that." André shook his head. "Too much pressure, bud."

Sean clipped him with his stick as he danced out of the way. They stood at attention for the anthem, then got in position for puck drop.

Sean crouched low at centre ice, stick blade flat, eyes locked on Jordan Wheatfill's smirk across the dot.

"Thought you'd have retired to the golf course by now."

Sean grinned. "And miss another chance to watch you choke under pressure?"

Behind Jordan, Cam banged his stick against the boards. "Careful, bud, his girlfriend's watching. She likes it when he's rough."

The ref motioned them in. "Sticks down, boys. Enough love letters, let's play some hockey."

Sean leaned forward, his eyes locked on Jordan. The barn buzzed as the puck dropped. Their sticks clashed as they both surged, and the war was on.

Brett scooped up the puck and shoved it up the ice, but immediately got stapled into the boards by Steele.

Brett grunted as he peeled himself off the glass. "C'mon, bud, you're not going to lick it clean?"

Sean cut across the dot, angling to intercept, and Cam tried to hip-check him late. Sean felt the shove, twisted, and let Cam's own momentum send him sprawling to the ice. The crowd was equally split between cheers and boos, the one con to playing a home team at home.

The first period was down and dirty, slogging through the mud. It didn't improve his mental game that Pucks Deep got a goal with two minutes left off a breakaway Sean should've cut off.

In the second period, the game stayed ugly. Pucks Deep clogged the neutral zone like they were laying bricks, every dump-in turning into a war in the corners. Brett got shoved face-first into the dasher and came up with a bloody lip. Country super-glued a cut on André's brow after a scuffle.

Thankfully, the Snowballs tied it late in the second. Tyler hammered home a rebound after a scramble in the crease. The crowd stomped on the metal bleachers until the whole barn rattled.

Jordan skated past their bench, tapping his stick in mock applause. "Congrats, you finally hit water falling out of a boat."

By the end of forty minutes, it was 1-1, and every bruise on Sean's body throbbed like a second heartbeat.

The third was survival.

The pace cranked up. Sean threw himself into lanes, blocking one slapper that rattled up his shin pad and numbed his leg to the hip. Boyd stood on his head in the net, sprawling, sliding, and stacking pads.

With three minutes left, Curtis broke free on a two-on-one. He deked, fired, and clanged it off the post. The sound knifed through Sean's ribs.

Wheatfill came back the other way, snapping one from the circle. Boyd gloved it, popped to his feet, and held the puck high like a trophy. The horn blew on a tie.

Overtime was pure chaos. Three-on-three that felt more like an open-ice combat than hockey. Brett and Wyatt collided at centre, gloves flying before either of them thought twice. The refs dove in, wrestling them apart while the benches weighed in with shouts and stick taps. Minutes later, Darcy hauled down Sam on a breakaway and got whistled for tripping, sending the Snowballs to a nerve-shredding penalty kill. Sean's pulse thundered in his ears as Boyd sprawled, stoning two point-blank shots. When Country finally cleared the puck the length of the ice, his lungs filled with air.

He'd never admit it, but it felt like they barely squeaked through until the horn blew. He hated shoot-outs, but after fifteen minutes of that shit, he'd rather bend over his mother's knee and take a spanking than volunteer for another shift.

They took a quick break, got water, and made their selections. Nobody talked to Boyd. He was locked in, and they didn't want to disrupt that.

Then there was nothing to do but wait.

Sean tapped his stick on the ice, chest heaving as Cam came in slow for Pucks Deep, trying a fancy toe-drag. Boyd was patient and robbed him with the paddle. The Snowballs' bench erupted, sticks hammering the boards.

Tyler was up next. He faked glove side, went blocker, and scored. 1–0 Snowballs.

Steele followed, barreling in like a freight train. Fired high glove. Boyd bobbled it, and the puck dropped over the line.

Sean cursed under his breath.

Country deked three times and scored on an empty net, 2-1, but then Jordan lined up. The crowd hushed. He skated in slow, patient. Why did he always have to look so steady?

He took the puck, angled left, cut right. Jordan faked a wrister, pulled wide, and tucked it backhand under the crossbar.

Sean's head dropped. He dragged in a slow breath, not wanting to look up and see Jordan's smart-ass expression.

"It's you, cap." Tyler clapped him on the back.

Sean skated to centre ice, the barn thundering so loud the boards trembled. He rolled his shoulders once, loosened his grip on the stick, and tried to ignore the thought bubbles. *You're not good enough. You can't make this under pressure. You're not as good as you were supposed to be.*

Horror stories. Well. Tonight he wasn't paying admission.

The ref dropped the puck at the dot. Sean tapped it forward and surged across the blue line.

His family was in the stands. His dad, who'd given up everything for him, stood with his hands in the air. His teammates were there behind him, believing in him even when he whiffed it.

Sean cut left, then snapped right, the goalie sliding with him.

Kelty was watching, and he needed her to know that he wasn't done fighting. He would not let these seconds slip away.

At the last heartbeat, he pulled the puck backhand, lifted it just enough, and cracked it under the bar.

The red light blazed. The crowd detonated, and just like that, the ending was different.

Snowballs flooded the ice, piling onto him. Sean gasped for air, laughing like he hadn't in months.

They'd taken down Pucks Deep in the shootout. And it felt damn good.

As soon as he pulled himself free, he scoured the stands, scanning the faces. His mom, dad, Crystal, Logan. He kept going, over his sisters, Curtis's family, Penny and Emma. He went back over the section, then made a third pass. Where the hell was she?

"She's not there, bud." Tyler hoisted him up from the ice.

"What?"

"Kelty."

Sean tore off his helmet. "What the hell are you talking about?"

Tyler held up his hands. "She's packing. Leaving tomorrow after—"

"What do you mean she's leaving tomorrow?" The blood drained from his head, making him dizzy. "She said after playoffs."

"I don't know. Emma told me on the way here. She's planning something for her tomorrow on the hike. A card or—"

"She doesn't need a damn card!" Sean bolted toward the gate, skipping the handshake line. Tomorrow? The hope that filled him at the beginning of the game crumbled to ash.

She'd meant it. *This can't happen again.* Was that why she was leaving?

Sean stormed into the locker room, threw his helmet and gloves on the bench, and tore his phone from his locker. Then he bolted back out to the empty hall on the backside of the tunnel. He dialed her number.

With all the adrenaline in his system, he knew it was stupid to talk to her, but how could she do this? Not even tell him and just take off?

The phone rang out, hitting her voicemail message. He hung up and dialed again. Then again, and again.

He slid down the wall and sat, and when the voicemail started a fourth time, he threw his phone across the floor. It skittered across the concrete and hit the far wall.

"New kind of celly, but I'm open to it."

Sean's head snapped up. "Don't." If it wasn't Jordan Wheatfill. There were a couple of other four-letter words rolling through his head, but he'd already gotten chewed out by Rhonda once.

"Can we talk?"

"Hell no."

"Cool. I'll start."

JORDAN STALKED FORWARD. "I'm not going to talk about you losing your way to the handshake line, but you know that was shitty."

Sean scoffed, but couldn't argue with him. "Yeah. That was shitty."

"Perfect. Not exactly equally shitty, but you didn't respond to my message."

Sean frowned. "What message?"

"On the boards. Last week." Jordan dropped to the floor, leaning against the wall across from him. He was still fully dressed besides his helmet.

"I don't check the boards during playoffs."

"That's what I figured. But Rhonda said texting you was a bad idea—"

"Correct."

"—so she talked to Jenna who talked to Country—"

"About what?"

Jordan leveled a stare at him. "Serious, bud?"

Sean glared right back. He had no idea why Jordan would need to get ahold of him. It wasn't to congratulate him for getting into the finals.

Jordan exhaled, pulling off his gloves. "About this whole thing Emma put together."

Sean's frown turned to a glower. "What thing?"

"She told Rhonda I needed to talk to you about . . . you know."

"You're starting to piss me off more than usual."

"Fine. I'll skip the foreplay. When I slept with Claire. I was trying to be gentle."

Sean's jaw locked. If he hadn't thrown his phone already, he would've chucked it then. *Emma was talking about his past with Jordan?* He hadn't had words with her after the whole Dusty Rose thing, but enough was enough.

He pushed off the floor. "Good talk."

"Sit your ass down. You won the game and skipped the glove taps. This is your punishment."

Sean ignored him, but then Jordan swept his phone off the floor before he could get to it. "You want to fight me for it?"

Sean could just imagine how that would look. Both of them walking out bloody from the tunnel after the Snowballs won in a shootout. He had half a mind to take him up on it and tell everyone he was a sore-ass loser.

But fighting Jordan wasn't going to solve his problem. For the past twenty years, he'd tried to deal with things on the ice. It had worked to a point. But now Kelty was at home packing.

"Let's get it over with, then. What did my sister tell you to say?" He still couldn't quite be cordial.

Jordan stood so they were at the same eye level. "She didn't tell me to say anything. She asked me if we'd ever talked about it. And I realized we hadn't."

"For good reason."

Jordan shook his head. "It wasn't. You were one of my best friends."

Sean had never heard him talk like this, and he didn't know what to do with it. They were good at chirping on the ice or at the bar when everyone else was there to mediate. But a real conversation? He didn't remember the last time that had happened.

"I shouldn't have done it. It was stupid and selfish. But Claire lied to me about you two being together. And that's kind of who I was, the guy you went to when you wanted a rebound. Not you specifically, but—"

"She told you we weren't together?" That was new information. Had he ever had a real conversation with Claire about it? She'd been cruel about the whole thing. Told him it was his fault she felt the need to look elsewhere. He doubted he'd have absorbed that information if anyone said it.

Jordan nodded. "I never would've done that to you, bud. But I was self-destructing, and I didn't know how to fix it. So when you didn't want to have anything to do with me, I gave up. I shouldn't have done that either."

"I wouldn't have let you fix it."

"That's true. Probably your fault, then."

Sean coughed a laugh, the whole situation circling into the present. It sounded eerily familiar. And back then, his whole life had been flipped upside down. It was easier to hate Jordan, to blame him, than admit he'd failed at everything that was important to him.

"That wasn't the only reason I hated you," Sean said.

"Mm. Tell me more."

"You're a dick on the ice." That was the easiest reason, but a deeper truth bubbled to the surface beneath it. They'd been the same back then. But Jordan had figured something out that he hadn't. Kelty was right. He'd noticed the difference when he was with Rhonda. How had he fixed himself when Sean couldn't?

Jordan grinned, handing him the phone. "You loved my dickery when we were on the same team." He took a few side steps.

"You're building a bad reputation."

Jordan shrugged, walking backward down the hall. "That's what they say about the Panthers. They seem to be doing well for themselves."

"Blasphemy."

Jordan laughed. "Shower. You smell worse than Chubs's pads."

Sean flipped him off, then inspected his phone after Jordan disappeared around the corner. Only a cracked screen. More importantly, he had no missed calls and no text messages from Kelty.

He hauled ass back to the locker room. Emma was going to get an earful later, but right now, he had to get to One Place. Fast.

———

Inside the locker room, Country had his arms around both Brett and Suraj, belting some old Shania Twain chorus completely out of tune. Darcy and André danced in circles with their helmets still on, slipping on the puddled floor. Boyd, still half in his pads, had his mask on backward and was twirling a towel like he was training for rhythmic gymnastics.

Sean should've been grinning ear to ear, soaking it all in. They'd just stolen the game in overtime, and he was the one who buried the final goal. Every guy in the room was flying high, but Sean's mind wasn't on the win.

He ripped at his skates with shaking hands. The laces snarled into knots, and he cursed under his breath. "Come on, come on—"

Tyler crouched next to him. "Missed you, bud."

"Yep." He yanked the lace on his left skate free.

"In a hurry?" Country's mouth quirked. At this point, they all knew something was going on with him and Kelty, and he'd been the last one to find out she was skipping town early.

"Just trying to get to One Place." Sean ripped off his jersey.

Tyler frowned. "But . . ."

"It's part of it. Promise."

Brett whooped. "Finally! Anything you need, bud. Just pop it on the group chat."

Sean dropped his pads on the bench. "Oh, like when I needed a spare tire? Or a ride home?"

The guys got quiet, their eyes darting to Tyler. Sean dragged a hand through his sweaty hair, realization dawning. "You ignored it on purpose."

"Did it work?" André waggled his brows.

"Did it—?" Sean slammed his locker shut. "That's why Kelty's leaving."

André tisked. "Because you didn't seal the deal?"

"No, because—" He let out an exasperated sigh. "Because I sealed it too well. I think."

Hoots and hollers followed him to the shower. Country laughed. "If it doesn't work out, that's what you should say on your dating profile!"

Sean was in and out in three minutes, hair dripping, steam clinging to his skin. He pulled on jeans and a hoodie and shoved his shoes on. He packed up and slung his bag over his shoulder, then jogged down the hall and took the stairs two at a time.

One Place sat lit up across the street, the neon signs flashing in the windows. He sprinted across the street, not even stopping to drop his bag, and when he pushed through the doors, the place exploded.

"THOMPSON!" someone bellowed, and the cheer caught on. People leapt to their feet, raising glasses. A round of applause broke into whistles and shouts. Pat pointed a finger at him from behind the bar, mouthing, *"On the house."*

He lifted a hand but didn't slow. Normally he'd bask in the glory, but tonight, none of it mattered. He made a beeline for the back table, heading straight for his dad.

"Hey, there he is!" Rob stood to embrace him, but Sean stopped, dropping his bag at his feet.

"Dad, she's leaving tomorrow, and I can't let her go. I need to fix this, but—" He swallowed hard, catching his breath. "I don't know how."

Emma pretended she wasn't eavesdropping, but he heard her lean into Rhonda and whisper, "Ghost of playoffs past." She was lucky there were witnesses at the moment.

Rob's smile widened as he glanced down first at Logan, then Chase. "Buckle up." His friends stood up beside him. "Because we do."

KELTY COULDN'T STAY at the game. It was too hard. Too sad. She thought she'd be able to stay until the end of the series with Pucks Deep, but after Sean stayed at the house . . . after their night together, it all just felt impossible.

She'd completely broken down when all the girls showed up at her house after celebrating with the team at One Place, and now they all showed the signs of staying up past two in the morning.

The group stood slumped at the trailhead of the hike that nearly did her in the week prior. Emma leaned on Rachel's shoulder, eyes half-shut. Eliza hid her bloodshot eyes behind dark lenses that weren't fully necessary with the sun barely up. Not their greatest moment.

Kelty's heart stuttered as Sean walked up, setting up their folding chairs for the day. She'd heard all about the game, about his shoot-out goal, and she regretted everything about not being there. But telling him that or talking about the game, the team, or the playoffs felt like pressing her thumb into a bruise.

"Alright, don't get comfy." Carter's hiking shoes crunched on the gravel. "You four." He pointed at Emma, Tyler, Sean, and Kelty, "You don't get off that easy." He held out two envelopes.

Kelty's stomach dropped. "I'm not doing this hike again." She shuddered and could've sworn Sean coughed to cover a laugh.

"Not the hike." Carter winked. "We didn't want you to miss out on the fun, so today, you have your own challenge."

Kelty pursed her lips, her blood rushing in panic. Would they do this challenge with the four of them? Or just her and Sean? "I'm not sure how long I'll be able to stay."

"You were going to take the times, right?" Carter motioned at the group stretching a few paces away.

"Yes, but—"

"This won't take you any longer. Promise. And we'll take the times here, so no need to come back."

Kelty scrambled for any other argument, but came up empty. She took the envelope from Carter, realizing Emma and Tyler had already read theirs and were jogging to the car.

She swore under her breath and ripped it open.

Glide to the place you compete. Puzzle out your path to earn your next clue.

"The Ice Centre." Sean peered over her shoulder.

"Has to be, right?" She looked up at him and instantly regretted it. He'd showered the night before and slept on it, which always made his hair look like they'd just taken a roll in the sheets.

"Carter, honestly, how long is this going to take?" she asked.

He blew out a breath. "Two hours or less." He glanced over his shoulder. "Less for Tyler and Emma."

Kelty did the mental math. It would be forty minutes back

into Calgary, but she'd have to drive that anyway. "We don't have to come back here?"

Carter shook his head. "Nope. End point is in the city."

She groaned, "Fine," then grabbed her bag and sprinted to the car with Sean. Why was she letting them—well, mostly Carter—talk her into this?

It was easy to rationalize it. She could deal with this crazy because this was her last day. With how emotional everything had been, it was probably good to have an over-the-top distraction.

Sean didn't say a word when she chose her car instead of his truck. Maybe the tire episode from the other night had spooked him. Thankfully, she was able to pick up her car from the shop the night before, right before the game. She was sick of asking for rides.

But Sean hadn't said a thing about the challenge either. Besides weighing in on the first location. "Do you want to do this?" she asked.

Sean settled back in the seat, looking awkward as a passenger instead of being the driver. It was like he didn't know what to do with his hands. "Carter's just trying to do something nice."

Not an answer, but okay.

"Music okay?" Kelty's heart hammered against her ribs. She shouldn't have asked. What if he said no? What if he wanted to talk the entire way back to Calgary?

"Sounds good."

She breathed a sigh of relief and turned on her playlist for road trips. Lots of banjo and mandolin.

Sean stared out the windshield. It wasn't that he was talkative normally, but to have no objections? No opinions on this drastic change in plans for the day? That set off every alarm bell in her head, and she couldn't stay quiet for more than five minutes.

"You won last night?"

Sean looked surprised to hear her voice. "We did."

"In overtime."

He nodded. "Yep."

Kelty was going to die. She wanted to pull the car over on the side of the road, step out, and crawl into a ditch. "Can you just, I don't know, tell me about it?" She'd never had restless leg syndrome, but she was fairly certain she was acquiring it.

Sean sat straighter. "Sure."

For the next thirty minutes, he walked her through the plays, gave her every detail of the penalties and the crap Pucks Deep spouted at them at face-offs. It was the kind of gossip that fed her soul.

By the time they pulled into the Ice Centre parking lot, she no longer wanted to scratch off her skin. She parked and scoured the lot for Emma or Tyler's vehicles as they ran inside. Nothing.

"Do you really think we beat them?"

Sean shrugged. "Maybe they took a different road through the city?"

The doors of the building were unlocked. They burst into the atrium with zero clue what came next until they saw Nora standing in front of the ticket booth with a plucky grin. She motioned for them to follow her, leading them down the stairs to the silver rink.

She pointed at a series of giant-sized Boggle cubes with letters on all sides. "Spell the word. Then I'll give you your clue."

Kelty nodded. Okay. This should be easy. There were five cubes. How hard could it be?

She stepped out onto the ice and slipped, almost biffing it before grabbing onto the boards. "How are we supposed to do this without—" She caught sight of the two pairs of skates sitting next to the bottom row of bleachers. Right. She was an idiot.

Sean helped her back to the rubber mats, and they both

laced up. It had been a while since she'd skated, but wasn't it like riding a bike?

She was careful on the ice until she got her bearings. When she felt confident, she moved away from the boards to check out the letters. H, T , R, E, and A.

"This has to make more than one word," Sean muttered. He was probably right. "R-H-E-A-T. Does that exist?"

Kelty snorted. "Sounds like a brand of oatmeal. Ooh! What about Earth?"

Sean considered this, then moved the blocks into place. They both stepped back, squinting at it, then glanced up at Nora sitting in the stands. She peered down, then went back to scrolling on her phone.

Okay. Not it. Kelty blew out a frustrated breath.

"What about heart?" Sean suggested after a beat.

Kelty's eyes lit up. "Yes! That has to be it!" She helped him rearrange the letters. When they were all in a line, Nora stood and blew her whistle.

"Ha!" Kelty clapped her hands to her mouth. "That wasn't hard at all!" She wobbled on her skates, and Sean grabbed onto her elbow.

He nudged her forward. "I'll get you back to the boards."

She didn't argue. When they returned to the mats, Nora had another card for them.

"Where are Tyler and Emma?" Kelty hissed.

Sean just shrugged and opened the envelope.

Clue #2 – Roadblock

One of you must eat the dish that started it all. Where late-night Calgary kitchens hum, recreate your date.

Kelty's throat tightened. What was this challenge? Carter

knew she was leaving today, didn't he? Why would he send them back to the place where they first fell in love?

Sean tapped the envelope against his palm. "Is he talking about that Thai place?"

She shook her head. "How would he know about the Thai place?" How would he know about any of it? "What do you consider our first date?"

Sean thought for a moment. "Probably The Med."

Kelty's pulse tripped. The night they went out after everyone left the office. Sean's whole diatribe about garlic. Neither of them had said it was a date. But they both knew even then.

Kelty shuffled over and sat on the bench to remove her skates. "Alright. Let's go."

———

The Med hadn't changed. The lettering was still the same, the gold paint chipped on the edges. Inside, the air was thick with roasted spices. Cumin, cinnamon, charred meat. Smells . . . they always got to her.

The light from the tall windows illuminated walls hung with faded photographs of seaside towns. It felt different in the daylight.

The hostess gave them a curious look when they asked about a clue, but she gestured them toward a two-top in the corner. The same corner where they'd sat that first night.

"This is a little creepy," Kelty whispered as they sat. "Did you tell him about this?"

Sean picked up the menu. "Once. A long time ago." Kelty looked skeptical. "I called him. Asked him for advice."

That shut her up.

Sean focused hard on the text in front of him. "Garlic chicken, then, right?" His eyes sparkled as he finally made eye contact.

Kelty nodded. "Has to be." She stared at her napkin and fork, emotions swirling like a bad cocktail in her stomach.

Being here, it was too easy to remember. That night, she'd memorized everything about him. The way his mouth moved, the way he mixed his food on his plate.

They put in the order, and Kelty excused herself to the washroom. Could she ask Sean to drop her off at home? Could he finish this by himself?

When the time away was approaching unexplainable, she made her way back to the table. Their server was on his way over with two steaming plates, the garlicky aroma so strong it seemed to already seep into her skin.

And there, tucked just beneath Sean's plate, was another cream-coloured envelope.

⌒

———

Their next stop was Prince's Island Park. They were supposed to find a specific tree based on the instructions given.

"I'm getting escape room flashbacks," Kelty said as they walked down the path from the parking lot.

Sean laughed. "I thought you loved escape rooms?"

Kelty gave him a sidelong glance.

They followed the step-by-step directions, and it wasn't until they strode up to the tree that Kelty's chest seized.

It wasn't the tree. It was the bench next to it.

Her eyes filled with tears. "Sean, this isn't funny."

Sean frowned. "What are you talking about?"

She froze and pointed at the bench. "Are you kidding

me?" When she saw his blank expression, she had to walk the opposite direction so he wouldn't see the tears overflow. He didn't remember. This bench, that day, was one of the happiest days of her life. "Just get the clue."

There was an envelope attached to the armrest. She waited, not able to turn and look at it. *I love you.* The words pulsed through her.

It had taken Sean six weeks after she said it to say it back. When he had, they'd been sitting right there, feeding the ducks.

"It's just coordinates," he called out.

Perfect. Anything that would take them from here.

"Uh, sorry. Didn't understand the last part at first. Looks like we have to go by boat."

Thirty-Four

ORANGE PADDLE BOATS bobbed at the dock, ridiculous and cartoonish. Kelty yanked a life vest over her head, muttering, "Two hours my ass." Sean slid in beside her. He started to push the pedals as soon as she sat in the plastic bucket seat.

She reeled on him. "You're okay with this?" He didn't answer. "You make fun of paddle boats literally any time we see them. You said they were clown cars for people who didn't do real workouts."

Sean's mouth quirked. "We're not doing it for fun. It's the challenge."

She folded her arms, pedalling with him. "So that's all I had to do? Call it a challenge, and you'd be on board? Or should I have gotten Carter to suggest my ideas?"

Sean was infuriatingly silent. They paddled to the other side, then followed Sean's GPS through the park and onto the street. They walked three blocks before Kelty realized they'd backtracked. They passed The Med and turned right, and a pit of dread opened in her stomach, worse than when she saw the bench. When Sean slowed and then stopped, she felt lightheaded.

Kelty stared at the facade of the building. *No.* She was not doing this today. She didn't know how Carter was getting his information. Clearly, he'd done his research when creating this challenge. Probably talked to Tyler and Emma. But this was the last place on Earth she wanted to be at that moment.

"Are you coming?" He took a step toward the door.

"No. You can do this one. I'll wait here." She folded and refolded the piece of paper with the coordinates on it, turning it into one of the fortune tellers she used to make in elementary school.

"I think we're supposed to do it together."

Kelty's eyes started to blur. They were supposed to do a lot of things together. "I'm not going up there. I think it'll only take—I'm not going up there, Sean." She finally looked up, not caring if he saw that her nose was turning red. "You can do it or don't do it. We can just let Tyler and Emma win. I didn't want to do this in the first place."

She had to get away from here or she was going to suffocate. Kelty launched herself down the sidewalk. North, south, she had no idea, but she had to get away from here.

"Kelty!" Sean called behind her.

"The building isn't even open. It's a Saturday," she yelled back, walking faster.

His footsteps pounded behind her, but her breath was coming in short gasps, and she couldn't make herself run.

"Kelty, stop." Sean put his hands on her shoulders, pulling her back. She didn't turn to him. "I know what happened last time—"

"It's not about what happened last time." She shrugged his hands off.

"Okay. Then what is it then? What is it about?"

"I just want to go home. I need to finish packing."

"Kelty, I think you're going to want to—"

"No! I don't want to! That building?" She pointed up at the windows of their old office. "That office? It was my favourite place in this whole damn city. I looked forward to walking in there every day when we were working on the acquisition. Not because of the work, but because you were there. That was the start of everything. And when we walked out of that building, we walked out together. And then Mason's party happened, and my very favourite rooftop turned into something I don't even want to think about. So can we please just leave that building be? Can it please just be the place that I loved?"

She took a few steps away from him, wrapping her arms around herself, trying to keep the gooey parts from spilling out. After seven and a half years, every place in this city was somewhere she'd loved. The Ice Centre, the Thompson House, the restaurants and bars, One Place, the Dusty Rose, the Saddledome, the Stampede Grounds, all of it was woven into a story that was now unravelling.

"Kelty," Sean's voice was low. "I know I have no right to ask anything of you. But I can tell you, if we walk in that building, we're not going into the office."

"Sean—"

"Please, Kelty." His voice broke, and when she looked up, tears pooled at the corners of his eyes. That knocked the breath out of her. Had she ever seen Sean cry? She scoured her memory, trying to find a single time when he'd stood in front of her like this, tears in his eyes. No. Sometimes she could tell he'd been crying, but only after the fact.

He swiped at his eyes. "I promise. This will be the last thing . . ." he paused. "The second to last thing I ask you."

"Second to last?" What in the world was he talking about?

He blew a breath out of his nose. "Maybe the last. Depends. On a couple of things."

"Sean. I need to go. I'm supposed to leave by two so I don't have to drive through the pass in the dark."

He nodded. "Yep. It will take three minutes. Tops."

Kelty gritted her teeth. "And you won't ruin the office."

He shook his head. "No. I promise."

"Fine," she snapped, striding to the glass entrance doors.

She should've stuck to her guns. She knew it as soon as she agreed, but how was that fair for him to cry like that? Why did this stupid challenge mean so much to him?

The doors were unlocked, and she walked inside to see a doorman at the elevators. Okay. Strange. Sean hurried in after her and nodded to the guy like he knew him. The hairs rose on the back of her neck.

They got in the elevator, and the doorman hit the button for the roof. Her jaw worked. Well, he did technically keep his promise.

Neither of them said a word on the way up. The elevator dinged, and they exited, walking toward the door that led to the platform. Sean pushed it open for her, and she walked out into the blazing Calgary sun.

"Okay. Here we are. What is it that—" She stopped, her eyes landing on a chair sitting in the middle of the deck. A wide cream envelope was taped to the chairback. As she got closer, blood started to rush in her ears. Her name was written on the front.

In Sean's handwriting.

Thirty-Five

Kelty,

Is this the first letter I've written to you? I think it might be. I can't tell you how difficult it was to write this. Not just because writing is hard, but because words are hard, too. I hate that this came after you told me you were leaving. I should have said all of this months, if not years, ago. I'm sorry it took the thought of losing you to kick me in the ass.

Let me say first, I've been in therapy. I announce that like it's impressive. I've only done three sessions. I'm not going to pretend it's some new amazing idea I had since you've been trying to get me to go for years. But I finally listened.

So far, I've learned that you're right about

everything. You probably already knew that. I did too, honestly. I just didn't want to admit it. Because that would mean I was wrong, and you know how much I love accepting that.

I've learned that it doesn't mean I'm wrong. it means I'm stuck. It doesn't mean I'm a bad person. It means I have some work to do.

Again, not news to you. But I learned one more thing sitting down and writing. It's easier for me to say how I feel on paper. Sometimes when you're talking or asking me questions, thoughts run through my head at a million miles a second, and it's impossible for me to get them out.

Here are some of those that I've struggled to say recently.

I love you. I love you so much I can't breathe when I wake up in the morning. The only night I've slept well in the past few weeks was when I came home for the night. Which, by the way, was a total set-up. I think my dad and Chase put that screw in my tire. I'll thank them later.

I didn't know how much the next life steps meant to you. I knew you wanted marriage and kids, but I didn't understand how much. I should've asked. I should've listened. I'm sorry.

Honestly, all of that still scares the shit out of me, but losing you scares me more. I don't want you to leave. I also understand how much you want to be with your parents. So, I have a plan to propose. Follow the instructions below and open the next envelope when you get there to see if it works for you.

Love,

Sean

SEAN SECOND-GUESSED his plan the entire way down to the main floor of the building. His dad and his friends swore that letters were the key to winning a woman over, but Kelty hadn't looked convinced. Maybe it was because it was his letter.

The elevator sighed at the lobby, and they stepped out onto marble that had been buffed to a gloss by a thousand weekday shoes. The doorman gave him a thumbs-up, jinxing him. Fantastic.

Kelty pushed through the doors. She didn't turn toward him, just held the letter with a death grip and started counting her steps.

He fell in behind and a touch to the side so she had room to pivot. She moved straight down the block. His heart beat at the speed of a scared rabbit. Had he counted correctly? It had been late when they came down here last night, and only his dad was sober.

At the corner, she turned and kept counting. He probably should've just said turn at the corner. Damn it, he was making it all too complicated.

Sean pulled his phone from his pocket, screen already

cued to the contact he needed, the tiny camera icon glaring up at him.

Kelty hooked another right. She took a few more steps and stopped. "Thirty-six."

The sidewalk in front of them was nothing much. Stained concrete, a skinny city maple tree in a metal grate, a narrow storefront with a high transom window reflecting the sky. No crowd. No fancy sign. Just a door with clean glass and tidy lettering.

Kelty frowned, finally turning to look at him. He could barely keep his grin caged. His thumb hovered over the call button.

"Read it."

Her throat worked. She slid her thumb under the flap. The paper rasped as she pulled out the letter and unfolded it. Sean pressed *Dial* and killed the sound, the video screen blooming to life on his palm. They answered on the second ring.

Kelty's eyes scanned the page. He watched the moment the words hooked her, holding his breath.

Her head shot up. She blinked up at the building's window, at the white lettering neatly applied there: Registry Agent in bold, and beneath it the list in smaller type: Vital Statistics — Birth | Marriage | Death. Alberta's crest tucked small in the corner. She looked back down at the letter. Back up at the glass. Finally, her eyes met his.

"I don't have a ring. I would've, but there's a reason," he blurted, because the words in his throat bottlenecked. This wasn't the speech he'd practiced in the mirror at two a.m. Just awkward-as-hell bare truth.

Kelty blinked. "What do you mean, Sean?"

He lifted the phone so the screen faced her and tilted it so the sunlight didn't blind it out. "They can explain better."

Kelty's mother leaned into the frame, as if she could climb through the square. "Hi, honey."

Kelty's face crumpled like paper. Tears jumped to her eyes, quick and hot. She took a step closer on instinct. "Mom? Dad?"

"We're here." Her father crowded into the frame.

She laughed and cried on the same breath, that wild little sound that always ate Sean alive from the inside out. "What is this?"

Sean's throat burned. He kept the phone steady.

Her mother answered gently. "Well, we got a phone call last night." The camera jostled as she adjusted it. "We got to talk with Sean a little more."

Kelty's gaze slashed to Sean, disbelieving.

He nodded once.

Her mother was still talking. "He wanted to know how to do this right, and I told him it was very important to us that you use this." She turned so only her profile showed as she reached off-screen and came back holding something small between her fingers. A ring. Thin yellow gold, an oval stone the color of late summer wheat, flanked with two tiny diamonds that winked in the light.

Kelty clapped her hands over her mouth. "That's—"

"I told him that your great-grandmother promised me this could be for my daughter. If she ever wanted it."

Kelty's shoulders trembled. A tear fell to the letter still curled in her fingers and blotted a word into a watercolour splotch. She dragged the back of her wrist across her cheek. "I don't understand. You said—"

"I know what I said." Sean thought about ending the call, but for the second time in a week, he didn't care who heard what came out of his mouth. "I was wrong, Kelt."

She shook her head, the tears falling faster. "I don't want you to do this because you think you have to."

He reached for her, pulling her against him. "I'm not. I promise, I'm not." She collapsed into his arms, burrowing into his chest. Her parents were either staring at the back of her shirt or the sky, but he didn't care.

The interminably long couple of weeks stacked inside him. Every misstep, every word he'd swallowed, every drafted late-night apology he couldn't send.

"I want to marry you. And we never talked about what that would look like, but they can issue a marriage licence here. We have our IDs. You have your ID, right?" Panic hit him in the ribs. He hadn't thought to confirm that.

"Yes," she choked out.

"Okay, then this office is open until eleven. I checked. We can find a commissioner this afternoon. My dad has a friend who can do it. We have witnesses—"

"Right now?" Kelty pulled back, tilting her chin to look at him.

The blood drained from Sean's face. Oh shit. Should he not have done this? Should he have only proposed and not gone full speed ahead? "Yeah. I was thinking . . . right now." He cursed under his breath. "I did it again, eh? Decided my way was best. I should've asked you—"

A laugh burst through her tears, helpless and hiccupped. She pressed her fingers against his lips and shook her head. Another laugh tumbled out and became a sob, and then she tried to speak and failed and tried again.

"I'm wearing joggers," she finally got out.

Sean could barely breathe through the burn in his throat. "Me, too." He worked to push the sting from his eyes, then finally gave up. "I was told there isn't a dress code."

Kelty coughed a laugh. She wiped her cheeks for the hundredth time and sucked in a deep breath. "Why now?"

Sean held her, still gripping the phone behind her back. He paused, waiting for the truth to coalesce between all the answers he would typically give. *You were going to leave. I didn't want to lose you.* Those were only a piece of the truth.

"It was something I learned in therapy."

Kelty groaned. "Is this how our lives are going to be now? You're going to be that guy?"

Sean barked out a laugh. He bent over her, kissing her neck. "Yeah. So, one time my therapist told me—"

Kelty smacked his chest. "If you say that at a party, I swear—"

"Never good enough for you, is it?" He grinned against her skin, heat flashing through him as her breathing hitched. "You were always the one I wanted. But I didn't want to fail again, Kelt. And what my *therapist* pointed out was I already was. By not playing, it was a hundred percent failure rate." He threaded his hand in her hair and tugged her head back so he could look at her. "I'm not worried about losing the game anymore. I just want to play. With you."

Kelty's nose turned pink, her cheeks damp and shining. "Okay."

Sean's heart flipped. "Is that a yes?"

"Yes."

Cheers erupted behind her, and they both jumped. Right. Her parents were still on the phone.

Kelty spun in his arms, pressing her back into him and snatching the phone from his hand. "I'm getting married!"

Sean wrapped his arms around her middle, kissing the top of her head. He was getting married. And for the first time ever, saying that word in his head only brought him peace.

Thirty-Seven

KELTY GRIPPED Sean's fingers so hard her knuckles blanched. The glass door hissed shut behind them. Fluorescent lights hummed. A laminated sign on a wire stand read: Registry Agent — Vital Statistics. Please take a number.

Sean reached across and plucked a ticket from the red dispenser: A104. The digital board on the wall blinked A103 in segmented orange numerals. Her eyes wouldn't stop leaking. Sean could've at least told her not to wear mascara.

"So this whole thing." She sniffed. "You planned it?"

Sean chuckled. "Kelt. You've known me for almost eight years."

She squeezed his hand. "Carter?"

"Nope. My dad, Logan, and Chase."

Her eyes widened. "You told them?" That was more shocking than anything she'd witnessed in the last three hours. Sean was setting and breaking records by the second.

"Yep. Last night at One Place. When you weren't there—" His voice broke. She leaned her head on his shoulder.

"I can't believe you were going to leave without saying goodbye."

Kelty groaned. "I would've said it. At the hike this morning."

"With my entire family there?"

"I don't think I could've done it on my own." Her shoulders shuddered. "I was too sad."

Sean curled his arm around her, pushing her hair back and exposing her neck. "I'm sorry."

"No, I didn't mean it like—"

"Kelt. I'm sorry."

She drew a shaky breath and exhaled. "I love you." She tensed like she always did when she said that, waiting for his hesitation, but there was none.

"I love you, too."

Nothing about this felt real. It was everything she'd wanted and everything she'd already grieved. Not just the idea of marriage and a family, but breaking down the walls that had always sat between her and Sean. They hadn't been a dealbreaker until they were.

"That's always how it is," she whispered.

"What?"

"That things don't come back to you until you're willing to lose them."

Sean stroked her hair. "Or until you're not."

The numbers on the board flipped to A104.

"Number?" The clerk peered out, cheerful and unhurried from behind a plexiglass shield. She wore a cardigan with tiny daisies. A ballpoint pen sat tethered to the counter by a silver chain.

Sean held up their ticket, and she motioned them forward. They stood and walked up to the counter together.

"Hi. Uh, we're here for a marriage licence."

———

. . .

They burst through the doors to the street, and Kelty sucked in a lungful of air. Sean held their paperwork snug inside the sheet protector. She was about to start retracing her steps to the paddleboats when a long, glossy black limousine pulled up to the curb.

Her jaw dropped. "Sean. Did you—?"

He didn't have to answer. The back door flew open, and Emma hopped out to the sidewalk. She was crying before she could make it to them, her arms thrown wide. After squeezing Kelty tight, Emma stepped back, sniffing. "Give me your keys."

"What?" Kelty wiped her cheeks for what felt like the thousandth time that week.

"I'm taking your boat back to get your car. Give me your keys and get in!" Emma gestured to the limo.

Kelty laughed and searched in her purse. She'd barely handed off her key ring when Sean pulled her into the back seat.

"This was Carter," Sean admitted as the soft leather interior swallowed them.

"I figured." Kelty landed in his lap, and the door thumped shut. She didn't even check to make sure the glass was up. The moment they were enclosed, she was on him, hands wrapped at the back of his neck, mouth hungry. He made a sound that was half laugh, half surrender, and kissed her like he'd been drowning and she was a hundred percent oxygen.

"What about kids?"

Sean kissed her quick and hard. "What about them?"

"Are they still off the table?"

He shook his head, seeming desperate for more of her mouth. "I don't know, Kelt. I'm open to it. This is all new to me."

"Okay, yeah." She dragged her fingernails through his hair. "I just—I want to keep talking about it. You can't shut down."

"I know. I won't."

"And if you do?" She sat back, her breath quick and shallow. "What if you do?"

Sean gripped her waist. "If I do . . . don't let me get away with it. Don't settle, ever again. I can't promise I'll be perfect at this—"

"I don't expect you to be perfect."

"I know, but it still scares me. I don't want you to ever—"

"I know." Kelty pressed a palm to his cheek. It took him a second to find words.

"I promise I'll never stop trying."

That was all she needed to hear. She kissed him slowly, her body aching for more of him. His strength, his weight.

Sean stretched out on the long side bench, pulling her on top of him. "I missed this so much."

She tore at his T-shirt, slipping her hands against his bare skin. "What, the other night didn't count?"

"It made it worse." His breath was ragged as his hands plunged beneath her waistband, cupping her backside, pulling her flush to him.

"How long is this limo ride?"

"Long enough."

She'd never been so grateful she carried a small pack of personal wipes in her purse. Kelty groaned against his mouth, heat flashing down her centre as his movements became jerky and desperate. "Sit up."

He pushed off the seat, panting. Kelty leaned back, threw her feet straight up in the air, and yanked off her joggers. When he was upright, she settled on his lap, her thighs snug against his hips. "You've always liked no armrests."

"I love you," he rasped.

She grazed her teeth over his jaw. "I don't trust it. You're compromised."

Sean huffed a laugh, spreading both of his large, rough hands under her shirt and across her back. "I'm marrying you, aren't I?"

Thirty-Eight

BY THE TIME the limo eased to a stop at the Thompson house, Kelty looked like she'd been in a fight with a raccoon. Sean didn't look much better, but at least his shirt was on right side out. He pointed out the tag, and Kelty quickly pulled it over her head and flipped it.

He couldn't keep the smile off his face. Mostly because Kelty had a drunken, sleepy grin, and he knew he'd put it there.

The limo driver opened their door, not meeting their eyes. Good man. Sean handed him a hundred-dollar bill as they passed.

Kelty stood on the driveway, waiting for him. He grabbed her hand and pulled her toward the side gate.

"Sean . . ."

"Hm?"

He fought to keep his expression even, but it was impossible. This part was his mom, and Sharla Thompson and her friends were incapable of half-assing anything. Even on short notice.

"Sean."

"Yeah."

He pushed the gate open, and Kelty sucked in a breath. A series of simple arches had been planted into the winter-compressed grass. Birch poles lashed together with twine and draped with guazy white fabric.

Kelty was crying again. She pulled him to a stop. "Sean, I want to do this—I want to marry you. And I know you called my parents, but I can't do this without them here."

Sean nodded. "It's a good thing I gave that caveat." She frowned, and he lifted her hand to his lips, kissing the tips of her fingers. "This is the last thing I'm going to ask you. Will you walk into the yard with me?"

She swallowed. "But if I go back there, they'll think—"

"Just walk with me."

Kelty drew in a breath and exhaled. She nodded. Sean pulled her against his side, walking slow to match her stride. The yard opened up to crisp white linens on round tables along the edges of the yard, set with bundles of tulips tucked into glass jars. Another arch stood against the fence, this one wound with branches and fresh blooms. White folding chairs were set up in rows, leaving an aisle open down the centre.

Everyone was there. Hiking shoes. Puffy jackets. Toques and backward hats. The girls looking much more perky now that they had their hands on massive amounts of coffee, and the guys already cracking open beers from the cooler on the patio.

But it was Sean who pulled to a stop as his eyes landed on the man standing at the end of the aisle. Fly was there, in a navy blazer over a graphic tee that read *THIS IS MY COMMISSIONER SUIT* in bold white letters.

Rob appeared next to them, his eyes sparkling. "I told you I knew a guy."

Fly looked up. "There he is!"

That's when Kelty noticed who was sitting in the front

row. Her body jerked like she'd been struck by lightning. "What? How—?"

Her parents stood and followed Fly up the aisle, her dad's face lit up with pure mischief. "We were on the phone here! In the Thompson's living room!"

That was more excitement than Sean had ever seen from the man. His soon-to-be father-in-law might like sitting in a chair with a book and a blanket over his legs, but when Sean asked for Kelty's hand and laid out his plan late last night, he'd gotten in the car with his wife and driven all the way to Revelstoke before stopping for the night. They arrived that morning at ten. He was earning his two afternoon naps.

Once everyone realized Sean and Kelty were there, the backyard turned into a tornado of hugs, laughter, and tears. Jenna presented Kelty with a pale pink strapless dress she was gifted by some brand wanting to sponsor their YouTube channel. Logan handed over a blazer he was planning to wear to the event at the Saddledome the following week. It still had the tags on and fit Sean perfectly.

In less than twenty minutes, Kelty's hair was pulled up in a pearl clip, her makeup was done, and she stood at the back door waiting for everyone to take their seats. Sean stood next to Fly, his hands clasped in front of him, the whole Snowballs team lined up on his right. All the women lined the left side of the fence, Ryan's girls trying to wrangle Hope into standing still by offering her Smarties.

When they were as settled as they could be, Delia carried her guitar to the stool set up next to Fly. She started to strum, and the whole world slowed.

Sean waited for the tightness in his chest, the sinking pit in his stomach. But all he felt was the breeze against his cheek, the sun warming his left side as it peeked through the branches of the large oak.

And all he saw was her.

Kelty glowed as she walked down the aisle toward him. She took her time, her eyes shimmering.

Love and grief tore through him in equal amounts. He'd been duped. For years, he'd believed he was keeping himself safe when really, he'd been missing out. Holding himself back from this full, vibrant thing he'd forgotten, or maybe never knew, existed.

Kelty stopped in front of him. "Fancy seeing you here."

Sean wrapped a hand around her hip, the fabric of her dress slippery under his fingers. He kissed her forehead. "I'm so glad you came."

"You're an asshole, just like your dad." She grinned. "Asking me when everyone knows so I can't turn you down."

Sean glanced over at his mom and dad sitting on the front row, his throat thickening. "Like father, like son."

Kelty ran a thumb over his cheek. "I think at this point, you're writing your own Thompson family lore."

Sean held his breath to keep from tearing up again. He'd cried more in the past two weeks than in his whole life combined. Was this what it was to let himself love? Did it always feel so volatile?

Fly walked them through a simple ceremony. Neither of them had prepared vows, but Sean made it clear he'd won on that count with the letter. His dad, Logan, and Chase cheered the loudest for that.

When they were pronounced husband and wife, Sean pulled her into him, not waiting for Fly to give him permission. He kissed her deep and hard, willing her to feel what he felt, to sink into his heart and know what she meant to him.

I love you, I love you, I love you.

Now that the floodgates were open, he couldn't stop thinking it. Saying it. Wanting to prove it.

Cheers rose around them, and Kelty pulled back just enough to whisper, "Babe, don't get me pregnant in public."

Sean laughed, scooping her close by the small of her back. "Stay right there. I need a minute."

She threw her head back, grinning. "You're wearing sweats. Everyone's going to see it."

Sean choked on a laugh and reeled her back in. "Best damn compliment you ever gave me."

Epilogue

KELTY SAT shoulder to shoulder with her parents on one side and Emma on the other at the Ice Centre for Game Five against Pucks Deep. It was standing room only at the back with the aisles about to be reported to Nora as fire hazards. They were tied 2-2 in the series. Pucks Deep had clawed their way back in Game Four, and now this battle was for all the marbles. It helped knowing there was still a pot for second place. But no player on the Snowballs was ready to accept anything but the Rose Cup. Especially not Sean.

The first period had barely started, and the noise already vibrated in Kelty's ribs. Her mom flinched when the puck ricocheted off the glass, eyes wide as though it might leap straight into their row.

The whistle blew for icing.

"Do they get a point for that?" her mom asked, leaning close so Kelty could hear her over the thunder of the crowd.

"No." Kelty smiled to herself. How did her mom still know so little about hockey after living with her dad for so long? "It only counts if it goes in the net. That was a whistle for the puck going too far without being touched."

She could almost see Sean smirking at her. *I'll show you going too far without being touched.*

Her mom frowned, asking why the players streaked back to the bench so quickly after coming on.

"That's a normal shift," Kelty explained, keeping her gaze trained on the breakout forming at centre ice. "They're skating flat-out the whole time. It's like sprinting. You can't do that for long without burning out."

The crowd cheered, jumping to their feet. Her mom tugged on her sleeve. "Why is everyone standing up right now?"

Kelty shared a look with her dad. "Because now we're on a power play." She pointed toward the opposite side of the rink where Jordan skated behind the glass, glowering in the penalty box. "They did something illegal, so we have one more skater than they do."

"Oh." Her mom nodded with understanding. "So it's like a freebie?"

"Hopefully. Gives us a better chance of scoring." She leaned forward, steepling her fingers against her lips. On the ice, the Snowballs set up at the blue line.

Sitting there felt surreal after the last week. A shotgun wedding followed by a celebration for the last day of their Amazing-ish Race. Rachel and Eliza ended up winning by a landslide. They were still wearing their crowns, their prize after Carter knighted them with a kitchen spatula and dubbed them race queens. Nate was convinced they cheated on the hike. Rachel insisted they only interpreted the trail creatively.

Logan's jersey retirement had sucked the last of her emotion, especially knowing Sharla and Rob's history with him and Crystal. The icing on the cake had been hearing that her parents were planning their move to Calgary. Turned out, they were just waiting for her to settle somewhere so they could move close.

It was a relief for all of them. Her mom wouldn't have to care for her dad alone, and Kelty would get to be there for all the seconds he was still with them. They'd already virtually met with a doctor in Calgary on Rhonda and Jordan's recommendation.

"Go!" Emma screamed as Sean gathered a seam off the half wall, shoulder faked, then feathered a pass through a window to Curtis. He didn't waste time being cute. He sent the puck low glove, hard. The net popped, and Kelty shot from her seat. 1-0. Six minutes in, and her voice was already thrashed.

Emma turned to her, beaming. "O Captain! My Captain!"

Pucks Deep tried to bully the middle in the second. The Snowballs made them skate for it. Boyd swallowed a rebound whole with a square body and good angles. The next save came off his chest protector. He plucked the puck out of the air with his glove like he was Mr. Miyagi, catching a fly with chopsticks. He flicked it to Tyler, who burned hard to centre and hit Darcy on the fly for a give-and-go that turned into the quietest, prettiest goal Kelty had seen in months.

It was 2-0, and her heart was in her throat. Then three on a power play courtesy of Country, Curtis, and Brett. Madelyn had talked with the boys about faster passes in the centre. Something about the limitations of the human eye and shot percentages. Whatever voodoo math she was calculating, it was working.

Kelty couldn't stop beaming whenever Sean took the ice. *Her husband.* The word was like candy on her tongue. He was solid. Commanding. Everything she loved about him. She couldn't get enough.

In the third, Pucks Deep scored one and then lost their patience. That sealed their fate. They took a roughing penalty in front of Boyd. Then two for high sticking and hooking.

Kelty caught Rhonda's eyes and made a heart with her hands. They knew this series would be rough for her no matter who won, and their Snowballs people always came before the scoreboard.

Three to one with five minutes left. Pucks Deep pulled their goalie at two minutes. Country immediately lobbed a shot from his own blue line that tracked centre but missed by an inch.

These were the dying seconds.

Kelty screamed until her ribs hurt. She hopped rows and linked arms with Penny, Aelin, Jenna, Grace, and Emma, screaming until the horn at the end chased them all into relieved, ridiculous joy. Gloves flew. Helmets hit the ice. White puff balls rained down from the stands.

But it was Sean who caught her attention. He dropped his helmet and found her in the crowd, then waved at someone or something to her left. She frowned, trying to decipher the signal. Then Rob leaned forward and passed something down the row.

"What is it?" she called out.

He laughed. "No clue! Sean said it was for you!"

Kelty took the tin in her hands. Strange. She'd never seen it before.

She opened the lid and gasped. Her head shot up, searching for him. Sean stood on the ice, still watching her, a stupidly big grin on his face. She dropped her gaze and rifled through the items. The matchbook from The Den, a river rock she immediately recognized as being from Vancouver Island. A shell. How long had he been collecting these? How had she not known?

Kelty flipped over a small slip of paper and read, "I owe you one miniature piece of sushi. Currently in use for game wins."

She laughed out loud, tears springing to her eyes. Sean Thompson loved her. He may not have been able to say it from the beginning, but he'd been collecting proof from the moment they met.

Kelty slid the lid back in place and clutched the tin in her lap. She found Sean again on the ice and mouthed, *"I love you!"*

He moved further away from the team so she could see his face better, and mouthed back, *"I love you too!"*

Kelty's mom leaned in. "Why are they talking to the referees? Do they have a problem with the calls? I thought the game was over."

Kelty sighed. "It's just because they're friends, Mom. They see each other at games every week. Now the season's over, and they'll probably miss each other over the summer."

Her mom frowned. "But they were so mad before. When they blew their whistles."

Kelty stifled a laugh. "I know. Funny, isn't it?" She stood and motioned for her parents to walk with her to the stairs. She drew in a breath of crisp, cold air. The same rink air she'd breathed for nearly eight years, and yet tonight it felt completely different.

Life could be beautiful at the most surprising moments.

For no reason at all.

———

See Rob and Sharla's story in Campus Confessions Book #1:
The Breakaway

Rob Thompson has always hated Sharla, but when her
boyfriend and his best friend, Logan, leaves for World
Juniors, Rob is still living under their roof.

She has to figure out how to make living with her enemy
work. But then every glance, every late-night argument, every

charged moment feels more like crossing a line she can't come back from.

Click here to buy Book #1 in Campus Confessions, *The Breakaway*, to see how long they can ignore the tension . . .

Tropes:
- Enemies to Lovers
- Boyfriend's best friend
- Comfort/Healing
- No Cheating
- Witty Banter
- Slow Burn

Bonus Scene

PRESENT DAY

KELTY SAT on the Thompson's couch with her ankle propped on a pillow while six people—seven, including Sean—ping-ponged around her. She'd expected sympathy for rolling her ankle on the hike with Sean, but she hadn't expected full-blown palliative care.

"I swear by Epsom salt soaks," Sharla announced, handing her a glass of water. "Every night. Twenty minutes. You'll feel brand new."

"Compression wrap's more important," Logan countered, searching in the cabinet Sharla had directed him to for an ACE Bandage. "Keeps the swelling down. I can grab one from my truck."

Crystal opened the drawer next to him. "Don't let him wrap it, though. He'll cut off all your blood supply."

"Not true." Logan scoffed.

"Guys, it's just a sprain," she tried to argue, but nobody was listening. It was kind of adorable. Sean insisted on piggybacking her in from the car, even though he was clearly exhausted from dragging her down the trail to the truck. Thankfully, it had only taken a little more than twenty minutes for them to get back to the parking lot, but he'd spent the first five minutes of the drive trying to get feeling back into his hands.

Madelyn lifted the ice pack from the side of her ankle. "Need a break?"

Kelty nodded. She couldn't feel anything, but that was probably a good thing.

"Found it!" Rob held up the bandage proudly as he descended the stairs. He handed it to Sean. "You want to do the honours?"

Sean's eyes flicked to Kelty's, a silent question. She gave him the go-ahead, and he dropped to the carpet, kneeling next to her.

Needing a distraction as Sean lifted her foot, she honed in on the photo albums fanned across the coffee table. Sharla, Rob, and their friends had been knee-deep in nostalgia before the ankle debacle hijacked the afternoon. Albums with cracked leather spines and torn plastic sheets showed college parties, road trips, and holidays with everyone jammed into tiny apartments.

"Did all of you go to school together?" She ran a finger over a picture of Sharla when her hair was cropped short.

"That we did." Sharla sat on the couch and opened a smaller album. Maddie shrieked when she saw a photo of her hair poofing around a thick, white headband. Chase wheezed at Logan's frosted tips, and Sharla flushed pink at a picture of her and Rob kissing in his truck.

"Get it, Sharla." Kelty nudged her, and she giggled.

Picture after picture, yearsof memories and inside jokes. Her chest burned. This was what she wanted. A life that left evidence in boxes and albums, people who knew who she was at thirty, forty, and fifty. She wanted to sit in a living room like this years from now and laugh until her sides hurt.

Sean finished wrapping her ankle. "Too tight?"

She shook her head. He leaned back on his heels, then stood and walked into the kitchen. Almost eight years. She'd spent almost eight years with him, and what were they going to have to show for it?

———

Kelty shuffled into her workday with only a slight limp. Her ankle throbbed, but at least she could navigate her kitchen and home office, which was really just a desk and an ergonomic chair she'd splurged on last year.

She made it through the morning on autopilot, calendar blocks and email chains blurring together. She'd transitioned out of acquisitions two years ago, when the company restructured post-COVID. Too much burnout chasing deals, too much pressure on volume. Now she handled vendor compliance. It was a world of spreadsheets, contracts, and detail-obsessed tasks that most people found maddening. For her, it was clean. Predictable. She loved when the numbers balanced and everything was tied up in a pretty little bow.

It paid better, too, and gave flexibility. She'd been remote since the pandemic, her boss too practical to argue against her productivity from home. The quiet suited her most days, but today her focus was shot. Probably everything to do with the nihilistic thoughts running through her head since Sunday Supper at the Thompsons'.

She worked later than she meant to and made a simple meal of buttered noodles with parmesan for dinner. When the dishes were done, she pulled out her notebook. There were only a few more challenges to plan for the race, but they only had until Friday to get them sorted.

Sean was supposed to debrief their hike with Emma and Tyler, so she moved on to scribbling down the ingredient list for the lemon ricotta pancake bake-off. A family favourite. They wouldn't buy ingredients until next week, but—

She froze, her pen bleeding ink onto the page. Was that—? Movement outside caught her eye. A shadow skimming past the kitchen window.

Her pulse spiked.

Kelty set the pen down slowly and peered into the back-yard. Just the dark blur of bushes and the outline of the trees. If this were a movie, she'd be screaming at the screen for her character to shut off the lights and hide in her room.

But had she seen something? She needed to know. Her heart thudded as she unlocked the sliding door and poked her head out.

"Hey."

Kelty jolted, smacking her head against the door and stumbling over the lip onto the deck. Her ankle didn't hold, and she fell to her knees with a thud.

There was a string of muttered curses, and when she looked up from the wooden boards, Sean hovered above her.

"What the hell are you doing here?" she hissed.

Cindy Gunderson is a voice actress and award-winning author. Since she has commitment issues, she writes both sci-fi and fantasy, as well as contemporary romance and women's fiction under the pen name, Cynthia Gunderson.

When she is not typing away in a quiet corner of her local library, you can find her traveling with her family, narrating audiobooks, or happily digging in her garden. She loves acting and performing, beating her kids in card games, and playing ultimate frisbee with her handsome husband, Scott.

Cindy grew up in Alberta, Canada, but has lived most of her adult life between California and Colorado. She currently resides in the Denver metro area. Cindy holds a B.S. in Psychology from Brigham Young University.

Cindy's first novel Tier 1 was awarded First Place in Science Fiction at the 2021 CIPPA EVVY Awards and her women's fiction novel Yes, And was honored with the Indie Author Award's first place prize for the state of Colorado, 2023.

Also by Cynthia Gunderson

Standalone Novels

Yes, And

I Can't Remember

Let's Try This Again

Holly Bough Cottage

The New Year's Party

Sugar Creek Series

One Last Christmas, Love in Audio

Canadian Played Series

Against the Boards, Called for Icing, Stickhandle with Care, On the
Power Play, Guarding Home Ice, Offside Attraction, Drop the Mitts,
The Dying Seconds

Campus Confessions Series

The Breakaway, The Save, The Comeback

Smash Point Social Series

The Big Dink

Find signed books and discounted bundles at

www.CindyGunderson.com

Instagram: @CindyGWrites

Facebook: @CindyGWrites

TikTok: @CynthiaGWrites